CITY
OF A
THOUSAND
DOLLS

MIRIAM FORSTER

HARPER TEEN

An Imprint of HarperCollinsPublishers

HarperTeen is an imprint of HarperCollins Publishers.

City of a Thousand Dolls
Copyright © 2013 by Miriam Wiedeback
All rights reserved. Printed in the United States of America.
No part of this book may be used or reproduced in any manner whatsoever
without written permission except in the case of brief quotations embodied
in critical articles and reviews. For information address HarperCollins
Children's Books, a division of HarperCollins Publishers, 10 East 53rd
Street, New York, NY 10022.
www.harperteen.com

Library of Congress Cataloging-in-Publication Data
Forster, Miriam, date
City of a Thousand Dolls / Miriam Forster. – 1st ed.
    p.   cm.
Summary: "Nisha lives in the City of a Thousand Dolls, a remote estate
where orphan girls in the Empire become apprentices as musicians, healers,
and courtesans, her closest companions the mysterious cats that trail her
shadow. When girls begin to die, Nisha begins to uncover the secrets that
surround the deaths–jeopardizing not only her own future within the City
but her own life."–Provided by pub.
    ISBN 978-0-06-212130-1 (trade bdg.)
    {1. Fantasy.   2. Orphans–Fiction.}   I. Title.
PZ7.F7765Ci   2013   2012004289
{Fic}–dc23   CIP
                                                                         AC

Typography by Erin Fitzsimmons
12 13 14 15 16 LP/RRDH 10 9 8 7 6 5 4 3 2 1
❖
First Edition

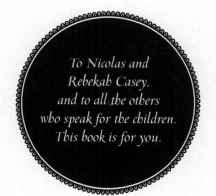

To Nicolas and
Rebekah Casey,
and to all the others
who speak for the children.
This book is for you.

DRAMATIS PERSONAE

in the

CITY OF A THOUSAND DOLLS

NISHA ARVI

The City Council
MADRI, The Matron of the Houses
AKASH TAR'VEY, the new Head of the City Council

On the grounds
ESMER, wild spotted cat, leader of the cat tribe
JERRIT, wild spotted cat, Nisha's best friend
RASHI, wild spotted cat
BRILL, wild spotted cat
VALERIANA, wild spotted cat

At the House of Combat
JOSEI, House Mistress
TAC, Josei's assistant

At the House of Flowers
INDRANI, House Mistress
TANAYA, novice, betrothed to the High Prince
MAYRL, tutor

At the House of Beauty

RAJNI, House Mistress
LASHAR, novice
LILAMAYI, novice

At the House of Jade

JINA, novice
SASHI, novice
DANNA, novice
ZANN, bond slave, former novice at the House of Music

At the House of Music

VINIAN, House Mistress
BINDI, novice

At the House of Pleasure

CAMINI, House Mistress
ATIY, novice

At the House of Discipline

KALIA, Mistress of Order
CHANDRA, Kalia's assistant

At the House of Shadows

THE SHADOW MISTRESS
MAYANTI, novice

THE BHINIAN EMPIRE

From the Capital

THE EMPEROR
HIGH PRINCE SUDEV, heir
DEVAN TAR'VEY, courier
UDITI, healer

The Kildi Camp

STEFAN, *KYS* OF THE ARVI CLAN
AISHE, Stefan's mother-in-law
SONJA, Stefan's daughter
MARET, Stefan's son
EMIL ARVI, Nisha's father (deceased)
SHAR, Nisha's mother (deceased)
ISITA, camp healer

THE CASTES

Flower, for the nobility
Jade, for the learned
Bamboo, for the merchants
Hearth, for the farmers
Wind, for the wanderers

It was the storyteller Elina who spoke for the children.
She sat before the Emperor,
the Second Lotus Emperor,
jangled the bells of her bow,
and sang of girls unwanted,
of babies left to die,
of a future where women were scarcer than gold.

And the Emperor listened and heard
the words of the singer
and her song of sadness.
The Emperor listened,
and he built a city.

All who wanted could bring their daughters to this place,
where they would be taught,
cared for,
and kept safe.

And the people honored the Emperor for his wisdom.

From *The Song of Stone and Blood*, a story-song of Elina the Bow-singer

"DON'T MOVE, NISHA." The words were playful, but the sharp slash of light along the blade of the throwing dagger was not.

Nisha Arvi forced herself to go still. Splinters dug into her shoulder from the wooden target wall behind her, but she didn't twitch.

A few paces away, her friend Tanaya twirled her dagger with careless grace. A smug and confident smile curled the edges of her mouth. "Don't look so frightened, Nisha. Trust me."

"You always say that," Nisha muttered, trying not to move the muscles of her face. Sweat from staff practice dampened her legs, and her loose cotton trousers clung to her skin like cold hands.

"And I'm always right." Like Nisha, Tanaya practiced her fighting skills in the rust-brown tunic and trousers of the House of

Combat. But Tanaya's tunic was of a finer weave than Nisha's, gold embroidery circling the neckline and sleeves. She polished her dagger on the edge of her tunic, and Nisha closed her eyes.

Swish–thunk.

Nisha cracked her left eye open. The dagger hilt quivered a finger's length from her cheek. Beyond the wooden handle, she could make out the copper-trimmed brick of the House of Combat and the smooth roof of gray sky.

Nisha sagged against the target wall. "You're getting better," she said weakly.

Tanaya gave a mocking imitation of an Imperial Court bow. "Why, thank you. You should see me performing the Dance of Fans and Daggers."

Nisha heard the shouts of instructors and the clangs of curved swords from inside a nearby building. Novices–and the outsiders the House Mistress brought into the City to help train them–practiced archery in the broad field behind them, the snap of their strings echoing across the flat ground. The sounds were straightforward, simple, comforting.

Nisha stepped away from the wall and pulled the dagger out of the wood. It was unexpectedly heavy, and she offered it hilt-first to Tanaya.

"I thought you were going to faint for a moment," Tanaya said. She sheathed the dagger in the hidden belt under her tunic. Tanaya was two years older than Nisha and wore every inch of her eighteen years with authority. Her light hair shone like polished beech wood, and her smooth hands danced like butterflies.

Nisha had the charcoal hair and amber skin so common in the Bhinian Empire, and her hands were rough and callused.

"You wouldn't laugh if you ever dared to spar with me," Nisha said, picking up her practice staff and lunging at Tanaya.

The older girl jumped back. "Careful! You know I'm not allowed to do anything that could cause bruising." Tanaya's voice was playful, but the smile slid from her eyes.

She dusted off her hands and started walking down the gray stone path that led to the House of Flowers, Nisha behind her.

"Besides, think how it would look. The future wife of the High Prince attacked by an assistant." The good humor returned to Tanaya's face, and she giggled. "Do you remember the first time you came to my House to deliver a message? You were so shy, all big, scared eyes and dark, dark hair hiding your face."

Nisha grimaced. She'd been so nervous, but also proud to deliver messages to the grand House of Flowers. Her satisfaction had lasted only as long as it took for a group of Flower girls to decide she was an easy target in her plain gray asar and untidy braid. It was her first experience of the dangers that lurked in the corners of the City of a Thousand Dolls. But it hadn't been her last.

The back of her neck prickled. Nisha's steps slowed as the prickle spread from her neck to her shoulders. It was the feeling that had become all too familiar in the past few days, the feeling that someone was watching her. She stopped.

"What is it?" Tanaya asked.

"Hold on," Nisha said, holding up a hand. She turned slowly, scanning the buildings around her. Then she saw the figure standing in the shadows of the armory.

It was Josei, the Mistress of the House of Combat, her hard stare fixed on Nisha.

Nisha whirled around and started walking.

Tanaya quickened her pace to keep up. "Nisha, what's wrong?" she hissed.

"Look over by the armory," Nisha said. "The House Mistress is watching me again."

Tanaya looked around, and her eyes widened. "So she is. I wonder why she seems to be spying on you? Is she trying to get you into trouble?"

"I don't know why she'd want to," Nisha said. Without looking around, she could imagine the House Mistress perfectly, her rust-brown asar wrapped so it came only to her knees, the short sword at her side. Josei was lithe and muscular and moved like a wolf. Just being in her presence made Nisha feel clumsy and anxious.

Tanaya laughed. "She frightens you."

"If you had any sense, she'd scare you, too." But there was a very good reason why Tanaya wasn't scared of Josei, or anyone. Tanaya was important.

Nisha's fingers crept to the base of her neck. There was a mark that looked like a stylized tiger just under her collarbone, and she rubbed it absently.

"I know what will make you feel better." Tanaya took her arm, and Nisha caught the delicate scent of the night-queen flower,

Tanaya's favorite scent. "I'll let you borrow you one of my asars for tonight."

Nisha felt her cheeks flush. "But your House wears Imperial Court asars. If Matron finds out, she'll be furious."

"So don't tell her. Come on. You can wear the overrobe to hide it until you're outside the walls. Don't you want to wear something *pretty* for Devan for a change?"

Nisha looked down at her dirt-streaked tunic and felt herself waver.

"I suppose—"

"You can come and change into it now," Tanaya said. "I have some time before my next lesson, and I can show you how to wrap it just right. Then you just have to stay out of sight until it's time to meet Devan." Tanaya's voice was rich with confidence, the same confidence that she had shown on the day Nisha first met her.

The Flower girls had surrounded Nisha like a pack of wolves, teasing her for the plainness of her clothes and the untidiness of her hair. She remembered biting the inside of her cheek, trying desperately not to cry. And then . . . Tanaya, swooping down like a guardian spirit. Like the other girls in the House of Flowers, Tanaya was training to join the nobility. She wore a vivid yellow Court asar patterned with butterflies, and her mere presence seemed to bring light and heat to the courtyard as if there were a flame burning inside her.

Even then—before she'd ever been spoken for—Tanaya could command a crowd.

Don't you girls have something better to do than stand here chattering like common starlings? she'd asked, cold disdain in her deep-brown eyes. Tanaya had taken Nisha's hand and pulled the astonished little girl away.

I'm Tanaya, she'd said with a smile that flew straight into Nisha's lonely, uncertain heart. *But you can call me Tani.*

Nisha had adored her from that moment on. Even now, ten years later, she found it hard to refuse her friend anything. Tanaya made people want to please her. She would charm and tease until she got what she wanted, and she never, ever gave up.

"All right," Nisha said. "But not a fine one. I'm going outside the walls, and I don't want the dirt to ruin it."

Tanaya waved a hand. "As if I would care about that," she said. "And don't worry, I have the perfect one." Her smile widened. "Trust me."

The asar Tanaya lent Nisha was beautiful, a deep lotus pink with white jasmine flowers, skimming her hips and falling in a graceful curtain around her feet. But it was also hard to walk in. Nisha tripped over her hem for the third time, stumbled, and almost dropped her bag of scrolls. She cursed under her breath, then looked around to make sure no one had seen her.

Despite its grand name, there wasn't much that was citylike about the City of a Thousand Dolls. In fact, it wasn't really a city at all, but a large private estate ringed by a high stone wall. The six Houses—Flowers, Beauty, Pleasure, Combat, Jade, and Music—each had their own grounds arranged loosely around a central point. A variety of gardens filled the grounds between them. In the city's center there was a large round hedge maze with six different points of entry and a hidden fountain at its heart.

A wide main road ran from the double gates that allowed entrance to the estate up to the maze, with the House of Flowers on one side and the Council House–the administrative center of the City–on the other. The remaining Houses were connected by paths of smooth, flat stones lined with benches and shaded by huge banyan trees.

And always, the City was filled with girls. While each girl was formally trained at one House, she often went to others for lessons. Between lessons, they gossiped in the gardens, played chase games in the hedge maze, and drank tea out on the wide stretches of lawn. There were tall girls, thin and graceful as herons, curvy ones whose hips swished like a dance when they walked, playful ten- and eleven-year-olds, wide-eyed children just out of toddling. The girls had skin of copper, amber, and gold, their eyes every rich shade of brown, and their laughter filled the City.

But the City was at its quietest at mealtimes. The river of voices was muted, hidden behind House walls. And there was no one to see Nisha as she slipped down the road that led out to the main gate.

Almost no one.

What in the name of the Long-Tailed Cat are you wearing? A spotted wildcat came padding up, his golden eyes visible through the thick grass that edged the side of the road. His voice was like tanned leather in Nisha's mind, strong and soft at the same time.

Nisha smiled at him. "Tanaya let me borrow it," she said, opening her overrobe and twirling in place. "What do you think, Jerrit?"

I think it could get you in serious trouble. Jerrit was thin and sleek, with longer legs than the cats Nisha knew were domesticated in the capital city. His golden-brown fur was streaked and spotted with black.

If you get caught in that—

I'm not going to get caught, Nisha said silently. She liked talking out loud to the cats as if they were people, but some conversations were better kept private. *Everyone is getting ready for lunch. And I'm not sneaking out, either. Devan's a courier. He delivers letters for Matron and picks up her outgoing mail. I'm supposed to bring it to him.*

That's not the only thing he picks up.

Don't be such a sourpuss. Nisha started walking again. *If I want to ask him to speak for me, I should look as sophisticated as I can.*

Jerrit kept pace with her at a lope. *I don't understand what you see in Devan. I don't trust him.*

Nisha rolled her eyes. It was an old argument between them. *Devan's not like most of the nobles we know.*

All nobles are the same.

How would you know? Nisha asked. *You've never been out of the City, not since you were a kitten. And I've been here just as long. Besides, we've only met the nobles on the Council. I'm sure all nobles aren't that . . .*

Arrogant? Scary?

I was going to say unfriendly.

Sure you were. Jerrit growled and trotted along in silence for a moment. *Do you love him?*

Nisha let out her breath. *I don't know*, she admitted. *Sometimes I think so. But then I wonder . . . how would I know if I did? Maybe I just like the way he kisses.*

Well, you'd better make your mind up. The Redeeming is in nine days. And if you're discovered before then–

I know.

Devan tar'Vey was a nobleman's son and a member of the high-ranking Flower caste. Nisha was . . . well, Nisha wasn't sure what she was, besides an errand girl. She was certainly no noble. And the story-songs were full of cautionary tales about what happened when someone from a higher caste and someone from a lower caste fell in love. If they were lucky, separation was the only punishment. But if the disgrace was severe enough for a family to become very angry, the lover from the higher caste could be banished to a remote part of the Bhinian Empire. The lower-caste lover in the story was usually killed.

The only exception to the rule was the City of a Thousand Dolls. If Devan spoke for her at the Redeeming, their relationship could be recognized as legitimate. But if they were caught before then, it was Nisha who would bear the brunt of the punishment.

Those are just stories, Nisha told herself. But she couldn't quite listen. In the Empire, power was everything–and if you had enough of it, you could get away with anything. Even murder.

Nisha, someone's coming, Jerrit sent. He sniffed the cooling air, fur raised. *Better hide.*

Jerking herself from her daydream, Nisha wrapped the folds of her overrobe around her and slipped into the abandoned guardhouse next to the gate. Guards had been stationed here a long time ago, to protect the walls and the girls inside, but the old Council Head had decided they were expensive and unnecessary. No girls had tried to run away for over a decade. And with the Emperor's soldiers keeping order on the roads, it seemed foolish for the City to have an armed force of its own.

Nisha had heard rumors that the new Council Head was reconsidering that decision. She hoped it wasn't true. Guards would make it almost impossible for her and Devan to see each other.

Peering over the windowsill, Nisha saw a servant in pale brown, an empty platter in her hands, hurrying toward the House of Flowers. She was probably borrowing it from the Council House. Even with all the Council Members to feed right now, the Council House kitchens could spare it.

As if alerted by Nisha's eyes on her, the girl glanced toward the guardhouse. Nisha ducked down, her heart pounding.

That brown tunic meant that the servant was with the House of Flowers. And like their mistresses, the staff at the House of Flowers loved to gossip. If word got around that Nisha was acting suspicious near the gates, Matron would start asking questions.

Nisha didn't breathe again until Jerrit told her the servant was gone.

That was too close, the cat sent. *Go. I'll keep watch here.*

Nisha impulsively bent down and kissed the top of her friend's slender head. *Thank you.*

You're welcome, Jerrit sent, the hint of a purr under his grumpy tone. *Just go, all right? And don't get caught.*

Nisha darted for the gates.

Devan was already waiting, his brown-and-gold courier's tunic glowing against the darkness of the woods. Nisha felt her own smile widen as she ran into his arms. His eager mouth found hers in a kiss. Here was one of the few places where she felt like she belonged, one of the few places she could forget about her work, the City, and the entire world.

And she did, until she heard the first scream.

2

THE SCREAM WAS so faint, it might almost have been mistaken for the cry of a bird.

Nisha slid her face away from Devan's and turned her head, scraping her ear against the stone of the city wall.

"What was that?"

"What was what?" Devan's hands slipped her overrobe off her shoulders, letting it fall to the ground.

Nisha listened, but she didn't hear anything else. "Nothing. It's probably nothing."

"Mmm-hmm." Devan's fingers moved to Nisha's jaw and brought her mouth back within reach. The tension ran out of her in a long sigh. She melted against the wall, giving herself up to Devan's kiss–

Another scream. Louder.

Nisha pushed hard against Devan's chest, giving herself just enough room to slide away from him. She scanned the silent teak forest, the high mossy wall that surrounded the estate, the flat gray sky. "Did you hear that?"

Devan smoothed his tunic, then his black hair. "I heard something," he said, after a moment. "But it might have come from the forest. I've heard a band of Kildi has moved into the area. I'm sure they make quite a lot of noise."

"It came from inside the walls," Nisha said, frowning at Devan's mention of the nomadic people who traveled the Empire. The City was so far from any other settlement. Why would the Kildi camp here? "At least I thought it did. . . ."

Devan lightly stroked Nisha's arm. His sleeve slipped back, exposing the tattoo that marked the smooth skin of his inner wrist. A kanak blossom, the mark of Flower caste. All noble children except for those from the Imperial family were marked with the sign of the golden flower at birth. The Imperial family's sign was a white lotus.

"Tell me about the Redeeming," he said unexpectedly. "I know it's a big annual party, and girls are bought as wives and things, but how does it work?"

"Not bought," Nisha corrected, pushing down the flutter in her stomach. "You can express your intention to claim a girl by Speaking for her. There's a redeeming fee to pay, but it doesn't mean you actually own the girl afterward."

"So can you reserve a girl? If you want a specific one?"

Nisha had to swallow before she could answer. She tried to

sound casual. "Matron likes to say there are as many ways to be Redeemed as there are girls in the City. You can pay in advance and have a girl trained to meet your specifications. Or you can come to the Redeeming and pick from the girls available. Why do you ask?"

Devan shrugged and gave her a smile that seemed full of possibilities. "I'm just wondering. What happens to a girl if no one speaks for her?"

"Most of the girls go to their first Redeeming at sixteen," Nisha explained, trying to ignore the way Devan was playing with the hair at the back of her neck. "If a girl doesn't find someone to speak for her by the time she's eighteen, the City gives her a small amount of money and a Wind caste mark and sets her free to earn her own living."

"I see," Devan said, pausing to brush his thumb along her jaw. "You know, that asar you're wearing suits you. I don't think you've ever looked so lovely. Or so elegant."

Nisha ran her hands over her borrowed asar. The silk felt like ripples of water under her fingers and made her feel reckless and exotic. Smiling, she stepped into Devan's arms.

Nisha! Jerrit came streaking along the wall. *You need to come in now.*

This isn't a good time, Jerrit. Nisha very carefully did not look at the cat. *Go away.* She lifted her face to Devan's kiss.

I wish I could, Jerrit sent in a disgusted tone. *But it's an emergency,* He wove himself between Devan's and Nisha's legs, meowing loudly.

Nisha sighed and stepped away from Devan, who scowled. "I don't understand why this place has so many cats," he said. "Or why you spend so much time with them. They're just animals."

"You only say that because you're allergic," Nisha said, picking up the long-bodied cat. She knew from long experience that no one else heard the cat's voices, and she didn't expect him to understand. "You know the stories say that spotted cats are good luck. It's good fortune to have a tribe here in the City."

Devan's eyes began to water. "If you say so," he said, sniffling.

Nisha, I'm serious. The cat struggled in her arms. *Something's happened, something terrible. Matron might send someone to look for you. If you're caught out here, with–*

All right, Jerrit. Nisha set the cat down and straightened the folds of her embroidered silk.

"Do you think there'll be any letters tomorrow?"

"Probably," Devan said. He picked up the bag of scrolls Nisha had given him and rattled it. "I know the Emperor is waiting for these letters from Matron. I don't think there has ever been so much correspondence between the City of a Thousand Dolls and the Imperial Court before. Normally the Emperor is the calmest person in the court, but now . . ."

Devan shook his head. "With the appointment of a new Council Head, and Prince Sudev marrying a girl from the City, there's a lot of political jostling. Even the Emperor's getting snappish, and that's not like him. I might have to invent an errand just to get away. And to see you."

Devan's smile creased the corners of his mouth and lit up his liquid, dark eyes. The warmth in those eyes flowed over Nisha like heated honey and melted her stomach into her sandals.

"See you tomorrow then, same time?"

Nisha! Jerrit ran a few steps toward the gates and looked back expectantly, the tip of his tail twitching. *Come on!*

With a last smile at Devan, Nisha turned and ran after the cat. The thick stone walls reached out and embraced her as she raced through the tunnel of the main gate. As she ran farther back into the City, Nisha heard another scream–then another, clanging and jangling like a box of high-pitched bells.

"What's happened?" she asked, her thin rope sandals slapping the dirt path to the hedge labyrinth at the City's center.

Jerrit ran beside her, the hair on his back raised. *I don't know. Whatever it is . . . it smells of death.*

Nisha's heart began to pound with more than exertion. Once, when she was young, she had tried to run away from the City, only to stumble over the body of a dead outlaw. The sight–the smell–still haunted her nightmares and had left her with a fear of the forest that she'd never been able to shake. The thought of seeing another dead body made her hands cold. But she kept running. Matron might need her help, and it couldn't be worse than the pictures her imagination was painting for her.

The hedge maze was a tangle of dim, narrow alleys. Nisha tripped, barely keeping her footing. Court asars were *not* designed for running.

Turn right, Jerrit sent. They broke out of the maze at a south corner and kept going. Flowering bushes grew in neat rows along this path. In one of the side gardens they passed, a fig tree dropped leaves into a shallow pool. Nisha followed the running cat past the figs and onto the private grounds of the House of Pleasure.

A flat-roofed building of weathered red brick, several stories high with copper-framed doors and windows, rose in front of her. Girls in black robes with their hoods pulled over their heads milled about like a flock of crows.

Nisha and Jerrit pushed through the small crowd. Nisha cursed herself for forgetting her overrobe as she tried to ignore the stares at her back. Without the black-hooded overcloak that novices were instructed to wear between Houses, Nisha's pink asar stood out like a candle flame at Darkfall.

Nisha wove her way to the clear area near the base of the building. She ignored the stricken faces around her, the whispers with undertones of fear. If she thought too hard about what might be in front of her, she would turn around. And Nisha wanted to see for herself.

A very still girl in red silk lay sprawled on her back next to the wall. Her asar was finer than Nisha had seen on anyone aside from Tanaya—a thin, fluttering fabric woven with gold that wrapped several times around the girl's broken body. Her eyes had the glassy stare of a painted figurine, and her head was tilted at an extreme angle, her limbs flung around her. If it hadn't been for the dark blood matting her light hair, she could have looked like a doll thrown by an angry child.

Nisha swallowed the bile that suddenly burned in her throat.

Jerrit's mind voice sounded shaky. *Who is she?* he sent.

"I didn't know her," Nisha whispered.

The girl next to Nisha pushed back her hood, revealing an attentive face and thick glass lenses held by twisted wire. "I think her name was Atiy."

"Jina," Nisha said, surprised. "What are you doing here?"

The girl didn't take her eyes off the body. "I've been researching love poetry in the Empire, something I can present at the Redeeming to show my skills as a scholar. I just conducted an interview with the House Mistress and some of her girls."

"With Atiy?"

"No." Jina scratched her forehead. "I wasn't allowed to see Atiy, since she wasn't being trained with the others. But they talked about her. Pale complexion, hair like lamplight. There aren't many girls of that description in the City, or in the Empire. The House of Jade has none."

Nisha nodded. Just as the House of Flowers trained girls as wives for noble families, the House of Jade trained apprentices as disciplined healers and scholars. Fair coloring was so rare in the Empire that any light-haired girls in the City were already spoken for, and the Council would never waste those girls in a House where looks were unimportant. Not when they could train her in another House and fetch a far higher price for her. That was the point of the City of a Thousand Dolls in the end. You could get any kind of girl here as long as you had the money to pay for her.

How much had someone been willing to pay for Atiy?

Nisha looked down at the body. A red, angry-looking welt encircled the girl's throat, as if she had yanked something from her neck, and there was a tear along the side of her asar.

"What do you think happened there?" Nisha asked, waving her hand at the tear.

Jina tapped her charcoal writing stick against her lips. Her hands were smudged with the charcoal, as black as her hair, and more streaks marked her green cotton asar.

"It looks like she jumped from the roof." Jina peered over her glasses, as if Atiy was a beetle in a jar. She made a note on a small piece of rice paper. "Maybe she didn't like the man who had spoken for her. Or she didn't like what she was being trained to do . . . or maybe the Shadow-walkers got her."

Nisha frowned. That Shadow-walkers lived in the City of a Thousand Dolls was the rumor that bothered her the most. Lethal assassins who could blend in anywhere and become invisible were the stuff of children's tales. "The Shadow-walkers are a legend, Jina."

"Not according to the archives," Jina said, still taking her notes. "Apparently, there's a whole family of assassins in Kamal. If the capital city has them, then why not us?"

"How on earth do you know that?" Nisha asked, amazed.

Then Jina did look up, a hint of rare mischief in her unusual sand-colored eyes. "I can't tell you how I know," she whispered. "But did you know that there's a shelf of restricted scrolls in our Mistress's private study? They're not off-limits exactly, but we are . . . discouraged from looking at them. One of them is about the Shadow-walkers. That they have a training House here, on the estate." She paused. "Some girls do vanish, you know. No one knows where they go."

"So someone came and redeemed them early," Nisha said. "That does happen."

"But very rarely. And it's never a secret. These girls don't say good-bye or tell anyone where they're going. And there's no record of them being redeemed. Besides, you know that most of us begin going to the Redeeming after our sixteenth birthday. The girls who vanish are usually younger."

Nisha shrugged. If there were anything like that happening in the City, Matron would have told her. "I've known girls who were redeemed earlier than sixteen. You just have to get special permission and pay a little more. There are craftsmen and Jade scholars and healers who prefer to do advanced training themselves. And I'm sure it's written down somewhere. There's probably a special scroll for that sort of thing that we haven't seen."

She would have said more to make her case and to convince herself there was nothing to Jina's wild idea, but Jerrit interrupted.

Nisha, this girl smells like fear. His black-tipped ears swiveled forward as he sniffed at the corpse.

Nisha crouched by the body but couldn't smell anything. *We've never seen anything like this on the grounds. It would be only natural if some of these girls were scared.*

Jerrit's tail twitched. *No, it's clinging to her. This girl died frantic, terrified.*

Nisha stood up. "Maybe this was an accident," she murmured, thinking out loud.

Jina looked up. "An accident would explain why her clothes are torn and the body is lying on its back. She slipped, tried to catch herself or pull herself back up, and fell. Interesting."

Interesting? Jerrit echoed.

Nisha shook her head at him. *It's not her fault. You know how the House of Jade is.*

I suppose I can't blame her for her training, but . . .

"An accident *is* more plausible than the assassin theory," Jina said, twirling the writing stick in her fingers. She sounded almost disappointed. Despite the gravity of a corpse before her, and what Jina had suggested, Nisha couldn't hold back a snort.

"Trust me, Jina, if there were a House training assassins, I would have noticed."

Jina shrugged and wrote something else down. "Well, you are Matron's shadow." Jina's words were bland, but Nisha heard a knowing amusement underneath them that startled her.

There was reason for Nisha to know the City of a Thousand Dolls and everything that happened within it. Besides her expected tasks as Matron's assistant—delivering messages between the Council House and the other Houses, keeping Matron's living and working areas tidy, running errands for the Council—Matron always instructed Nisha to record the gossip, in case anything unusual arose, and to report any serious problems she heard about. Such as anyone dissatisfied or deeply unhappy with her training, with her life in the City.

In return, Matron granted Nisha an unusual privilege for a servant: learning dancing at the House of Music and practicing staff skills at the House of Combat along with permission to wear the colors of both Houses. Matron had even given her a small workspace in the greenhouse at the House of Jade when Nisha expressed an interest in herbs.

Not many people knew about Nisha's secret role as Matron's informant, and Nisha liked it that way. Things had been hard enough when she was younger, the other girls teasing her about her unruly hair, her plain clothes, her uncertain status. If it became widely known that Nisha was Matron's spy, the snubs would only get worse.

Jina's attention had returned to her piece of rice paper, her face intent on the notes she'd scribbled down. Nisha studied her for a moment and then decided not to worry. Jina liked to know things, not so she could act on her knowledge or to change anything, but to simply know. She collected knowledge like other girls collected bird feathers or pretty stones. Even if she suspected something, Jina wouldn't tell anyone.

Matron's here. Jerrit's voice broke into her thoughts. He lifted his head, ears alert, and his eyes flashed gold.

Nisha looked up in time to see the Matron of the Houses walking toward them, her silver asar parting the black like the gleam of a fish in dark water. The silver was a symbol of Matron's authority under the Emperor, the higher color to the sky-gray asar that Nisha wore as her assistant. The asar she was supposed to be wearing right now.

3

PANIC ROSE IN Nisha's throat, and she slid behind Jina, out of sight. It would be bad enough to be caught wearing an Imperial Court asar, but if Matron figured out why she was wearing it–

"Jina, can I borrow your cloak? Please?"

"What?" For the first time, Jina looked fully at Nisha, who was nearly crouching on the ground. Her eyes followed Nisha's to Matron, who was speaking softly to the girls around her.

"Oh," she said. "I see." Without hesitating, she slipped out of the black overrobe and handed it to Nisha, who clutched it in gratitude.

"Thank you," she whispered.

Jina smiled wide, and it struck Nisha that this was not the peaceful, calm smile she was used to seeing from the girls of the House of Jade. Jina's smile lit up her clear eyes and made her unexpectedly beautiful. "Don't worry about it. We all have secrets." Then she slipped away through the crowd.

That *was interesting*, Nisha sent to Jerrit as she pulled the black robe tight around herself.

You're always startled when people are kind to you, Jerrit sent back.

Nisha turned to make sure that no glimpse of colored silk hung below the black of Jina's overrobe. *That's because most people aren't kind. I wouldn't have expected Jina to be so friendly. Maybe I should get to know her better. . . .*

Matron spotted Nisha before she could finish her thought. "Nisha! What's happened here?" Silver threaded the heavy, dark hair that framed Matron's oval face. Her eyes were the smooth brown of river rock, and Nisha felt like those eyes were seeing straight through her cloak to the borrowed asar underneath.

She resisted the urge to rub her ear, still stinging from its scrape against the wall outside the gates. Fidgeting would make her look as if she had something to hide. Matron didn't know yet that their old courier, Yerek, had recently been replaced with a nobleman's son, and a very young and attractive one. It wasn't that Nisha was hiding Devan, not exactly. But if Matron suspected that her assistant was flirting with nobility, or that she had caught the eye of a noble, she would never let Nisha retrieve the mail again. Although her courtship–if it was even a courtship–with Devan was only a few weeks old, it had come to feel like her strongest connection to the world outside. And it had become her biggest hope of reaching that world one day.

"I don't know, Matron," she said, lowering her eyes in a gesture of respect. "I heard the screams and came to see. It appears that she fell."

"What's going on here?" Camini, the Mistress of the House of Pleasure, pushed her way through the crowd and stopped at the sight of the girl on the ground. "Oh, no." She knelt by the body and ran her hand over Atiy's soft, pale hair. "Oh, Atiy, my little rock dove, what has happened to you?"

Before Matron had sent Nisha with her first message to the House of Pleasure, Nisha had pictured Camini as an ethereal, seductive beauty. But the mistress was a short, plump woman with a thick braid of dark hair that reached almost to her knees. She was quick with a laugh and with her anger, and Nisha had never seen her cry.

Camini was crying now, soft, wounded sobs that tore at Nisha's heart. Matron knelt down next to the mistress, placing a hand on her shoulder and speaking in a low voice. "I feel your sadness. But the girls are terrified. We need to stay in control, for them."

Camini wiped her tears, smearing the kohl that lined her eyes. It was such a vulnerable gesture that Nisha winced. For the first time, she saw the dead girl not just as a terrible accident, but as a loss, a hole ripped in the lives of the people who cared about her.

That she hadn't thought of Atiy as a real *person* yet, just as a dead body, made Nisha nauseous. The borrowed asar seemed to burn her skin, and she itched to get it off, before anyone else saw her discomfort. She wanted away from this place of death.

Gesturing to Jerrit to follow her, Nisha edged away from

Matron, Camini, and the small crowd around them. The girls who remained were from the House of Pleasure, their red asars showing underneath their open cloaks, hoods pushed back as they whispered in low, distressed voices. A few cried silently as other girls tried to comfort them.

Nisha walked quickly until she reached the sheltering shadows of the hedge maze. She stopped and took a deep breath, rubbing her hand over her face. "Poor Atiy . . ."

Who's Atiy? And what was all that screaming for?

A cat with spotted fur the color of iron and a mind-voice like smooth steel slipped out of the hedge. *All that commotion ruined a perfectly good hunt.* She licked her lips, revealing the gleam of sharp teeth. *It was a nice fat wood swallow, too.*

Hello, Esmer, Nisha sent. *A girl just jumped off the roof at the House of Pleasure. Or fell.*

Or was pushed, Jerrit sent.

Nisha ignored Jerrit. Girls had been hurt in the City before, but no one had ever been murdered. The founding principle of the City was that it provided a safe place, a refuge, for unwanted girls. The idea of murder in this place was unthinkable, and more than a little frightening.

"I've never seen Camini cry before," Nisha murmured. "It was so sad."

Someone died? That explains the screaming, Esmer sent, flicking her tail. *Poor child.*

"But it has nothing to do with us," Nisha said, surprising herself with her own vehemence. Something about Camini crying over Atiy's dead body had shaken her, made everything feel dangerous and fragile.

"I have to go see Tanaya," she said quickly. "I need to give her this asar back before I get into real trouble with it."

Nisha started walking again, using the high wall of the hedge to shield her from Matron's sharp eyes. She heard the cats' voices buzzing in the back of her mind, but she didn't bother listening. Nisha often wondered why no one else heard the cats' soft mental voices. She had asked Esmer about it when she was younger, but the gray cat had just said they didn't want to talk to anyone else. And Nisha had stopped asking. It felt as if the cats were here for her, protecting her, and as unlikely as that was, she preferred it to any other explanation.

Nisha tripped yet again over the hem of her borrowed asar and let out a grunt of frustration. "Why did I let Tanaya talk me into this?"

She was still grumbling when she left the maze and headed for the House of Flowers. It was much like all the other Houses on the outside, with the same weathered red brick and the same copper-framed windows. But there all resemblance ended.

Nisha pushed open the heavy doors. Spotless marble stretched beneath her feet like a carpet of frost, cold and smooth under her thin sandals. The high foyer ceiling shimmered with inlaid stone, vivid blues and greens in the pattern of a peacock's tail. A broad marble staircase dominated one end of the room, with two smaller staircases branching out on either side.

The hall had an imposing quiet that always made Nisha feel

overly tall, with too many hands and feet. She adjusted her over-robe and crept toward the stairway.

Glimpses of opulence whispered behind half-open double doors. On one side, a mirrored ballroom reflected endless Nishas as she passed. The adjacent banquet room held a table that gleamed like water. On the other side was the library and a throne room, its practice throne made of polished teak and carved with flowers.

On the night of the Redeeming, the City hosted an elaborate masquerade right in the House of Flowers. It was the culmination of the long day, a grand party designed to show off the remaining novices in the best possible light. The mirrored hall would hold musicians and dancers, the long table would be covered with the finest food, and the House would be full of all kinds of people: nobles, healers, merchants, and of course, dozens of novices in masks and special asars, each one waiting for the formal announcement that she had been spoken for.

This year, Nisha would be one of them. On her sixteenth birthday, Matron had told her that it was time to attend the Redeeming, to try to find someone to speak for her. Nisha briefly wondered what price the City Council would post for her, an errand girl with little formal training within any one House. It couldn't be much. Some people came to hire, knowing they would find well-trained girls eager to work. Those fees were reasonable. She could be spoken for as an apprentice or an assistant—

Or as a wife. Nisha put a hand to her face, remembering the way Devan had touched her cheek earlier. Yes. This was the year she'd finally get away from the heavy walls of the City, find a life of her own somewhere. Even though Nisha felt safe in the City, it wasn't enough. She felt restless here, confined inside the high walls. She wanted to find someplace to belong, someplace where she could be free.

"What are you doing?"

Nisha almost jumped through the roof, she was so startled. She whirled around to see a House of Flowers tutor emerge from the library, a rice-paper scroll in her hand. She wore a brown silk asar patterned with fig leaves. Nisha knew there was a message in that particular pattern—there were messages hidden in all House of Flowers asars—but she had no idea what it was.

The woman's hair was pulled back tightly. She looked at Nisha's feet, and a scowl creased her face.

Nisha looked down and realized Esmer and Jerrit had followed her inside. *Out!* she scolded them in her mind. *You're not allowed in here!*

Jerrit's eyes blinked once. *Sorry.* He exchanged a glance with Esmer. The cats trotted away, and right before they slipped out the door, Nisha heard Jerrit send *I don't like leaving her alone.*

I know, Esmer sent, her mind-voice so low that Nisha barely caught the words. *But we can't draw attention to ourselves. Not with the Council crawling the City. Be patient.*

Nisha had only a moment to wonder what they meant before the tutor cleared her throat. Nisha bowed, palms pressed together at her chest.

"Forgive me for not closing my eyes against the glow of your wisdom, Wise One. How may I best serve you?"

The tutor didn't return the greeting but demanded, "What are you doing in that asar?"

A JOLT OF anxiety shot through Nisha. Looking down, she saw that her overrobe had fallen open to reveal the lotus-pink silk and white jasmine flowers of Tanaya's asar. The white blooms were the same color as the marble floor. The asar was perfectly suited to the elegant hall.

"I don't understand," Nisha said, stalling for time. The woman was new here, someone she'd never seen before. Maybe Nisha could bluff her way out of this.

The woman's lips tightened further. "That," she said, "is an *invitation* asar, worn to flirt with potential suitors. It is inappropriate to wear it for everyday tasks."

Nisha's mouth opened, but no words came out. Despite her relief at not being recognized, she could feel her skin turn a dark red. When Tanaya had offered her an asar, she had assumed that the design would, if anything, communicate happiness or affection. But *invitation*? She was about to turn and run out of the building when Tanaya's golden head appeared at the top of the stairs.

"Why, Mayrl," Tanaya murmured with a finely honed sweetness. "Did you not tell me just this morning that courtesy is the jewel of the high castes? That only those of low breeding and training return politeness with blunt speech? Yet here you are, rudely scolding a student not your own." She clucked her tongue. "Such a poor example you're setting."

The tutor opened her mouth, then closed it again. A flush touched her cheeks, and Nisha felt sorry for her.

Tanaya glided down the stairs, her fingers touching so lightly on the copper banister that they left no mark. She had changed from her Combat clothing into one of the elaborate costumes of the House of Flowers, a black silk asar embroidered with red flower petals. Tiny mirrors flashed and twinkled from her hemline, and thin copper bracelets jangled on her wrists. Against the pure white of the stairs, the older girl glittered like a mosaic made of jewels.

"Why don't I speak with her?" Tanaya asked. "Surely you have more important things to do than concern yourself with this trivial thing." She flicked the folding bamboo fan she carried, an obvious gesture of dismissal.

The tutor bowed. "Of course, Tanaya. I leave her in your capable hands." Turning her back on them, she left, her asar swishing the marble floor.

"Quick, Nisha, come upstairs, and put on something else!"
Tanaya took Nisha's arm. "Did you see the look on that woman's
face? She couldn't have been more horrified if you'd come dressed
as a Kildi." She dragged Nisha up the satin-smooth staircase and
opened the door to her bedroom, shoving Nisha inside.

"A flirting robe?" Nisha whispered furiously. "You gave me a
flirting robe?"

Tanaya sank down on her narrow reclining couch, set down
her fan, and pulled off her ruby-spotted sandals. "It's *so* nice to
sit down." She caught Nisha's eye and laughed. "Of course I gave
you a flirting robe."

Sick with embarrassment, Nisha pulled off her own sandals
and collapsed onto the thick woven rug. "This is awful. How will
I ever face him again?"

"You worry too much," Tanaya said with assurance. "I gave
you the robe that communicates flirtatious intent and affection, not the one that indicates that you might have an affair
with him. I thought it might help."

"Help what? Help embarrass me?"

"Of course not," Tanaya said, a sharp edge to her voice. "I just
thought Devan could use a push or two. If he's serious, he's
being terribly slow about telling you." Her face softened, and she
reached to put a hand on Nisha's shoulder. "I'm sorry if I was
presumptuous. It's just . . . if he speaks for you, you would come
live at court, with me. We could still be friends. Wouldn't that
be nice?"

Nisha let her gaze wander around Tanaya's room and tried to

collect her scattered thoughts. Parrot-green silk draped the walls, and an open window let in fresh air. A hint of cinnamon incense floated in from outside. Nisha thought of her own window-less room with its rough floor and peeling walls. If she became a noble–like Tanaya would be soon–she could have a room like this, a sky outside her window, and a carpet thick as grass under her feet.

"I do wish you had told me, Tanaya."

Tanaya opened the carved chest in the corner. She pulled out Nisha's Combat tunic and handed it to her. "If I had told you, you would have said no. And I am sorry. But what happened? Did you ask him if he'd speak for you? What did he say?"

"I never got the chance." Nisha thought about the blood in Atiy's pale hair and swallowed hard. "There was an accident at the House of Pleasure, and I had to leave."

"An accident?" Tanaya's hands played with the necklace at her throat, a web of lacy gold set with rubies that the High Prince had sent for her birthday. "What happened?"

Nisha slid the combat tunic over her head. Someone–probably servant–had brushed the dirt off it and perfumed it with rose extract. The fabric felt smooth and cool against her skin, and the smell was worlds away from the rough soap Nisha used to wash her own clothes.

"A girl fell off the roof at the House of Pleasure. Or jumped, we don't know yet." She closed her eyes. "I saw her. It was awful."

"Oh, Nisha, how terrible. Are you all right?"

"I'm fine. But can we talk about something else?" Nisha

indicated the golden chain that wove through Tanaya's hair and the ruby that hung over her forehead. "I see you get to play empress tonight."

A flush stained her friend's light skin. "Oh, you know," she said with a forced laugh. "Playing empress is all about receiving supplicants and directing servants, and leading at dinner. It's almost as boring as etiquette lessons."

Nisha grinned. Most of the girls in the House of Flowers loved pretending to be empress. But most of them were being groomed as the wives of lesser noblemen and second sons, men who had nothing to do but play palace games, attend balls, and attend to the provincial affairs of their own estates. All they would need to learn was how deeply to bow to each member of the Imperial family, and the intricate languages of dress, fan movements, and poetry.

Tanaya was different.

"Only you would prefer economic history to playing empress," Nisha teased.

Tanaya shrugged her graceful shoulders. "High Prince Sudev requested a well-read and intelligent woman. I don't want to disappoint him."

"You won't," Nisha said. "How could you? No girl in the history of the City of a Thousand Dolls has been trained in every House before. You know more of the intricacies of history and court customs than anyone in the City, novice or tutor. You could even defend the prince with daggers if you had to. How could he *not* love you?"

"Love has little to do with anything, Nisha. Especially since the prince and I have never met." Tanaya settled into her reclining couch and tilted her head back. "Sudev is taking a wife from the Houses because the Emperor wishes it. The grumblings against the two-child system are getting louder. Our marriage will show the Empire that the system works, that the City of a Thousand Dolls is a good place for unwanted and orphaned girls. But the prince won't take a City girl who is inferior to him, not even to please his father. I have to prove that I'm his equal."

Nisha shook her head. She couldn't imagine the prince thinking Tanaya was inferior.

Tanaya let out a breath and rose from the couch in one fluid movement. She extended her hand to Nisha and helped her up. Nisha caught her friend's wrist, frowning at how thin and brittle it was, how light and quick the pulse felt against her fingers.

"Tani. Is everything all right?"

Tanaya gave a little laugh. "I'm fine. I just haven't had much of an appetite lately, and sometimes it's hard to sleep. The excitement . . ."

There was a loud knock at Tanaya's door. "Mistress Tanaya, the House Mistress wishes to speak with you before dinner," a servant called.

"I'm coming!" Tanaya snapped.

She picked up her fan. To Nisha she said, "I'm sorry. They just won't leave me alone. There's an envoy from the palace coming tomorrow. I'm supposed to spend the whole day in the Council House, serving tea and making polite conversation about my lessons. House Mistress Indrani probably wants to go over what I'm supposed to say. And what not to say."

Tanaya picked up her sandals and smoothed her asar. "The prince might have requested an intelligent woman, but if I appear *too* smart, it might scare the prince's councillors."

"I should be going anyway. I–"

"I'll be all right, Nisha," Tanaya interrupted, widening her fixed smile. "Once the masquerade is over and Prince Sudev and I are together, everything's going to be perfect. For both of us. Trust me."

Nisha rolled her eyes. "You always say that."

"And I'm always right," Tanaya shot back as she walked out the door.

When Nisha looked down to slide her sandals back on, a scrap of rice paper just by the door caught her eye. She scooped it up, noting the scalloped edges. Tanaya loved scalloped paper. She used rice paper with these borders to write poems on, the highest form of communication in the Imperial Court.

Nisha tucked it into her tunic without reading it and bit her lip. Her fingers still held the memory of Tanaya's pulse, rapid and soft, like the wings of a trapped bird. No matter what her friend said, Nisha couldn't help but worry about her. About both of them.

Esmer and Jerrit waited for Nisha outside the House of Flowers, but they weren't alone. A girl about Tanaya's age with cropped hair and the bronze wrist cuffs of a bond slave stood with them.

Her pale-green tunic marked her as tied to the House of Jade; it was a lighter shade than the asars worn by Jade novices.

The girl looked up, her eyes narrowing, and Nisha breathed a prayer of thanks to the Ancestors that she wasn't still wearing Tanaya's court asar.

Of all the people Nisha could have been caught by, Zann had to be one of the worst. Zann would be only too glad to report Nisha's infraction to Matron, or worse, Kalia, the Mistress of Order.

But Nisha was back in her House of Combat clothes now, and she had nothing to fear.

"Hello, Zann."

The girl scowled, resentment radiating off her like heat from a cookstove. "I've been looking for you everywhere. Matron sent me to tell you she wants you in her study right now."

Nisha bit her lip, trying not to respond to the girl's snappish tone. Zann had been a novice once, a brilliant student in the House of Music. Now she was bound to the estate by a debt it would take her decades to repay. She blamed Nisha for her downfall, and sometimes Nisha wondered if she was right to.

"Why does she want to see me?"

"She didn't tell me. I'm just a bond slave, remember?" Zann spit out the words. She touched the bronze cuffs at her wrists, the engravings that told the world what she owed. "But if you think that getting to go to the Redeeming this year means you can shirk your work, think again."

"I'm not shirking anything," Nisha said, stung. "I have free time for myself before dinner."

"Not today you don't. Like I said, Matron wants to talk to you. Maybe she's thinking of making you earn your keep for once."

Nisha ignored her and started walking toward the Council House. When she realized Zann wasn't following her, she turned around.

"Aren't you coming?" she asked Zann, unable to resist a dig. "I thought you'd be anxious to see me in trouble."

Zann narrowed her eyes again, her scowl replaced by a smug look of self-satisfaction. "I have a meeting of my own," she said. "And it's far more important than yours."

Nisha watched Zann turn on her heel and stride away toward the hedges.

As her eyes followed the angry girl, she caught sight of something else. Josei, leaning against the side of a gardener's shed, eating a fig.

5

ESMER HISSED AT Zann's retreating back. *That girl can hold a grudge like no one I've ever known. What happened to her wasn't your fault.*

Nisha sighed. *If it's not my fault, then why have I always felt so guilty?*

Esmer didn't answer.

They maneuvered their way through the maze, Nisha running over the things Matron could want to talk to her about.

"I cleaned the study and the library today; it's not that," she muttered, talking mostly to herself. "And I've already given her mail to Devan. Something has come up that needs to be done for the Redeeming, maybe." She wasn't usually needed at this time of day. What was the emergency?

Someone did *just die*, Esmer sent. That's *emergency enough*.

True. Nisha conceded. *As long as Matron hasn't found out about Devan . . .*

Fear touched her spine. The trouble she would be in if Matron thought she was flirting would be nothing compared to the danger she'd be in if it was discovered she was in a relationship. If Devan uttered a word about them to anyone, it was Nisha who would suffer.

Silence was critical, at least until the Redeeming. Nisha hadn't even planned on telling Tanaya, but one day, hoping for a letter from Prince Sudev, Tanaya had insisted on coming along to pick up the mail. She'd said nothing, just watched Devan and Nisha awkwardly try to carry on a casual conversation in front of her. But as soon as Devan rode out of sight, she'd pounced on Nisha and demanded to know what she thought about the handsome courier. Nisha had confessed that she found his personality as charming as his appearance–and that the previous week, he'd kissed her. Ever since, Tanaya had been pushing the two of them together any chance she got. She was confident that if Nisha only said and did the right things, and showed him how she felt, Devan would agree to speak for her. Nisha wasn't sure it would be that easy.

In the privacy of her own thoughts, she could admit to herself that she hadn't asked Devan to speak for her yet because she was afraid: afraid of the tar'Vey family, favored above all the other noble families by the Emperor; afraid that she'd misunderstood Devan somehow. Could a Flower caste noble want to marry a girl of mysterious parentage? A foundling?

Nisha touched the tiger mark under her collarbone and the questions that had haunted her for her entire life came tumbling back. Had her parents inked the mark into her skin? If so, why? Was it a connection to her lost family, or as Matron claimed, was it just a birthmark that meant nothing and that happened to look like a tiger? Whatever it was, it was strange, not like any caste mark she'd ever seen.

Don't do that, Jerrit sent, brushing her leg.

Don't do what?

Jerrit sniffed. *Every time you touch that mark of yours, I know you're wallowing and feeling sorry for yourself.*

I am not, Nisha sent.

You are. Esmer's words were sharp. *And it's not doing you any good. You need to think about what's ahead. Things don't smell right. Haven't you noticed how closely the tribe is following today?*

Nisha had seen that the other spotted cats were pacing alongside them, blending into the trees and bushes along the path like watchful shadows. She stopped, a shiver of unease creeping down her back. *Esmer, what's going on? What do you smell?*

Change and trouble, Esmer sent. *Things are shifting. We all smell it. The balance is changing. I don't like it. And I don't like you being in the middle of it.*

Nisha's shiver turned into full-blown chills. The cats' sense of smell was unbelievably sharp. They could smell fear and tension, sense danger better than any human she'd ever known. Besides Jerrit and Esmer, the dozen or so cats in the tribe seemed to tolerate her with gentle amusement, but they rarely involved themselves in her life, in the life of the City. If what they sensed had the whole tribe worried . . .

Jerrit gave her leg a light scratch. *We won't let anything happen to you, Nisha.*

"How can you be sure?" Nisha asked out loud. Worry threw thorns into her voice. "You can't fix this, Jerrit. You're just a cat."

Jerrit lowered his head, his tail drooping. Remorse choked her before she even finished speaking, and Nisha dropped to her knees, gathering the cat into her arms.

"I'm sorry," she whispered into his soft fur. "I say such stupid things when I'm scared."

Esmer nuzzled her arm. *Jerrit's right. We won't let anything happen to you.*

Nisha scratched around the bases of Jerrit's ears. *I know. Forgive me?*

Jerrit looked up, his golden-brown eyes light. *On one condition.*

What is it? Nisha asked, almost falling back as Jerrit leaped from her lap.

Race you to Matron's!

He took off low across the ground, as Nisha scrambled to her feet. *Cheater!* she sent, and ran after him, laughing.

They ran all the way to the Council House, a sprawling building several stories high. It held Matron's set of rooms as well as Nisha's tiny sleeping space. There were spacious kitchens, rooms for visiting Council members, and a chamber where the Council sessions were held. There was even a large library with a fireplace, the favorite napping spot of the old Council Head.

The previous Council Head had been a white-haired elderly man, stooped and gentle. To no one's surprise, he had passed peacefully in his sleep not long before. Nisha didn't know who the new Council Head might be, but she hoped he'd be like the old one, content to let the City run on its own, under Matron's watch.

The high, sharp-cornered Council House towered over the rest of the estate. Nisha slowed her steps as she approached its broad stairs. She felt suddenly vulnerable, as if the building were reaching for her, threatening to crush her under its weight.

Two Council members walked down the stairs. The man wore a knee-length tunic of fine linen and a matching vest worked in tan and silver. The woman was dressed in a blue-gray asar with a hem design of black lions, and she carried a sheer silver scarf. Their steps were hard and certain. Nisha kept her head down, hoping to slip past unnoticed.

She didn't succeed.

"Girl." The hook-nosed man held out a hand, palm down, and gestured her to them. "Come here."

Nisha turned, eyes still down, her posture bowed and submissive. The City Council made her nervous. The appointed nobles normally lived in the capital city of Kamal and came to the City only a few times every year to discuss important business. But this year marked the first time a member of the Imperial family would claim a girl from the City of a Thousand Dolls. The Council members seemed determined to oversee everything personally.

"How may I serve you, sir?" she asked.

The woman lifted Nisha's chin. Her fingernails were long and pointed like the claws of an eagle.

"Are you Matron's girl?" she asked.

Nisha nodded, willing her emotions to stay hidden.

The woman looked at the man. "Akash is right. She's young and she looks strong."

Her companion walked around Nisha, looking her up and down. "She's not a great beauty by any means. But she's not painful to look at either. And Matron says she's willing to work, and very efficient."

The woman dropped Nisha's chin and wiped her fingers with a handkerchief. Then the pair continued on, leaving Nisha trembling on the steps. "Her price won't be enough. But I suppose it's a start. . . ."

Jerrit, hiding in a nearby bush, leaped up beside her. *What was that? They usually ignore you, don't insult you to your face. They inspected you like you were a horse going to market!*

Tears burned in Nisha's eyes. *They're just discussing my Redeeming fee,* she sent. *Go with Esmer. I'll call you when my meeting with Matron is over.*

They are wrong, you know. You are *beautiful.*

Jerrit's words erased the last of Nisha's urge to cry. *Well, as long as you think so.* She reached down and ran her fingers through the short fur of his head. Jerrit rubbed his nose against her hand.

What do you suppose Matron wants? he asked.

I don't know, Nisha sent. Out of the corner of her eye, she thought she saw a flash of rust-brown asar around the corner. But when she looked again, there was nothing there. *But with a girl dead, I'm guessing nothing pleasant.*

As Nisha approached Matron's study, she heard low voices. One was Matron's.

"Are you sure you have no other girls in your House who might be suitable?"

"No." The other voice was Camini's, and it sounded clogged, as if the House Mistress was still fighting tears. "Not for this. Not to be a secret mistress."

Nisha ducked into a nearby side hallway, out of sight of anyone who might come through the study door. Atiy was training as a secret mistress? Nisha's sympathy for the girl deepened. Secret mistresses were girls chosen for their beauty, and trained in all the arts of pampering and pleasing men. They lived in isolation, could be cast aside for the smallest infraction—and when they were cast aside, they had no one. Because they were trained and kept in secret, it could happen that no one knew a secret mistress existed. Atiy must have been kept completely isolated, living in her room alone.

I might jump off a roof myself, Nisha thought.

Matron and Camini exchanged a few more words, so low that Nisha couldn't hear them, and Camini left. Nisha waited until the woman's footsteps had died away, then stepped back around the corner and headed for Matron's study.

Matron sat at her low writing table, her head bent. Nisha tapped her finger on the doorframe.

"Come in and shut the door, Nisha," Matron said, waving her in, palm facing down.

Nisha did as she was told and stood in front of Matron's desk, waiting. Matron's study was a comfortable room with low chairs, a wall of shelves, and a woven rug of black and cream. A birdcage in the corner held a gray parakeet. The room smelled strongly of ground sandalwood, incense that Matron used only when she was disturbed or upset. It made Nisha's nose twitch, and she tried not to sneeze.

Matron moved her papers to one side of the desk, then after a few seconds moved them back to the other side. Her hands trembled. Nisha watched her curiously. She'd never seen Matron like this.

Matron finally placed her papers together in a neat pile and took a deep breath.

"Nisha"–she paused–"Nisha, do you know why I chose you as my assistant?"

The question was so unexpected. All the theories she'd had since she was a little girl flew out of her head. "You always said I was too old to train," she said slowly. The words stung as they left her lips.

Nisha closed her eyes, remembering the day she'd come to the City of a Thousand Dolls. The cold stone at her back and the smoothness of a carved toy cat in her hands. *A gift,* her father had said. *Spotted cats are good luck. This one will look after you.*

Then he had kissed her on the forehead and told her to sit near the gate and not go anywhere while he gathered mushrooms.

He had never come back, and Nisha hadn't seen her mother again either. Eventually Nisha had accepted that she, like the other girls, had been abandoned. Sometimes she wondered what her parents had found so awful about her that they'd left her here.

Once Nisha realized that her parents weren't coming back, she had begged Matron to let her go into a House as a novice. To dance at the House of Music, or to train at the House of Combat, anything to give her a place to belong. But Matron had always said that the Council's decision was that she was too old to make a proper novice. If she'd come to the City as an infant, like most of the girls here, it would be different. But Nisha had been six when she came to the City.

Nisha opened her eyes, chasing the memories away. "I don't know, Matron. I thought it was the only place you could find for me."

Amusement flashed across Matron's face. "I could see why you would think that," she said. "But we could have given you to one of the House Mistresses as an assistant too, or put you to work in the kitchens."

"But I served you," Nisha said, wondering at the exchange. "Why?"

A momentary bitterness twisted Matron's mouth before her face smoothed into her normally placid expression. "I didn't have much choice," she said. "For reasons I can't discuss, I was forced to be your advocate. But I don't regret it. You have been invaluable to me as an assistant and as a source of information." She hesitated. "And I'm afraid that your value to me has put you in danger."

Nisha burst out with a nervous laugh. "Who cares about me?"

"No one, usually," Matron said with blunt cruelty. "But the new head of the Council, Akash tar'Vey, does."

Nisha held herself perfectly still, masking the jolt of surprise she felt at hearing the tar'Vey name. The new Council Head was a member of Devan's family?

Unease crawled like a long-legged mantis over her skin. This appointment gave the tar'Vey family even more power. Made it even *less* likely that they would ever let Devan speak for her, even if he did want to go to his family with the idea.

Nisha held her breath and waited for Matron to mention Devan. But instead, Matron said something completely unexpected.

"Nisha, today the City lost a novice, one who was spoken for by a very wealthy and powerful man. A man who has already paid us a great deal of money. If we cannot find a girl to replace her, then we will have to pay him back. Akash tar'Vey believes he has found an easy way to quickly get some of the money we need." She took a deep breath. "Nisha, the Council wants to sell you."

Three things should never be trusted

The scales of a rival

The gold of a Kildi

And the smile of a nobleman

Bamboo caste merchant's proverb

6

"SELL ME?" THE words echoed in Nisha's head like the ring of a gong. For a moment, she thought she had heard wrong. "They don't own me."

"No," Matron said, "they don't. But you have no caste or family, like most of the servants do, and you have not been accepted as a novice in the City. You can claim the advantages of neither novice nor servant. Akash says that makes you the perfect choice."

"You mean no one will miss me. They can just take me and sell me, like they do slaves, and no one will care." Fear roared in Nisha's ears. "But I'm supposed to go to the Redeeming!"

"The Council thinks they can sell you for more money than you would bring in at the Redeeming," Matron said firmly. Then she sighed. "Nisha, listen to me. This isn't about you. Akash is trying to get rid of me. He wants to replace me with another tar'Vey to increase his family's power. but first he has to convince the Emperor that I'm incompetent. And taking away my eyes and ears in the Houses is the first step. So far, he hasn't had any way to get to you, but today . . . that changed. If the Council wants to take you and sell you as a bond slave, no one will stop them. Unless–"

Nisha dug her fingernails into her palms, grabbing at the words. "Unless what?"

Matron leaned back and steepled her fingers. "I've been researching the old House rules, and I found one, written long ago, that states a novice with no formal training can get an endorsement from a House Mistress. It was meant to help us place older girls who were sent to us untrained." Again the tiny hint of bitterness tightened Matron's mouth. "The Council decided years ago that we could no longer afford to take the older children, but this rule was never revoked."

"But how does that help me?" Nisha asked, wiping her sweaty palms on the fabric of her borrowed overrobe.

"A House Mistress's word counts for much in our world, Nisha. It's unusual that assistants go to the Redeeming at all–if one decides to leave the City, she usually wants to go home. Your eventual price is an unknown, and Akash is taking advantage of that. If the Council thinks they can profit by letting you go to the Redeeming, they may not sell you now."

If I can get to the Redeeming, Devan will speak for me, Nisha thought. The idea didn't comfort her as much as she hoped. She didn't know what Devan intended. She might have to find another way.

"How long do I have?" she asked out loud.

"There's a Council meeting tomorrow afternoon. If you can find someone to endorse you by then, I can offer that as a solution. But you need to hurry."

Nisha left quickly before Matron could see her shaking. Once in the hallway, she leaned against the wall to steady herself and closed her eyes.

Sell her. They wanted to sell her. The idea filled her chest and paralyzed her muscles.

No. Oh no.

Free servants—like her, like the assistants who served other House Mistresses and worked all over the City—could theoretically come and go as they liked, hire with different masters, and keep all that they earned. Free servants belonged to Wind caste, the lowest in the Empire. But at least they were treated like people.

Bond slaves like Zann were criminals or people with so much debt that they couldn't repay it. Until they paid the price set on them, bond slaves were property.

Even if she somehow had the luck of a good master, Nisha would not be able to walk where she wished, wear what she wished, or say what she wished. And if the price set on her was high enough, Nisha might never be able to pay it back.

She'd never be free again.

I won't let that happen, Nisha vowed to herself. *I'll run away again if I have to.* The idea made her feel sick inside. The woods were full of wild animals, outlaws, and slave traders—slave traders who could claim her as property to sell anyway. Until Nisha took a caste mark, and not a mysterious mark that no one recognized, she was fair game to anyone who claimed her. And if she waited too long, and her bond was sold, she would be considered a runaway slave. She could be sent to the copper mines, a death sentence in itself. Or they could execute her. She would be dead either way.

What was she going to do?

The cats were waiting when Nisha staggered out of the Council House.

What's happened? Esmer asked. *You look like you're about to faint.*

Nisha knelt and pulled both cats close to her for comfort. She couldn't make the words come, so she just let the memory of Matron's news flow from her mind to Esmer's, along with the rapid images of her own fears, and hoped the cats could make sense of her cascading thoughts. Her breathing eased as she let go of the memories, and by the time she finished and stood up, Nisha felt almost calm.

I have to find a House Mistress who's willing to endorse me before tomorrow afternoon, Nisha sent, as she started walking. Her rooms were back inside the Council House, of course, but she didn't feel like going anywhere near there right now. Instead she instinctively walked to the large, winding hedge maze. Nisha often walked through it when she couldn't sort out her thoughts.

If I don't find someone– The fear rose in her throat again, sharp as a knife. *I don't know what will happen.*

Esmer, running along beside her, pulled her ears back. *I can't believe they would do this. This place is changing.* She was silent for a moment. *But it's getting close to Darkfall, and you can't do anything tonight. Go to the greenhouse and make yourself some lemongrass tea. Then come back, eat your dinner, and try to get some sleep.*

It sounded like a suggestion, but Nisha knew it wasn't. Esmer was the closest thing Nisha had to a mother, and when the gray cat spoke firmly like that, she expected to be obeyed.

All right, Esmer, Nisha sent. *I'll try–* Just as she was about to say more, she heard raised voices from deeper inside the maze. She couldn't hear what they were saying, but it sounded like an argument.

Nisha looked down at the cats and laid a finger on her lips. Then she crept forward, trying to follow the sound.

It wasn't easy; the twisting passages tangled like threads, taking you one way just when you thought you were going in another. But Nisha had spent hours in this maze as a child and now, and it took only a few turns before she could hear the words more clearly.

One of the voices was Zann's, raised in protest. "I'm telling you, it won't matter! Vinian won't let me near her House. They'll never let me in there again, not after what I did."

Nisha slid farther down the passageway. The voices were on the other side of the hedge now. If she peered around the corner, she would be able to see who Zann was talking to.

There was a thin, rustling sound, and Nisha realized that the second person was whispering. She couldn't make out the words, but from the way Zann was sniffling, whatever she was being told wasn't good. She sounded near tears.

The girl drew a ragged breath. "All right, I'll do it. But you'd better keep your promise."

Nisha edged around the stiff branches and peered out just in time to see . . . nothing. Whoever Zann had been talking to had disappeared, leaving only a rustling hedge behind.

Zann herself was sitting on the hard dirt, knees drawn up, head buried in her arms. She was crying. Nisha felt a burst of sympathy, and without thinking, she took a step toward her. A twig broke under her foot, and Zann looked up.

"*You*," the girl spit, her face contorting with fury. "This is all your fault." She pushed herself up and ran deeper into the maze.

Nisha, Esmer, and Jerrit looked at one another.

What was that about? Jerrit sent.

A headache pounded at Nisha's temples, and she rubbed her forehead. *Who knows? She clearly doesn't want to tell me.*

She turned her steps toward the House of Jade and the greenhouse. Esmer was right. She needed tea and sleep.

While she could get tea in the Council House kitchens, Nisha didn't care for the strong black mixture the other servants drank. She preferred to make her own herbal teas. *Besides,* she thought, rubbing her arms against the chilly air, *at least the greenhouse will be warm.*

The greenhouse was nestled next to the House of Jade, a beacon lit in the dimming light. It was almost Darkfall. Nisha pushed open the door, and the heavy warmth enfolded her like a cashmere blanket.

She felt some of the tension leave her shoulders. She wasn't good at growing things, but something about being surrounded by the plants made her happy. It was better than being within brick walls any day.

When she was younger, Nisha had tried meditating in the greenhouse to achieve the calm detachment of the House of Jade novices. Sometimes Sashi, one of the Jade girls, would sit with her and offer advice on how to focus on breathing, giggling at Nisha's grunts of frustration.

When Sashi meditated, her face radiated peace. Nisha had never been able to figure out how she did it. Sitting still made Nisha twitchy, and no matter how hard she tried, she couldn't seem to find the same kind of detachment. Next to Sashi, Nisha felt like her emotions were leaking out of her skin.

She plucked a few slender stalks of lemongrass for her tea and made her way to the long back workbench. Sashi was sitting there, as Nisha had suspected she would be. The girl's dark-green Jade asar was wrapped simply, and her dark hair slipped down over her graceful golden neck as she bent over the herbs on her workspace. Her calm expression never changed as she sorted the herbs by touch.

Nisha liked being around Sashi. She had been born blind, but never showed any hint of bitterness about it. If Sashi had been born a noble, a Flower caste girl, she would have been an embarrassment and tossed away. No noble could possess a physical defect so obvious. Had Sashi been born in one of the villages, she would probably have been seen as a burden. But in the House of Jade, the discipline of the mind was more important than the weaknesses of the body.

Nisha took a deep breath and tried to slow her anxious heartbeat.

Sashi straightened up and turned her unseeing eyes toward Nisha. "Who's there?" she called.

"It's just me, Sashi," Nisha said quickly. "Sorry, I didn't mean to scare you."

Sashi relaxed. "Oh, hello, Nisha. Just let me finish up with this lavender. I have to take a new batch of perfumed sachets to the House of Beauty soon." She shook her dark head. "Those girls always ask us for the silliest things. Do they really need every piece of clothing to smell like lavender?"

Nisha found herself smiling. "Well, you know what the Beauty girls would say to that."

"Beauty is *serious* business," Sashi finished, then laughed, a sweet sound, like the echo of a sitt-harp. "I'll be glad to become an official healer's apprentice so I can spend more of my time making medicines." She picked up another slender stem of lavender, stripping off the tiny flowers and adding them to her pile. "Lavender smells pretty, but smelling nice isn't the most important thing in the world."

A hint of sadness strained her words, and Nisha looked more carefully at her friend. "Sashi?"

Sashi's fine, silky hair was coming loose from its tie. It fell over her eyes as she turned away. "It's this last year of healer training," she said. "The master healer tells me that I excel in every area except one. My emotions are not completely under control yet."

"What?" Nisha was too surprised to hide her reaction. "That's crazy. You're the calmest person I know."

Sashi gave an almost imperceptible shrug. "You know what the canon of Jade caste says: 'Two things cause unrest: the accumulation of wealth and the accumulation of affections.' I'm too attached to people."

"You care," Nisha said. "How can that be a bad thing?"

"Because it clouds judgment," Sashi said, with complete conviction. "Just as the infatuation of romantic love makes it hard to see the person you love clearly, too much compassion can get in the way of helping others." She shook herself, and her calm smile returned. "Enough about me. Your step is so tense that I can feel it through the floor."

Nisha fought the urge to tell Sashi about Matron's news. There was nothing Sashi could do about it anyway.

"I am upset," she said instead. "Something awful happened today." In a few quick words, she told Sashi what she'd seen outside the House of Pleasure.

Sashi listened in silence. Her hands played with the lavender stem, breaking it into pieces. "What an unfortunate thing," she said with forced detachment. "The loss of a life is magnified when it's by the person's own hand."

Nisha stared at her. "Unfortunate? Sashi, you don't have to be a healer with me."

"I have to be a healer with everyone. And it's true. Everybody dies. Young and old, rich and poor, we all face the same end. And you can't help if you're paralyzed by the sadness of it."

"But doesn't it *matter*?" Nisha asked. "She was alive and she was important, to Camini, even if to no one else. Just because it's something that happens to everyone doesn't mean we should accept how it happened."

"Nisha . . ." Sashi sighed. "Never mind. I'm sorry. I'm making it worse. It just . . . hasn't been an easy day for me, either." A small, rueful smile flickered across her face, and for a moment, Nisha saw the young girl Sashi used to be. "Forgive me?"

"Of course," Nisha said. "I thought I'd slice up lemongrass for tea. That usually helps."

"That's a wonderful idea." This time Sashi's smile warmed the room. "If you prepare the lemongrass, I'll warm the water for you. I'll add my special ingredient. It's guaranteed to calm the nerves."

Nisha slid her hands into the pockets of her House of Combat tunic, and a piece of paper fluttered to the floor. It was the poem she'd picked up in Tanaya's room. Nisha unfolded the thin rice paper and scanned Tanaya's precise, perfect handwriting.

A frost flower blooms
Beauty is irrelevant
To eyes unseeing

The imagery of the poem tugged at Nisha. Frost flowers were white flowers with red centers that grew during Earthsleep. They were rarely seen, because they grew in out-of-the-way places, alone.

Nisha tucked the poem away. She knew how lonely the frost flowers felt. The words *the Council wants to sell you* still pounded in her brain. And there was no one who could protect her.

No one.

THE NEXT MORNING Nisha began her quest for an endorsement at the House of Music. Wrapped in her saffron-yellow Music asar, Nisha made her way down the thin path that connected the Council House to the House of Music. Despite the seriousness of her mission, she found herself practicing dance steps as she walked. She loved the way her Music asar flowed and swirled around her.

Nisha's steps slowed when she reached the open area where the men were setting up the Redeeming pavilions. The large eight-sided tents consisted of panels of embroidered silk and brocade and were put up early so the House Mistresses and novices could spend days decorating them in the manner they wished. The decorations varied each year, sometimes following rumored fashions from the court, sometimes in entirely unexpected ways to highlight how unusual, how special each House's novices were.

Usually Pavilion Field was just a large swath of grass dotted with nodding white, purple, and yellow flowers. But now the field rang with shouts and mallet blows as builders from the capital city of Kamal erected the thin, strong frames of wood that held up the tents. The flowers and thick grass were hidden by stacks of wooden poles and heaps of colored fabrics. Nisha saw a pile of deep-green brocade with a pattern of swans that she knew would transform into the Jade pavilion. Next to it was a heap of shimmering ruby silk embroidered with parrots that belonged to the House of Pleasure.

On the day of the Redeeming, this field would be even more crowded. House of Music novices would dance and sing stories, Beauty girls would paint delicate ceramics and pour tea, and Combat novices would spar next to their pavilion, all watched by strangers. The chatter and laughter, the swirling crowd—it was the closest thing to a festival that Nisha had ever known.

The only House that would be missing from the fun was the House of Flowers. The House of Flowers alone conducted its demonstrations at the Redeeming masquerade. Over the course of the evening, every Flower novice would demonstrate a full formal Imperial Court bow before the wooden throne. The throne was reserved for whichever noble was overseeing the Redeeming that year. The girl would touch the noble's feet with her fan, bring the fan to her chest, and then give the formal bow with hands pressed together. Everything about it had to be perfect: the message of the novice's asar, her fan movements, the precise angle of her head. There could be no flaws.

The House of Flowers always strove for perfection, since the noble Flower caste it serviced valued flawlessness above all other things. There could be no scars, no permanent injuries among the girls. Nisha had even known girls who were transferred out of the House of Flowers after an accident left them unsuitable in some way.

This year Tanaya would be presented to the High Prince in a ceremony at the height of the masquerade. Nisha imagined it: everyone–nobles, servants, and Mistresses–lining the hall, eyes watching Tanaya's long, slow walk to the base of the throne, waiting as the prince passed his judgment.

It was enough to terrify anyone.

You're deep in thought, Jerrit sent, trotting up next to Nisha. A few bits of bird feathers clung to his whiskers.

"Have a nice hunt?" Nisha asked.

Jerrit sat and began to wash his face with one tawny paw. *An excellent one. And you're dodging.*

Nisha waved her hand at the Pavilion Field. "That," she said. "All that. A place for everyone, and everyone exactly where they belong."

Except you.

"Except me."

Well, I know where you belong, Jerrit sent. *You belong with us.*

Nisha laughed. "Of course I do. But where do *we* belong?"

That's a different question. And I wish I had the answer, Jerrit sent, unusually serious.

"I was afraid you'd say that," Nisha said. "Can you at least help me figure out what to say when I meet Devan? I need to practice."

I suppose, Jerrit sent. *If it will help.*

"It might," Nisha said. "It can't make me more nervous." She sat down on the grass, put Jerrit on her outstretched legs, and looked into his golden-brown eyes.

"Devan," she said, "I want to ask you about the Redeeming."

What about it?

For a moment, fear closed Nisha's throat, the words too heavy to say. But Jerrit's gaze calmed her. If she could say this to anyone, it would be Jerrit.

"I care about you," she said in a rush. "I love the time we spend together. I love how kind and funny you are. I want you to come to the Redeeming and speak for me. If you want to."

Jerrit's oblong pupils were wide and dark. He blinked, breaking eye contact. *That sounds good*, he sent. Then, *If I were Devan, I'd never say no.*

"Unfortunately for me, you're not Devan," Nisha said. "I know he likes me, and that he cares about me, but it takes more than that to want to marry someone."

Jerrit made a low and unhappy sound and jumped out of her lap. *He's not the one risking his life to . . . If he doesn't realize how special you are, he doesn't deserve you. Not that he deserves you anyway.*

Nisha felt her face grow warm and coughed. "We'd better hurry," she said. "Today of all days, I can't be late for my lesson."

She ran the rest of the way to the House of Music, Jerrit running easily beside her. The front entry of the House led straight into the concert hall. It was propped open, allowing the sounds of rhythmic percussion to flow through the half-open door. Under the drums, Nisha heard the faint jingle of ankle bells.

Sounds like they're in the middle of something, Nisha sent to Jerrit. *Let's go around back.*

Through one of the House's long, wide windows, Nisha saw a girl in a yellow tunic and trousers practicing a dance that made her sway like a young birch. Through another, an older girl showed a younger novice how to mend her sitt-harp.

Nisha felt some of her worry ease. This was her favorite House, ever since she had discovered the way music wrapped around her while she danced, keeping out the world, making her feel graceful and free. She would never be as good as Zann had been at playing, but the House of Music—and its Mistress, Vinian—made her feel safe. Maybe she *could* get an endorsement here.

"Nisha!" House Mistress Vinian appeared in the back entryway in a flutter of saffron. Tiny and intense, the Music Mistress always reminded Nisha of a vibrating harp string. Vinian's dark-gray eyes glowed with affection as she reached out to hug Nisha. "Are you here for your lesson?"

Nisha felt Vinian's small, straight frame under her loose asar. "Of course," she said, glad to be there. "When do I ever miss it?"

At her feet, Jerrit mewed.

Vinian looked down and laughed. "Still popular with our local good luck charms, I see. I'm glad someone pays attention to them." She reached out for Jerrit, who ducked behind Nisha, bringing another laugh from Vinian.

"Nisha, after you're done, you must come into the kitchen and have tea with me. I want to know how your Redeeming plans are going."

Nisha knew she needed to jump at the opportunity. "I'd love to! I have something I wanted to talk to you about."

"Wonderful! I've got to oversee the next exam, but come to the kitchen when your lesson is done and we'll talk!" Vinian's intricate braid of black hair swung as she turned, and darted off.

She always overwhelms me, Jerrit sent. *Makes my claws itch.*

Nisha laughed and joined the other girls, who were already going through their stretches. She slid into place next to Tanaya, who gave her a smile. Nisha tried to clear her mind and focus on the warm, loose feel of her muscles, savoring the way her body did exactly what she asked when she asked for it.

Here at least, she was in control.

The dance began, and all she wanted was to lose herself in the rhythm and flow of the music. But as hard as she tried, she couldn't forget her anxiety or let go of the nagging tension in her shoulders. Her movements were blocky, her steps a hair too slow.

Frustrated, Nisha watched Tanaya next to her, envying her friend's easy movements, the way her silken fan danced like a butterfly. All the girls in the class were learning the dance, but only the girls from the House of Flowers danced with fans.

The dance was set to a story-song about the Sune, magical half-animal, half-human creatures that lived in the mountains and forests of the Empire. Nisha had never seen one—they were reclusive and stayed away from humans—but she knew they could switch from animal to human in the space of a breath. It was said they were fierce fighters and loyal to their tribe above all else.

This dance illustrated a fable, a story about a tiger-Sune who fell in love with a human man. She abandoned her tribe to stay with him in a village, but it wasn't long before she became homesick. At the end of the dance, the tiger-Sune returned to her home in the forest, leaving her husband and young son behind.

The steps told the tale, but the fans communicated its emotions. By the end, Nisha lost herself in the story, and when the girls' fans snapped shut in the final beats of the song, she felt her eyes sting with sadness.

She was almost glad to start the cooldown exercises. Dancing was hard work, and she was thirsty and sore.

The moment Nisha sat down in the House of Music's warm, open kitchen, Vinian appeared with two steaming cups of pale golden tea.

"How are you, dear?" she asked.

"I'm well, thank you, Mistress," Nisha said. She wrapped her hands around the warm ceramic and took a deep breath. "But I do have a . . . problem. I told you that Matron asked me to go to the Redeeming this year, but I . . . might not be able to go anymore."

"That's terrible!" Vinian said, her eyes warming with sympathy.

"I was hoping you could help me." Nisha's fingers pressed into the thin clay of the teacup so hard that she thought she might break it. "Matron said if I had an endorsement from a House

Mistress, I would have a much better chance to find someone to speak for me, and to speak for me at a sum that . . . pleases the Council. And I thought, since I love to dance . . ."

Nisha kept her eyes on the ripples of amber tea, afraid to look at Vinian. "Is there anything you can do?"

Now that the question was out, Nisha dared to raise her eyes. Vinian's mouth was very serious, and her fingernails tapped on the glossy surface of her cup.

"Nisha," she said gently, "I would love to claim you as one of mine." She paused. "But I must be honest with you. The market for dancers is getting more and more specific. At last year's Redeeming, I found no men to speak for my generally trained dancers. I had to send them to train at the House of Beauty so they would have a chance this year." The Music Mistress spread her hands. "If I could help you, Nisha, believe me, I would. But I have to save these chances for my own girls. They have no other skills."

The stone that had fallen in Nisha's stomach sank heavier than ever. She pressed her ankle against Jerrit's warm fur underneath the table. "I understand. Thank you."

"Of course." Vinian walked around the table and cupped Nisha's face in her hands. "Good fortune go with you," she said, touching their foreheads together. "You do have the spotted cats. Maybe they'll bring you good luck."

SHE DID SEEM *to* want *to help you,* Jerrit sent, once they were outside the House of Music.

I know. Nisha looked back at the building where she had spent some of her freest hours. *She's always been kind to me, even though I deprived her of her most gifted novice. Sometimes I wonder why she ever forgave me.*

Esmer slipped around the corner of the building. *The person who needs to forgive you is you,* she sent dryly.

And Zann, Nisha sent. *Let's not forget her.*

Nisha and the two cats walked in silence for a few minutes.

Now what? Jerrit sent.

"I don't know, but I have an errand to run for Matron at the House of Beauty first. I was supposed to do it yesterday, but with everything that happened, I completely forgot.

Then . . . well, I'm meeting Devan."

Nisha saw Jerrit look long at Esmer.

Will you ask Rajni for an endorsement? Esmer asked.

Nisha laughed but stopped when she heard the note of pain in her voice. She tried to make her tone light, as if she didn't care. *No chance. There's no place in the House of Beauty for someone like me. Someone like me . . .*

The words ran in a continuous circle in Nisha's head as she washed herself in the brick bathhouse and changed into her plain gray asar. She peered down at the reflection of her face in the waves of water. Heavy hair, wide-set eyes under thick, dark eyebrows, a full mouth. The outline of her tiger mark, half hidden under her asar. Was she pretty enough for Devan? Graceful enough?

Not for the House of Beauty.

But for Devan? He seemed to think so, at least when they were together. But–as Jerrit had reminded her–Devan wasn't risking his life by being with her. Not like Nisha, who was risking everything–

"Hello, Nisha."

Nisha jumped when a voice interrupted her thoughts, a voice like the slide of feathers over iron.

Kalia, the Mistress of Order, had slipped into the bathhouse while Nisha's thoughts floated elsewhere. The woman's pure-white asar set off her silky copper skin, making her glow in the shadows of the bathhouse, and her hair gleamed like a fish-owl's wing. Nisha dropped her head, unwilling to meet Kalia's eyes.

Kalia hovered over Nisha's only clear memories of her first

weeks in the City of a Thousand Dolls. Nisha had been hiding behind someone in a brown-and-gray tunic. She'd watched, frightened, as Kalia stormed out of Matron's study in a rage that she had not gotten the new girl for herself.

"I thought that was you," Kalia murmured. "How are you, Nisha? I wish that I saw you much more than I do."

Nisha had to swallow before she could answer. "I'm well, thank you, Mistress. I do have a lot to do. For the Redeeming." She tried to edge past Kalia and out of the bathhouse, but the woman put out a hand to stop her.

"I heard a rumor," she said. "My cousin Akash told me that your bond might be for sale soon."

Cousin? Nisha willed her fingers not to shake. "I . . . I didn't know you were part of the tar'Vey family."

"Oh yes," Kalia said, her wide mouth stretching in a grin. She lifted her long hair, revealing a small gold tattoo at the back of her neck. "I don't use the name, of course. The girls here have no last names until they are spoken for, so the House Mistresses don't either. They say it helps to curb discontent and status seeking. But I've been a tar'Vey since the day I was born."

A trickle of cold sweat traced its way down the back of Nisha's neck. This was worse than she could have imagined. Nisha would have to be very, very careful.

She pulled away from Kalia's hand, forcing herself to stand tall, hide her fear. "I don't know what Akash told you, but I don't have a bond. I'm a free citizen of the Empire."

Kalia laughed. "Such optimism, but then you are young. The

Houses have fed and clothed you for ten years. If they claim the money that supported you as your bond, who is there to stop them?"

Nisha's chest went hollow with fear.

No one.

Kalia tilted her head. "Maybe I could help you. I need a new assistant. The assistant I have . . . she isn't working. Come and work for me, Nisha."

Nisha suppressed a shudder. Kalia disciplined the House novices. The only time that Nisha had been beaten, it was Kalia who had done it. Nisha's back still bore the scars, a thin crosshatch of marks she would wear for the rest of her life.

"Thank you, Mistress. But it's not the right position for me. I'll wait and hope for the best."

Kalia's smile slipped a little. "Are you sure? You would still have the same status that you have now. I know you think Matron is all-powerful, but she's not." Kalia looked behind her, as if she were making sure they were alone in the dark bathhouse. "Nisha, Matron's time as the leader here *will* come to an end. The tar'Veys will see to it. If you were my assistant, you would still be free and I could protect you from Akash. He's really quite reasonable if you know how to ask. Besides," she said, giving the words a sharp twist, "it's not as if you have many choices."

As far as Nisha was concerned, any choice was better than spending more time in the presence of Kalia tar'Vey. "I appreciate the thought," she said with as much courtesy as she could summon. "But I have plans."

Anger pinched Kalia's thin face. "Be careful, Nisha. I'm not a safe person to disappoint. Think about my offer."

Choking down the refusal that sprang to her lips, Nisha fled out of the bathhouse–and bumped into a stocky figure wearing an off-white asar. Chandra, Kalia's assistant. The assistant who wasn't *working*.

Chandra cringed and looked away. Her eyes were the pale brown of dying grass. There was a beaten look about her shoulders.

"It's all right, Chandra," Nisha said. She bent and picked up Jerrit, waiting by the door.

When the girl saw Jerrit, her drawn face transformed with a smile that lit her up like a shaft of light through an open door. She reached out a hand, stopping just short of his fur.

"Hello, pretty one," she whispered.

"Chandra," Kalia said from the doorway. "Come here. Now."

The smile vanished and Chandra froze, quivering on the steps. Her eyes were huge and hunted. Then, head down, she hurried past Nisha and into the building.

"You see?" Kalia said, her voice conversational, when Chandra had disappeared. "She's far too timid for my liking. But you"–and with the speed of a snake strike, the Mistress of Order seized Nisha's arm, her eyes glittering–"you're different."

Nisha willed herself not to jerk away. Kalia's fingers dug into her arm, sending sparks of pain from her elbow to her fingertips. Jerrit hissed. His ears lay flat against his head.

Let me scratch her. Please.

No, Nisha sent. *If I do anything that could be interpreted as defiance, she could punish me. I can't go through that again.*

"Kalia." Josei, the Mistress of Combat, materialized out of nowhere. Her dark, red-brown hair was pulled back from her forehead, and her fingers twitched on the leather-wrapped hilt of her short sword. "Is there a problem here?" she asked, quietly but clearly.

Kalia dropped Nisha's arm. "No problem, Josei. Nisha and I were just discussing her future."

Josei didn't look at Nisha when she said, "I do not think Nisha's future is any of your concern. You are needed in the Council House."

"Of course." Kalia gave a tight smile, then turned to Nisha. "If you have work to do, go do it. You don't belong out here."

Without waiting to thank Josei, Nisha hurried away and spit to try and get rid of the helpless, sour tang that coated her tongue. She felt like a trap was closing around her, tighter every day.

I have to escape. Soon, or I'll be wearing bronze cuffs by dinner tomorrow.

Her wrists ached to think about it.

The House of Beauty girls were just sitting down to the lunchtime meal when Nisha slipped in. House Mistress Rajni was deep in conversation with someone, and Nisha didn't want to interrupt. Instead she pressed herself against one wall of the large dining room and watched the girls.

The novices sat in two long rows on either side of the table, and from a distance, they all looked curiously alike. Smiles showed straight teeth, careful nods accented dark hair that shone like candlelight on water, hands gestured with slender brown fingers.

Even the ritual of eating lunch looked like a dance as the girls delicately placed paper-thin chicken slices, fine-grained basil rice, and mangoes that had been cut into the shapes of flower petals into their perfectly painted mouths.

Nisha fought the urge to roll her eyes. Instead she listened carefully to the flow of words, the way Matron had taught her.

I found the perfect shade of sorrel paint for the tree branches on my fan. It will show up wonderfully against the ivory.

No, you have to put the bellflower stems in the middle. They droop too much if you put them on the side of the arrangement.

I'm supposed to serve tea to the Council tomorrow. I'm so nervous. What if I spill? You know the tea ceremony is supposed to be perfect.

Nisha focused in on the nervous girl, looking for undercurrents that might mean she was growing restless or discontented. But the girl didn't seem resentful, only anxious, so Nisha moved her attention back to the room at large. Most of the girls were talking about clothes.

What asar will you choose for the masquerade?

Deep blue silk with a pattern of white geese in flight. And I'm wearing milkstones in my hair.

I have a new asar, this gorgeous cream color with dark-blue and yellow embroidery and an edging of gentian flowers. They stand for sparkling conversation, you know. And the man who is speaking for me sent me a necklace to wear. Silver with topaz stones. I'll have to show it to you.

You're lucky. I have no idea who might speak for me yet.

But that just makes it more exciting! Think of all the handsome noble-men who will be there!

The conversation dissolved into giggles and whispers, and Nisha moved on.

The Beauty girls might sound frivolous, but they were artists, and skilled ones. If the House of Flowers was dedicated to per-fection and the House of Jade to discipline, the House of Beauty was devoted to loveliness in every form. Everything beautiful here came from the girls. All the food had been arranged by the novices, as had the bouquets of orchids and lilies that dotted the long table. Each novice was an expert in the art of creating beauty, especially when it came to her own. They were trained not to waste a word, a movement, a look, to present themselves in the best possible way.

Because of their ability to create flawless environments, girls from the House of Beauty were in high demand, and the House was full of novices. They were the favorites of wealthy merchants and noble families who did not need their sons to marry for polit-ical power. Every girl here was certain to be picked.

When Nisha caught Rajni's eye, the House Mistress waved her over.

An important part of Nisha's job at this time of year was mak-ing sure that every House Mistress had everything she needed in advance of the Redeeming. A House could underestimate the amount of supplies it needed. Nisha's task was to fix that, or bet-ter yet, to ensure that the supplies didn't run short in the first place.

 79

Fortunately, Rajni needed only a few small accessories that had to do with the girls' costumes for the masquerade: more ribbons to tie masks with, extra eye paint, and more hairpins. Nisha jotted the list down on a small piece of parchment and left to find Matron.

9

MATRON WAS STANDING in the largest of the Council House kitchens talking to the cook about preparations for the masquerade. She nodded to Nisha when she saw her. "I'll be right with you, Nisha."

The kitchen was large and bustling, with earthen ovens, a fireplace, and several cracked wooden tables. The back door was open as servants came in and went out, bringing food from the storage cellars. The heat from the ovens fought with the draft from the open door, making the air move on Nisha's skin.

Matron gave the cook her last instructions and approached Nisha. "Are all the Houses ready for the Redeeming, Nisha?"

"Almost." Nisha handed her the list of items that Rajni still needed.

Matron read the list, her brow creased in thought. "You might check the House of Flowers for ribbons. The girls at the House of Pleasure will probably have enough kohl to give some to Beauty."

Nisha nodded. "It's going to be the hairpins that are difficult. There are never enough this time of year."

Matron's smile crinkled her eyes and made her look years younger. "I know. No matter how many I order to be made, they always seem to disappear. It's as if you girls are eating them." She handed the list back. "Just do the best you can. If all else fails, we can tell Rajni that wearing your hair down is the latest fashion in the capital."

Nisha giggled. "She'll love that."

"And how are the girls?" Matron asked. "Are they all still excited about the Redeeming? Any problems?"

"Not in the House of Beauty," Nisha said, pushing down the usual niggle of guilt that came from telling secrets that weren't hers. "Just the usual nervousness. Lots of talk of clothing, giggling about who they might meet, that sort of thing. The girl who's serving tea in the Council House tomorrow seemed a bit anxious."

"Ah, yes. That would be . . . Lilamayi?" Nisha nodded. "I'll see if I can give her some encouragement before she goes in." She looked hard at Nisha. "You seem uncomfortable."

Nisha shrugged. "The eavesdropping bothers me. It's like I'm stealing something from them and they don't even know it."

Matron let out a sigh. "I understand. That's never been your favorite part. But what you do is important, you know that."

Nisha knew. Many times she had been able to spot an unhappy novice before she went too far in her training. In each case, once Matron knew about it, the girl could be sent to another House or her training would be adjusted to suit her personality and her strengths.

Before Nisha had come to the City, other girls had tried to run away. In one infamous case, a girl even committed suicide. But no one had run away or killed herself since Nisha had become Matron's eyes and ears, and Nisha felt good about that, even if she hated how she had to do it.

Suddenly Atiy's glassy stare intruded into Nisha's thoughts. She pushed it away, shuddering. She could not have helped Atiy. Atiy had been isolated from everyone, with no one to know of her unhappiness, apart from Camini and any other trainer working with her. If she really had killed herself, it was *their* fault.

"Have you found anyone to endorse you?" Matron's soft question interrupted Nisha's thoughts. "The Council meeting is this afternoon." Matron's eyes were on the kitchen staff and her words were was casual, but Nisha could hear an undertone of worry in her voice.

"Not yet," she murmured back.

Matron didn't look at her. "Have I ever told you that there's a school for older orphan girls in the capital? They teach basic trade skills. All the girls there are destined for a lower caste, but they're able to earn a living. And you have lots of skills already, Nisha, that would serve you well in the capital."

"That's . . . interesting," Nisha said carefully.

Matron turned away. "I'll leave that list in your capable hands, Nisha. We'll talk tomorrow."

After Matron left, Nisha sat down to warm herself by the fire. She leaned her head against the stone of the fireplace, taking comfort in the waves of heat that rolled over her. The fire snapped and sparked, the coals glowing like living jewels. Nisha closed her eyes, ignoring the bustle around her. The warm stone hearth was an island, a shelter in the midst of chaos.

But if she ran and the school didn't take her, what would she do then? Without a caste mark, she wouldn't be able to work in any city or town. She would starve, or worse, be captured by slavers. If she was able to join a Wind caste caravan, she might be able to get a mark. But in order to find one, she'd have to go into the forest, and the forest terrified her. Besides, how could she leave the cats, her friends, and Devan?

Nisha shook herself. Running away was too uncertain. She had to find someone to endorse her.

There was a commotion, and she looked up just as Tanaya swept in. Her hair had been gathered into an intricate pile of curls on top of her head, and she was wearing a black silk asar with tiny brown owls embroidered on it.

"Where are the *jeera* puffs?" she demanded. "The envoy from the High Prince will be here soon, and half the tea isn't ready!"

The cook gave Tanaya a hurried bow. "Forgive me, lady. I

thought House Mistress Indrani said the tea wasn't for another quarter hour."

Tanaya's lips tightened. "*I* am telling you that the tea needs to be ready at once," she snapped. "Now do your job."

"Of course, lady." The cook ducked her head, and Nisha felt a stab of pity for her. All the free servants on the estate were Wind caste, forbidden to settle in one place without a work permit. If the woman lost her place, she would have to become a nomad, sleeping in a different inn every night, or camping in the forest until someone hired her again.

"See that you do," Tanaya said. Then she turned and stomped out. Concerned, Nisha left her place by the fire and followed.

"Tanaya, what's happening?"

Tanaya whirled around but relaxed when she saw Nisha. "Oh, it's you."

Nisha just stared at her. "Are you all right? I've never heard you speak to a servant like that before."

Tanaya chewed her bottom lip. "I'm sorry. It's just . . . this is so important, and everything has to be perfect. I feel like everyone's waiting for me to make a mistake—"

She sighed and patted Nisha on the shoulder. "You're right, of course. I'll apologize to the cook later. I cannot *wait* for this to be over!"

"I know." Nisha reached up and squeezed Tanaya's hand. "Good luck."

Tanaya smiled at her. "Thanks. I'll need it." Then she turned and walked down the hallway.

A low mist rose as Nisha made her way down the broad stone path winding from the central gardens to the gates of the City to meet Devan. Dim, gray fog twined around her ankles like silver ribbons. Its touch was cold on her skin, reminding her that the season of Earthsleep was fast approaching. Nisha's future would be decided by then, no matter what it was.

She went out through the wide main gate, brushing her hand over the thick stone of the wall. She'd touched these rocks many times over the years, and every time she promised herself that someday she would climb the nearby stairs and stand at the top of the gate.

Novices were forbidden to walk on top of the wall around the Houses, and Nisha had never dared it. But she wanted to. She wanted to see the tops of the trees, watch the leaves rattle with birds and monkeys and see the gray threads of mist weave through the forest. As much as she feared the woods, she was also drawn to them by a longing she couldn't explain. Maybe if she saw them from above, her fear would fade.

Once outside the wall, Nisha took a few experimental steps toward the trees. The teak forest loomed ahead of her, threatening and dark. There was a faint sound that might have been a wolf call. The thought sent a jolt of fear through Nisha, and she turned to run back to the gate.

A twig snapped like the crack of a whip.

Nisha froze, as still and alert as any forest deer. Slowly, she turned. A dark shadow ghosted along the line of trees, then stopped. It was just far enough inside the forest that Nisha couldn't make it out clearly. But it was human-shaped and broad at the shoulders. As the shadow shifted, Nisha caught a flash of eyes.

Then it moved forward, resolving into a man. His face was in shadow, but his clothes were rough and worn, and there was a red scarf tied around his neck.

A Kildi.

Nisha shrank back, pressing herself against the wall. Devan had mentioned Kildi in the area, but she hadn't really believed him. There hadn't been any Kildi camped near the City of a Thousand Dolls for years. What were they doing here now?

The man stared at her for what felt like a long time. Then he waved and dissolved into the woods, vanishing so completely that Nisha could almost believe she had imagined him.

Almost.

NISHA PRESSED HERSELF against the damp wall and waited. For a long time she saw nothing but the swirling threads of mist, heard nothing but the restless rustle of branches, and smelled nothing but wet leaves.

Then her ears caught the trip of a horse's hooves coming down the road. A graceful white mare clopped into view, and a warm anticipation loosened Nisha's insides.

"Devan!" she called. "Over here!"

Devan pulled his horse up with a flourish. "I have crossed terrible wastes to give you this, my lady," he said, brandishing a leather bag of scrolls.

"You and your terrible wastes," Nisha said, smiling up at Devan's open grin. "Kamal is only a few hours away on horseback, and I've heard it said that the road between here and there is one of the best maintained in the Empire."

She reached out to rub the horse's silken nose. Devan laughed as the mare huffed a breath of grassy air into Nisha's face.

"My horse is jealous of you. She wants to be the only female in my life."

"Deservedly so," Nisha said. "She's lovely. Our last courier only had an old pony."

"Ah, but Yerek is not a nobleman's son," Devan said evenly. "He's the son of the Emperor's accountant, and he'll always be just a courier." He swung himself out of the saddle and tied the horse to a nearby tree. "No noble blood, no horse."

He lifted Nisha into his arms and whirled her around. "I'm so glad to see you. You wouldn't believe the morning I had. Everything stamped triple urgent, and the Emperor in a foul mood. The Court of Lesser Princes continues to shout about Prince Sudev marrying a girl who might have blood from the lower castes, the Merchants' Circle is complaining about trade prices, and the western farming villages sent another petition about repealing the two-child law. I'll be glad when Sudev and Tanaya are married so things can calm down again."

Suddenly he kissed her, deep and sweet. The strength ran from Nisha's knees like water. Devan pulled back and grinned at her. "That's more like it. How do you always manage to make my day better?"

"I do? Really?"

"It's true." Devan raised one hand. "I swear on the grave of my great-aunt."

"Your great-aunt? What kind of oath is that?"

"You never met my great-aunt," Devan said.

Nisha tickled him and he retaliated, starting a wrestling match that ended with his mouth warm and strong on hers. Their lips parted only for them to laugh.

In these moments, Nisha thought, it was so easy to believe she loved him, so easy to think that everything would be all right.

Half breathless, they sat against the wall, Nisha's head on Devan's shoulder, his arm wrapped around her.

"How is your family?" Nisha asked hesitantly. Maybe he would tell her about Akash tar'Vey, the mysterious new head of the Council and the man who wanted to get rid of her.

A shadow flickered across Devan's face. He shook his head without answering.

Nisha nestled closer and waited.

Devan leaned his head against hers. "My father is still angry that I ever took this position. He thinks being a courier is too base a job for a tar'Vey. After all, you don't have to be noble to do it."

Nisha held on even tighter to Devan. "But what do you think?" she whispered.

"I don't know," he said. Real anguish ripped through his voice. "I've had this job only a short time, but I love it. The peace of the road, the different places I get to see, the people I've met, it's so different from the Imperial Court. But my father . . . he's worried that my acceptance of this 'low' job could reflect badly on our family." Devan scowled. "I'm the personal courier to the

Emperor himself. Why can't that be good enough? If everyone has to give at least two years of service to the Empire, why can't mine be something I enjoy?"

He turned to Nisha, his face inches from hers, his dark eyes intense. "You're the only truly good thing in my life. You know that, right?"

Nisha wanted to ask him right then–about Akash, about the Redeeming, about everything–but her throat closed up and she could only nod. Devan kissed her lightly on the nose, and then pulled her close for a deeper kiss. His hands tangled in Nisha's hair, his palm slid over her waist, her hip, leaving a trail of heat behind. For a moment, Nisha wanted nothing more than to let go of her fear of being caught, to give in completely.

But if we get caught, I'm dead. Dead like Atiy.

The thought was as unexpected and chilling as a bucket of well water. Nisha stiffened.

"What's wrong?" Devan asked, pulling away to look at her. "Are you all right?"

Nisha was shaking. She couldn't speak for a moment. The risk she was taking had never seemed as real to her. Seeing Atiy, her young, broken body, made it sink in. If anyone discovered her with Devan, Nisha could be dead tomorrow, her body burned, and her name forgotten.

"Nisha." Devan was saying her name and shaking her lightly. "Nisha, what is it? Did I do something wrong?"

Nisha shook her head, pushing the tears away. "I'm sorry," she managed. "It's just . . . I'm scared."

"Of what?" Devan said. "Of us?"

Nisha swallowed. "Of what will happen if they find out about us," she said. "If they know . . . You're a tar'Vey. I'm a nobody. If they find out about us, I could be executed."

"Really?" Devan sat up straighter, and his forehead furrowed. "I didn't realize they still did that." He fell silent. "Nisha," he said at last, lifting her chin to look at him. "Nisha, do you remember the first time we met? I was late with my first mail delivery, and you had fallen asleep waiting for it."

Nisha rubbed her eyes on her sleeve. "You almost ran me over with that horse of yours. I thought I was being attacked by a monster."

Devan laughed deep in his chest and pulled her closer. "I'll never forget how you looked when you stood up, your hair flying everywhere, scared and sleepy at the same time. I thought you were a spirit of the woods at first. And then you started yelling at me."

"I didn't know who you were!" Nisha said. "I was horrified when I finally saw your mark. You could have had me punished for speaking to you like that."

"But I didn't tell anyone," Devan said. "Because I didn't want anything to happen to you, my beautiful wild girl." His thumb brushed the side of her jaw, and he kissed her softly on the forehead. "I protected you then, and I'll protect you now. I won't let anything happen to you, Nisha. I swear."

Nisha bit her lip. She wanted to beg Devan to take her away with him today, to take her to a place she felt safe. But she knew he couldn't. The only way they could be together was if he came and spoke for her at the Redeeming. "Devan, would you–" She swallowed. "I mean, have you ever thought–?"

Rerewww!

A high-pitched yowl cut the air, and Jerrit flung himself over Devan and into Nisha's lap. The noble swore as fur flew everywhere.

Nisha scrambled to her feet, trying to contain the cat. Jerrit jumped to her shoulder. His paws pulled at her hair, and he yowled again.

"What's wrong with him?" Devan yelled.

"I don't know." Nisha winced as claws dug into her shoulder. "I've never seen him like this!"

What in the name of the Ancestors are you doing? she sent.

Look. Jerrit's tail lashed.

Nisha turned just in time to see Zann come out of the gate, a large clay pot in her hands.

Oh. Nisha was suddenly glad to be grappling with a cat. It wasn't dignified, but now she had a good explanation for her mussed hair and rumpled asar.

"What's this?" Zann asked, her narrowed eyes flickering from Devan to Nisha.

Jerrit was still trying to climb Nisha as if she were an *arjin* tree. It was Devan who answered.

"Isn't it obvious?" he said, brushing the cat hair off his tunic. "This girl's animal went crazy and we were trying to contain it." He sneezed and rubbed his red eyes. "May I suggest that you cull your cat population?" he said to Nisha. "There are altogether too many of them, and they're very bad mannered."

Still trying to pry Jerrit off her shoulder, Nisha opened her mouth to answer and caught a whiff of the stuff in the pot that Zann was holding. It smelled horrible, like spoiled meat. Nisha almost gagged.

Devan covered his nose. "What in the name of the Ancestors is that? And why would you bring it out here?"

Zann scowled but kept her eyes down. "It's rotflower extract, sir. I'm supposed to dispose of it in the woods. It attracts too many flies to dump it inside the walls."

"I can see why," Devan said. "Well, I certainly don't want to wait for the flies to show up." He untied the horse and swung himself up into the saddle. "I won't be here tomorrow," he said, looking at both girls. "The Emperor has other work for me at court." His eyes lingered on Nisha for a heartbeat, a glance she felt like a physical touch on her skin. "But I'll be back in three days. Let your matron know that, won't you?" Then he turned and rode away.

With another yowl, Jerrit sprang out of Nisha's arms and ran into the woods.

Nisha turned to Zann, hoping desperately that the disgraced girl hadn't seen them talking or suspected anything if she had. But Zann no longer seemed interested in the retreating courier.

Instead she stared at Nisha, her lip curled with disgust. "Look at you," she said. "You're a mess." Without warning, she swung the pot at Nisha, splashing some of the foul green liquid onto her sandals.

"That's better," Zann said, and walked away.

Nisha was still staring after her when Jerrit poked his head out of the woods.

Is she gone?

"Yeah," Nisha said, wiping her foot on the rough grass. "But so is Devan. Now I'll have to wait three days to talk to him again."

I know, Jerrit sent. *But I saw Zann too late to warn you, and jumping on you was the only thing I could think of.* His tail drooped. *I'm sorry.*

"You're forgiven," Nisha said. "But for a moment there I almost killed you. I didn't even know you could shed on purpose."

I have no idea what you're talking about, Jerrit sent. *And I might not like Devan, but at least he can think on his feet. He might have more than hairballs for brains after all.*

Nisha scooped up the bag of scrolls. "Well, that's nice of you," she said, rolling her eyes. "Come on. I'll put these in Matron's study; then you and I can try to figure out what to do next. Council meetings always last forever; maybe there's still time."

After dropping the scrolls, Nisha and Jerrit walked through the hedge maze. Nisha kept a wary eye out for Zann, but the girl wasn't anywhere in sight.

Halfway through, Jerrit stopped, the hair on his back standing up. *Do you smell that?*

Smell what? Nisha sent. *All I can smell is this muck Zann splashed on my shoe.*

Jerrit growled, the sound sending a prickle along Nisha's spine. Then he crouched and crept forward. Stepping carefully, Nisha followed him to the center of the hedge maze.

The fountain at the heart of the maze was a round, three-tiered tower built of polished gray stone and inlaid with lapis lazuli surrounded by short velvet grass. Water danced over the edge of each pool. They stopped at the fountain's edge. Jerrit's growl intensified, and a whimper escaped Nisha's throat.

Not again.

A DARK-HAIRED GIRL lay crumpled facedown in the large bottom pool. Her overrobe was in disarray, and the dark green of her asar had fallen off her shoulder, revealing wet brown skin and thin shoulder blades. Her black hair drifted in the fountain's trickling flow.

Nisha took a step. "Is she–"

Jerrit crept a little closer and sniffed the air. *Yes,* he sent, his mind-voice more serious than Nisha had ever heard it. *But freshly dead, no more than a few minutes.*

Death is following me. The thought came out of nowhere, and Nisha backed away from the fountain. "Jerrit," she said, "stay here and don't let anyone touch her. I'll go get help."

Nisha darted through the maze, trying not to let her growing sense of panic overwhelm her. She didn't want to get lost. Once she broke out of the high hedge walls, she looked around for someone, anyone.

Luck was with her. Nisha had come out on the side closest to the House of Jade, and the first person she saw was Sashi. The blind girl was sitting outside the greenhouse with several other Jade girls, all engaged in repotting a collection of soft-leaved licorice plants. Sashi wore an emerald-colored long-sleeved tunic under her asar for warmth, and her face was intent as she carefully transferred her chosen plant from one clay pot to the other.

Nisha tried to look calm as she walked up. No need to frighten them, especially since she didn't know who the girl in the fountain was yet. She could be one of these girls' closest friends.

Sashi looked up, wrinkling her forehead. She smiled when Nisha placed a hand on her shoulder.

"Is that you, Nisha? Have you come to help us with these plants?"

"I wish I could," Nisha said, forcing her voice to stay light. "But I need a favor. Does one of you have a piece of paper I can use?"

All four girls pulled pieces of rice paper out of their pockets. Nisha fought a hysterical giggle. She quickly took the paper and a proffered writing stick and wrote a brief note.

Please come to the fountain at the center of the maze. Something terrible has happened.

Nisha signed her name and folded the paper several times. "I need to get this to Matron. Is there a servant around who can take it?"

"I'll take it," one of the Jade girls said. "I'm supposed to go to the Council House and drop off some blank scrolls for Matron."

"Thank you." Nisha forced a smile. "Can you make sure she gets this as soon as possible? It's important."

After the girl took the message, Nisha looked down to see Sashi's face turned toward her with a puzzled expression.

"I have to go," Nisha mumbled, biting her lip to keep herself from telling Sashi what she'd found. She turned and darted back into the maze.

Nisha ran all the way back to the body. She had the horrible feeling that she was going insane, that when she got there, the girl would be gone, vanished back into her imagination.

But the body in the fountain was still there, as dead as it was before. Jerrit sat by it like a guardian statue.

Anyone come by? Nisha sent.

The spotted cat shook his head. *No, but I did see a bunch of seeds scattered around.* Jerrit jumped down, sniffing through the grass. *Maybe she was eating them.*

Nisha squatted down. The seeds were almost lost in the grass, but she recognized them immediately as *mukhwas*, an after-dinner snack made of sugared anise, fennel, coconut, and sesame seeds. The red and green seeds also dusted the edge of the fountain.

Maybe she choked on the mukhwas mix? Jerrit sent. *Or slipped and fell?*

I don't know, Nisha sent. She turned away from the body. *I wish Matron would come. I should have gone myself. I just didn't want to*

99

leave the body far too long. . . .

When Matron finally came hurrying through the maze, she wasn't alone. Josei was with her. Matron made a small choking sound when she saw the body. Josei went very still.

"What happened here?" Josei asked quietly. Her direct stare made Nisha feel like a deer confronted by a tiger.

"I–I don't know," Nisha stuttered. "We found her like this."

"We?" Josei looked down at Jerrit, who was sniffing her foot. "Ah, I see."

Matron took a deep breath and stepped closer to the drifting death in the fountain. "What do you think, Josei?"

The Mistress of Combat knelt and brushed the girl's clinging wet hair aside. Ripples from the movement wrinkled the surface of the water, and the edges of the girl's asar bobbed like a dead leaf. The tips of her narrow fingers were puckered and wrinkled, like lizard skin.

Nisha took a deep breath. The air was getting colder, sending goose bumps over her arms. Jerrit jumped from the fountain's rim and rubbed against her leg.

Are you all right?

No, Nisha sent.

I need to find Esmer, Jerrit sent. *But I don't want to leave you alone.*

It's all right. Nisha bent down and ran her hand along his back. *Go on. I'll call you if I need you, I promise.*

Jerrit touched her ankle with his satin nose. *I'll hold you to that.* Then he turned and trotted away.

Josei looked up, her light-brown eyes pinning Nisha in place. "I need help lifting her," she said. "Can you handle it?"

Nisha swallowed, forcing down the sick feeling in her throat. "Yes, I'll help."

It was harder than she thought it would be. The body was slippery and limp, and the soaked asar clung to Nisha's arms as if trying to drag her down into the fountain. The girl's wet hair covered her face, and water dripped like tears from her fingers. Nisha tried not to think about who she could be holding as they laid the girl facedown on the grass.

"Did she drown? Slip and fall?" Matron asked, with a note of fear that Nisha had never heard before.

Josei shook her head. There was a patch of wet on her tunic, the rust-brown fabric reminding Nisha of dried blood. "No," she said. "This wasn't an accident."

"Not an accident?" Matron asked sharply. "How do you know?"

Josei gave a deep, sad sigh. "Because it looks like she was poisoned." To punctuate her words, she rolled the body over.

It took Nisha a moment to realize what she was seeing, and when she did—when she saw the staring, sand-colored eyes, the mouth permanently twisted with pain and the hands bent into rigid claws—she felt her throat burn, her stomach thudding into nausea.

Josei gave her a sharp look. "If you're going to be sick," she said, standing up, "try not to do it near the corpse."

"I knew her." Nisha forced the words out. "I saw her just yesterday."

Josei's eyes narrowed. "Yesterday," she repeated.

Nisha nodded. She felt weak and shaky, and the garden began to spin into a thousand mazes. "I saw her in the crowd, after . . . after we found Atiy. I spoke to her." She turned away from the body. "Her name was Jina."

12

NISHA LEANED AGAINST the brick walls of the House of Combat and took several deep, shuddering breaths. She welcomed the way the cold air burned her lungs, the hint of ice in the air. The ache in her chest meant she was alive.

Why Jina? she thought. *Jina never hurt anyone in her life.*

Josei came out of the back door of the House of Combat, holding a rough clay cup. "Here, drink this."

Without thinking, Nisha grabbed the cup and took a big swallow. The hot, bitter drink seared through her, giving her a short coughing fit.

Josei laughed, a harsh sound like a parrot's squawk, and took the cup back. "It's not tea, Nisha. You don't just gulp it down."

"What is that stuff?" Nisha asked, wheezing a little.

Josei handed her the cup again. "It's called *kafei*. The Kildi swear by it. They say it clears the mind and gives energy."

Nisha took the drink gingerly and sniffed at it. It definitely wasn't tea. The liquid was dark and glossy, and there were hints of ashes and earth in its rich scent.

The smell triggered a memory: a campfire, a wagon loaded with bags and boxes. A small, bubbling pot that gave out the same dark, spicy smell, a woman's sure hands on the handle. And her own little-girl self squatting back on her heels, her fingers drawing aimlessly in the dirt as she stared at the ribbons of white-orange flame . . .

A hand touched Nisha's shoulder, startling her.

"Drink up," Josei said, as if she hadn't noticed Nisha's distraction. "I need you alert."

Nisha sipped at the drink obediently, trying to force her mind back to the present. She rarely had those flashes of memory anymore. She rarely thought about the parents who had left her behind. But now the old feelings of loneliness twisted together with everything else inside her, and she felt like crying.

The *kafei* helped, the smoky, bitter taste sliding over her tongue. She focused on that, pushing everything else aside, and by the time she finished the cup, she was back on balance.

"Better?" Josei said.

Nisha nodded. "Much better," she said, taking in her surroundings.

They were standing behind the group of buildings that made up the House of Combat. A few steps away was the small, thickly wooded area that the Combat novices used to practice their woodcraft in. Nisha could hear starlings calling to one another from the treetops. The air was thick with the scent of hay from the nearby stables.

"Why are we here?" Nisha asked. She vaguely remembered Josei leading her away from the maze and the body, remembered stumbling over her own feet and Josei holding her up.

Josei started walking, forcing Nisha to run after her. "Matron is at the House of Jade, breaking the news of Jina's death to the House Mistress. We'll meet her there when we're finished. But right now, I need to know everything you know about Jina and about yesterday."

"I don't know much," Nisha said cautiously. "Jina and I spoke sometimes when I was at the House of Jade. She was training to be an archivist. She loved history more than anything and would talk about it for hours."

Josei turned down the path that led to the armory, Nisha still trailing behind her. "Did Jina ever seem depressed? Or likely to take her own life?"

"You mean commit suicide?" Nisha asked, startled.

"She was poisoned," Josei pointed out. "I don't know how yet. That's for the healers to determine. But I do know that poison is a popular choice for suicides."

Nisha's mind rebelled at Josei's assumption. "I can't imagine Jina wanting to die. She was too absorbed. I don't mean selfish," she added, remembering the other girl's smile as she handed Nisha her overrobe. "Just . . . preoccupied. Even finding Atiy's body yesterday didn't seem to sadden her. She was too busy taking notes."

Josei seemed to consider this for a moment; then she went into the armory. She emerged with two long *lati* sticks and tossed one to Nisha.

"Come on," she said, making the formal salute that Nisha recognized as both compliment and challenge. "I think better when I'm moving. Besides, I've been watching you practice. I'd like to test your skills."

Nisha made the ritual bow of acceptance. Her hands shook, and she gripped the bamboo staff firmly to make them stop. "This seems like an odd way to question someone," she muttered to herself.

Josei pretended not to hear her, but a wisp of a smile, like mist, passed across her face.

They ran through the forms of the fight, the sticks swirling around them like a dance.

"So Jina was there when Atiy's body was found?" Josei asked, moving into an attack form, both hands on the staff and her right foot forward. "Did she say what she was doing at the House of Pleasure?"

One end of Josei's polished staff whipped down and Nisha pivoted, twisting her wrist to bring the low end of her stick up in a block. Their sticks had barely touched before Josei was moving into a defense position, with her knees bent and hands spread apart.

"She said she was researching love poems," Nisha answered. "I think it was part of her Redeeming presentation." She brought her stick up, and Josei blocked it.

"Good," the House Mistress said, showing her teeth in a smile. "Now let's really fight."

Nisha's stick made a blur around her as she tried to get around Josei's defenses. She whirled, aiming for the House Mistress's knee, but Josei leaped away. She avoided the strike completely, and then swept her staff toward Nisha's feet. "Did she say anything else?"

Nisha stumbled out of the way, raising her staff to absorb the next blow. "She thought Atiy might have been killed by Shadow-walkers," she said, then froze in horror.

Josei aimed a blow at her head, and Nisha ducked too late. The metal-tipped staff struck her on the shoulder. Pain shot through her arm.

"Don't ever let down your guard while in the middle of a fight," Josei scolded. Then, "Did you believe her? About the Shadow-walkers?"

Nisha shook her head. "I told her they didn't exist. If there was a House like that on the estate, I would know." Nisha shifted into an attack stance and flung herself at the Combat Mistress, causing Josei to step back.

"Would you?" Josei asked, blocking Nisha's strikes as quickly as Nisha could make them.

A thin trickle of sweat ran down Nisha's temple, and she felt her respect for Josei increase. By keeping Nisha focused on the fight and distracted from Jina's death, Josei was getting more honest answers than she might have if Nisha had had time to think about what she was saying.

"Do you think Jina was poisoned because she found out something dangerous about the City?" she asked the Combat Mistress.

"I think nothing," Josei said calmly, pivoting gracefully. Her stick turned so fast that Nisha couldn't follow its line of movement. "I'm gathering information. Why haven't you tried to run away again?"

The abrupt shift from questions about Jina to her own story caught Nisha completely off guard. She almost dropped her staff. "What?"

Josei stepped into the gap Nisha had opened up, planted her front foot in the ground behind Nisha's left foot, and shoved.

Nisha fell, slamming into the dirt, and Josei flicked the tip of her staff to rest against Nisha's throat.

"I asked you, why haven't you tried to leave the city? You're getting restless, there's no place for you here in the eyes of the new Council Head, and you have no bond to pay off. Yet."

All the energy drained out of Nisha, as if the hard ground she lay on had sucked it up. Her cheeks felt sticky and hot. "You know about that?"

Josei pulled the staff away and sat cross-legged on the red dirt across from Nisha. Not a hair was out of place on her head. She wasn't even breathing hard.

"Matron told me," she said. "She's worried about you. She hinted to me that it might be better for you to leave now than to wait until after the Council meeting."

"She didn't tell me that," Nisha said. "Is that why you've been following me? Does Matron think I'm in danger?"

Josei shrugged. "Matron doesn't like to do things directly, especially when it's something that could put her at odds with the Council. She prefers more . . . subtle ways of working. But I think she might be right this time."

The thought of running away brought a panic back into Nisha's throat. There were wolves in the woods, wolves and bandits and slave merchants. Even the Kildi man she'd seen in the trees would be a danger.

"I can't," Nisha said. "I know what's out there. I saw it the first time I tried." She closed her eyes against the memory: the sight of the man's tattered flesh and torn tunic and the dark blood staining everything. "There's nothing out there for me but death."

Josei gave her a curious look. "You might be surprised. The woods are dangerous for children, but you're not a child anymore."

Nisha rubbed her shoulder, still stinging from where Josei had whacked her. *Maybe I'm not a child. But that doesn't mean I can survive out there on my own, either,* she thought.

She stood up. "Thank you for the practice, House Mistress. Is there anything else you wanted to ask?"

Josei gave Nisha a piercing look, and Nisha shifted her feet. She wanted to trust this woman, wanted to tell her the fears and worries that swarmed in her chest, but she couldn't. If Matron couldn't protect her, then Josei couldn't either. Nisha was on her own.

"I'll do it," Josei said, rising to her feet. "I'll endorse you. You're a good staff fighter, you pay attention to what is around you, and you have a nose for when something's crooked or off. I think you'd make a very good guard."

Nisha was struck dumb. She followed Josei as the woman returned the *lati* sticks to the armory. Through the open door of the building, she saw a young man repairing a bronze hand-shield. The youth's hair was a few shades darker than the shield he was working on, and it fell over his forehead, almost to his eyes. He wasn't anyone Nisha had seen before. Josei must have a new assistant.

Sometimes outsiders came to train with Josei; they helped her for a few months, learned from her, then moved on. Nisha didn't usually pay much attention to them. She wasn't interested in building a friendship with someone who was only going to leave.

As if he sensed her gaze, the young man lifted his head and looked through the doorway. When he saw Nisha staring at him, he winked.

Nisha felt her face grow warm. It was impolite for this stranger to make direct eye contact with a girl he didn't know. And it was certainly impolite to wink. Out of the corner of her eye, she saw him smile, and her face got hotter. She was only too glad to follow Josei down the flat stone path leading to the House of Jade.

This part of the City was devoted to lotus ponds. The calm water seemed to rebuke Nisha for her worry. Tiny green-and-black frogs hopped from glossy leaf to glossy leaf, croaking to one another.

After a few minutes of walking silently, Nisha couldn't contain her questions anymore.

"Why?" she demanded, not caring if it was rude. "Why do you

care what happens to me?"

Josei stopped on the path and held up one brown hand for Nisha to see. "Because I am also an outsider," she said. Her hand began to shimmer like a rock when seen through river water. It wavered and blurred into a paw with brown fur and dull black claws.

Nisha breath caught with awe. Carefully she reached out and touched the paw. The dark pads were dry and rough under her fingers.

Josei's eyes shone gold for a moment, and a fierce, wild pride crossed her face. Then her eyes darkened to gold-flecked brown, and her paw became a calloused hand again.

It was a moment before Nisha's tongue could form words. "You're Sune?"

In those days—before the Ending, before the Barrier—magic was everywhere. It was in the land, making it fertile. It was in the water, keeping it clear and full of fish. And it was in the people. Most people had some form of magic, even if it was only an awareness of the power that flowed through the world. But only a few people were powerful enough and driven enough to actually use it. The old magicians said controlling the magic was like trying to change the course of a cascading waterfall. One slip and the magic would break loose and spray everywhere.

From the scrolls of Naveen ka'Lyer, Jade caste historian

13

"HALF SUNE," JOSEI said, starting to walk again. "My mother belonged to the Shrilah-Sune, the fox clans. My father was a scout for the Imperial soldiers. They met in the forests of the south, on the slopes of the Mountains of the Dead. They might have stayed together, but he was killed when he stumbled on a nest of bandits."

The path turned to a wooden bridge over the largest of the lotus ponds. Josei stopped and leaned on the railing, looking out over the flower-spotted water.

Nisha copied her, studying Josei out of the corner of her eye. Now that she was looking for it, she noticed the Combat Mistress's's faint musky scent that lay under her normal smells of dirt and sweat.

"Well," she said finally. "No wonder you're so fast."

Josei threw her head back and laughed. "Sune are faster and stronger than humans, it is true. The magic makes our senses sharper and we heal more quickly. But I have trained hard as well. And I do know what it is like to be on the outskirts of every place you go, to have to choose your own future because no one else will choose it for you. Half Sune don't develop the power to change to animal form until they're fully grown. My mother was one of the wild Sune, and she didn't know what to do with a human child. When I was old enough to care for myself, she left."

There was no sadness in Josei's words, just acceptance. For a moment, she looked very animal.

Nisha thought about her own parents leaving her in the City. She hadn't been old enough to care for herself, so why had they abandoned her? And why couldn't she remember more about them?

"I wish I were Sune," Nisha said, looking down at the pond below. The lotuses' sweet scent rose up to the bridge. "Then I could turn into a fox and get away from here."

"It is a curse and a gift, just like anything," Josei said. She paused. "How much do you know about how the Sune were made?"

"Just what everyone knows, I suppose," Nisha said. She gestured at the unchanging gray sky. "The songs say that the Sune were formed five hundred years ago, when the Empire was cut off. The magic that made the Barrier splashed onto some of the animals."

"Is that what they're teaching these days?" Josei shook her head. "Interesting. You at least know how the Barrier appeared, don't you?"

"Of course," Nisha said, preparing to recite the old story from memory. "The magicians of the Old Empire worked a spell to see the future, and what they saw was destruction. They saw the river flood its banks, saw the earth shake and an invading army so vast that no one would be able to stand in its way. The magicians of the royal court–which included the Emperor and his sons–found a spell that would protect the Empire. But the spell was so large that it would take the life of everyone who cast it and would remove magic from the land forever. So they sacrificed themselves and died raising the Barrier. But with no magic and no leaders, the people fell into chaos until the First Lotus Emperor took power and restored order."

Josei burst out laughing, startling Nisha.

"Nisha, that's a wonderful tale," she said. "But it's not at all what happened."

"It's not?" Nisha frowned. She'd heard the story-singers in the House of Music sing the history of the Empire many times. She was sure she'd remembered it correctly. "What do you mean?"

Josei sighed. "Nisha, the Sune sing this tale too. According to them, the magicians of the Old Empire were careless and arrogant. They found a spell they thought would work and cast it without proper care. The Emperor wanted big magic, something that would make him memorable in history. The Emperor's councilors protested, but he didn't listen. The spell was cast, but it was far too big and burned out of control. When the dust settled, the Empire was cut off from the rest of the world and every magician was dead."

"So the magicians did die, like the songs say."

"But it wasn't just the magicians," Josei said. "What your songs don't tell you is that the spell also killed every man, woman, and child with a breath of magic in them and stripped the land of its own power. The Empire went from being a country where magic was everywhere and in everything to a barren place. Fewer than one in ten people survived. And in the mountains on the edge of the Empire, where the Barrier touches the ground and the magical backlash was strongest, all those who did not die were twisted into animal forms."

"Is that why no one goes into the mountains anymore?" Nisha asked. "They say there are monsters there."

Josei pulled away from the railing, her footsteps creating a dull echo on the wooden planks of the bridge. "I don't know about that." Nisha followed her, and Josei continued, "But I do know that it took that first generation a long time to learn to change from one form to the other without getting stuck. And some of them couldn't survive the change. But those who did became the Sune, doomed to live as both animal and human. The full Sune cannot hide their true nature, because when they are sick or injured, they revert to animal form. That's why most Sune keep to the wild places, preferring their animal bodies to their human ones. They want nothing to do with humans, because the arrogance of humans made them what they are."

The story Josei was telling was so far from what Nisha had been told her whole life that she found herself at a loss for words. How terrified the people must have been, after losing so much. Especially the first generation of Sune, struggling to survive in their new forms.

"Why don't they tell us this?" she asked.

Josei shrugged. "Probably because a story of sacrifice sounds better than a tale of mutiny. You see, the Old Emperor didn't die in the magical cataclysm. He was one of the survivors. But one of his own advisers took advantage of the people's fury and confusion and led a rebellion. The adviser's supporters overthrew the ruling family and established themselves as the new leaders of the Empire. The land was so damaged and wouldn't yield crops for years, and there weren't stores of food enough for everyone, so the new Emperor—the first Lotus Emperor—declared martial law and a two-child limit on every household."

And that's why the City of a Thousand Dolls exists. Nisha looked back at the lotus pond as they left the bridge for the stone path. This part of the story she knew as well as she knew her own. *We're here because no family can have more than two children, and because people want sons instead of daughters.*

"But why are you here?" Nisha blurted before she could stop herself.

Josei's face went still, as if she'd pulled a mask down over her features.

"I owed someone a life-debt," she said. "Working here, training these unwanted girls to be warriors, that was my payment."

"Really?" Nisha stopped in surprise. Life-debts were the most serious contract in the Empire. When Josei didn't stop, she ran to catch up, her mind spinning.

Life-debts were rare. You had to save someone from certain and immediate death, and the debt was only canceled when both people agreed that it had been paid. Who could have saved *Josei*? Nisha had just scraped up enough courage to ask her about it when they reached the House of Jade.

Matron was standing near the greenhouse, anger in every line of her stiff frame, and she wasn't alone.

The tall, severe man standing next to her was someone Nisha had never seen before. He was about Matron's age, muscular and flat bellied as a river crocodile, with some of the crocodile's waiting stillness. His black hair, with a touch of gray at the temples, was slicked back, and it touched the high collar of his brown-and-silver brocade tunic.

Josei's voice dropped to a whisper. "Remember this, Nisha. You cannot change what's been done, no matter how hard you want to. But you can go on."

With those cryptic words, Josei disappeared into the House of Jade.

Nisha turned to face Matron and the stranger. As she did, Nisha's eyes met the man's for just a moment. His gaze was flat, predatory. Adrenaline shot down her back, made her want to flee as far away as she could.

She bowed, trying not to let her anxiety show on her face.

Matron spoke in a controlled tone. "Nisha, this is Akash tar'Vey, the head of the City Council. He has . . . something to tell you."

Akash tar'Vey gave her the same evaluating stare the two Council members had given her outside the Council House the day before. "We have had an offer for your bond," he said, his voice cruelly like Devan's. But instead of flowing warmly over her, Akash's voice was cold and slimy, like the oil from a cart axle.

Nisha pressed her palms together and bowed again, hiding the sudden panic she felt. "Forgive my confusion, sir, but I was told that if I could get an endorsement, I might be able to bring in more money. And I *have* found someone willing to endorse me. The Combat Mistress has said she will do it."

Akash pressed his lips together in an imitation of a smile. "An admirable gesture, but where there is one offer, there might be more. The buyer is willing to pay a higher price than we expected. It's enough money to cover the cost of training a last-minute replacement for the girl, which will please our important client greatly. I can see no reason to risk that assured money by allowing you to go to the Redeeming."

Anxiety stiffened Nisha's spine. Who would offer so much money for her?

Matron's hands clenched into tight fists. "Akash, I have said already that we must bring this offer to the Council to discuss the right way forward." Less evenly, she added, "This high-handed behavior is completely unacceptable. I will make sure the Emperor hears of it."

Akash's voice grew colder. "Remember, Matron, there are

those in the court who would like to shut us down. I have no intention of seeing that happen. This City is a merchant's dream. Unwanted girls are worth nothing, but trained wives and mistresses, girls bred to please and obey, are far more valuable. With a few adjustments–more guards, stricter discipline–this City could be more than self-sustaining. It could be a source of riches and power like nothing you have ever imagined."

"That is not why we are here." Matron folded her arms, her words sharp. "You know that. That is not what the City is for."

"It might not be why you are here," Akash countered. "But the Council feels quite differently. They quite like the picture I've been painting for them. As long as we keep the City running, the Emperor doesn't care how we do it. And I am not the doddering old man that my predecessor was. He might have been content to let you run this place according to your idealistic notion of helping girls, but I am not. These girls are a source of income, a commodity like spices or tea."

Some of the fire died out of Matron's face with this assertion. Nisha's anxiety turned into pure, cold fear.

The gold of Akash's flower tattoo showed as he straightened his tunic. "We can discuss this later," he said. "In the meantime, Nisha's price will go some way toward replacing the money we lost from yesterday's unfortunate accident."

Then he walked away, leaving Nisha staring after him. "He's really going to sell me, Matron?"

Matron started to say something, then nodded once, a final, sad nod, like the closing of a gate.

Nisha couldn't breathe. It was really happening. The Council could just sell her, like a piece of furniture or a herd of cattle.

Kalia's words whispered through Nisha's mind. *If they claim that money as your bond and sell you to make it back, who is there to stop them?* And she was right.

Nisha thought of Zann, trapped in the City, forbidden to play music ever again, with no hope of a different life. Nisha's future was uncertain, it was true, but at least she had always held rights as a free citizen, and the possibility of a different future.

But now her rights were worthless, and she was the one who was trapped. If they sold her . . . she would be just like Zann, but worse, probably. The healers at the House of Jade were kind masters. They allowed Zann plenty of food and adequate rest. They didn't beat her. If Nisha was bought by a cruel master, she would be considered his property. He could do anything to her, even kill her, and no one would be able to stop him.

No one would care enough to stop him.

Bright Ancestors, no.

Her fear curdled rapidly into panic. "You can't let them do this." She hated the begging sound of her voice, but she could not stop herself. "Please. Please don't let them do this to me."

The lines around Matron's mouth deepened. "I've been trying to hold them off, at least until after the Redeeming. I told them I need you too much to give you up. Akash is very anxious to finalize a deal. But I won't stop trying–"

Nisha couldn't hear any more. Nausea and terror had her now, and without thinking, she turned and fled into the maze.

Behind her she heard Matron call her name, but she couldn't stop running.

The labyrinth closed around her, and Nisha dodged through the narrow alleys, running blindly until she hit a dead end. Leaning against the high hedge walls, she bent over, emptying her stomach into the bushes. Again and again she retched, her stomach clenching in pain.

No, no, no, no, no!

Kalia's words from yesterday pounded in her head, given a cruel new twist.

You don't belong here.

You've never belonged here.

You'll never belong anywhere.

NISHA! JERRIT'S CRY brought her out of a trance. She looked around to find herself surrounded by cats. Nisha wiped her mouth and sank to the ground, pressing her back against the prickly branches. The cats nuzzled close.

"They're going to sell me," Nisha said, the shape of the words making her feel sick again. "They're going to make me a bond slave."

The group exploded in startled growls.

They can't do that!

What are we going to do?

They promised!

Enough. Esmer's voice was as sharp as a sword's point. Her black-tipped tail lashed, and the other cats fell silent.

Esmer, we can't let this happen, Jerrit sent. He held his head low, ears back, and the fur on his spine stood up like the bristles of a paintbrush. *You can cast me out if you want, but I won't sit by and let it happen, no matter what secrets we swore to keep–*

Esmer hit him. The gray spotted cat struck so fast that Nisha barely saw it, burying her claws in Jerrit's scalp. Jerrit yowled but didn't strike back.

A low, ragged growl came from Esmer, and her lips pulled back to reveal her teeth. Her paw didn't move from Jerrit's head. *Don't you dare lecture me about what we swore to do. Or act like you're the only one who cares what happens to Nisha. You're not the only one who would bear the consequences of a broken oath. The tribe stands together, Jerrit. What happens to one affects us all.*

Nisha held her breath, her own fear momentarily forgotten. She'd never seen the cats argue like this.

Under Esmer's paw, Jerrit was still making small angry noises, but now his ears seemed more flattened in submission than in fury. The growl died from Esmer's throat, and she retracted her claws.

Her mind-voice was as sad as Nisha had ever heard it. *We aren't going to sit by, Jerrit. But we have to be careful.*

Jerrit sat up, his tawny fur still on end. His tail twitched. *I'll try.*

"But how can we stop it?" Nisha said. "What can we possibly do? The Council could come and get me at any time." Akash had free run of the Council House and the estate. Nisha wasn't safe in her room. She wasn't safe anywhere.

Esmer padded to Jerrit's side and licked his ear.

Can you sleep outside Nisha's door? she asked him.

Of course. Jerrit's ears were upright again and his fur was smoothing. He looked around at the other cats, silently watching. *I'll take a couple of the others.* He looked up at her, his sleek frame stiff with emotion. *We'll watch over you, Nisha. No one will get past us.*

The idea of having sentries outside her door made her feel a little safer.

But she also knew that nothing would ever make her feel completely safe again.

Nisha couldn't sleep. Despair wrapped her like a heavy shroud. She tried to drive it away with memories of the way Devan kissed her, the way he smiled just for her. But her mind's images of Devan kept morphing into visions of Akash's cruel smile. Then Akash's face twisted into Jina's, frozen in pain, then flattened into Atiy's wide, dead stare.

Nisha sat up. Her skin was damp with sweat, and her hair stuck to the back of her neck. Her tiny, windowless room was hot and suffocating. *Trapped.* She longed for the cold, sharp air outside.

It was almost time for the White Mist, the heavy cloud that would rise from the ground every morning and evening. Ever since the Empire had been cut off, the cold season had been marked by thick mist and frost. The people of the Empire would pull on woolen asars and long-sleeved tunics, wear soft slippers and boots instead of sandals, and keep their ovens lit for warmth. The parrots would fly to the warmest parts of the deep forest, the deer and monkeys would grow thick, shaggy fur. And everyone would wait for the warmth and life to return to the world.

The cold season was called Earthsleep.

But it had always made Nisha think of death.

Nisha gave up trying to sleep and swung her feet onto the floor. Tonight she didn't want to be alone. Rising in the darkness, she felt her way out of her bedroom. She thought about bringing one of the clay lamps she always kept by her bed, then decided against it. In the unbroken black of Darkfall, her tiny light would be visible for a long way, and she didn't want anyone wondering what she was doing outside in the dark.

The minute she stepped into the narrow back hallway that separated her room from the rest of the Council House, she felt a press of fur.

I hoped you'd come out, Jerrit sent.

I'll say. He's been staring at your door like a lost kitten since you went to bed, said one of the other cats.

Jerrit growled, but Nisha smiled for the first time since her encounter with Akash tar'Vey.

The night air was cool on her skin as she stepped out the side door, and Nisha stretched out her arms to the ink-dark sky. The world suddenly seemed open and less frightening.

Aided by the cats' soft pressure on her ankles, Nisha crept down the road to the hedge maze and found a sheltered corner deep inside the labyrinth. The dense grass tickled her skin as she lay down. Warm, furry bodies pressed against her as other cats joined them. Esmer murmured in her ear, and the purring creature on her chest could only have been Jerrit.

Nisha hugged him like a shield and slept.

She woke to cold, damp grass and wet air. A low mist rose from the ground, a white soup that soaked Nisha's night-robe and chilled her skin. Beside her, Jerrit hissed.

Isn't it too soon to have the White Mist? he sent, growling.

"I guess not," Nisha said as she rose to her feet, brushing twigs and bits of grass from her damp sleeping gown. The first morning of White Mist was always the thinnest, but it was still wet enough to make her shiver. "It's almost the season of Earthsleep."

The gray, even expanse of the sky glowed softly with a new day, and Nisha caught the fading scent of the night-queen flower on the fresh air. It made her think of Tanaya. Maybe when Tanaya was a princess, Nisha could ask her for help. And if all else failed and she had to run, she had the cats. Maybe the stories about their being good fortune were true. For a moment, the idea of going into the forest seemed a little less frightening.

Pah. Jerrit tried to lick the water off his thick fur. *The old cat legends say that water used to come from the sky, and all you had to do to stay dry was crawl under something.*

Nisha laughed. The idea of moisture coming down, instead of seeping up, was oddly funny to her. *Esmer told me some of those tales,* she sent. *I like the ones with fish as large as bears and lakes the size of the entire Empire.*

I like those too, Jerrit sent. He licked his lips, showing sharp white teeth. *And speaking of fish* . . . He gave Nisha a hopeful look, and she rolled her eyes.

Come on, she sent. *Let's get breakfast.*

Good. I'm hungry. Jerrit slipped after her as she headed reluctantly for the Council House. Some of the other cats rose, stretched, and followed.

You're always hungry, Nisha pointed out. There was gentle mind-laughter from the cluster of cats behind her, and Jerrit swiveled his ears.

It's because I'm a mighty hunter, he sent. *Takes a lot of energy.*

If you were a mighty hunter, you'd be off hunting your breakfast with Esmer instead of waiting for scraps, Nisha teased, and went in the back door of the Council House to scavenge for the cats' breakfast.

It was more of a symbolic chore than anything. The cats could—and did—hunt the mice, birds, and small game of the City. But spotted cats were considered good luck, and part of the ritual to maintain that luck was to give them an offering every day.

Plus, the cats loved the meaty scraps soaked in goat's milk that Nisha set out for them. By the time she got back, the shoving, mewing crowd was about twice as large. The cats waited with restrained eagerness until Nisha set down the large platter; then there was a rush for the food. The mews and growls were replaced by contented chomping. Nisha watched them for a moment, then smiled and went to grab some figs and a slice of brown bread for herself before her chores.

Nisha liked her morning chores. She liked dusting the shelves in Matron's office and polishing the low teak desk until she could see her reflection like a ghost in the wood. The Council House was quieter in the morning, and it was easier to think here, away from the crowds of girls.

This morning there was a map left half unrolled on Matron's desk. Josei's story about the Old Empire still fresh in her mind, Nisha took a moment to examine the map.

There was the long, platter-shaped valley that made up the bulk of the Empire. Dangerous mountains, and a wide black oval that designated where the Barrier touched the ground, ringed the valley. Five Sacred Rivers, spread out like a fan across the Empire, each branch joining the main river at a different point. There were the wheat and barley fields of the west, the copper and gem mines of the south, and the large spot on the central river that designated the capital city of Kamal.

Now that Nisha was actually looking for it, she could see that most of the Empire remained deserted. There were only three cities of any size on the map; Kamal was, of course, the biggest. Then there was Deshe, the city second in size to Kamal, overlooking the farmlands. Aranya, a fortress city, rose high in the wild forests of the east. Everyone else lived in towns or in the tiny villages that lay like scattered rice over the map.

And then there were the ruins. Nisha touched the dark marks that designated the abandoned cities, wondering what they had been like when they were new. When the Empire had been full of people and full of magic.

Her fingers moved to a small star inked into the woods not far from the capital. Someone–Matron maybe–had written *City of a Thousand Dolls* in flowing script next to it. And under that was a small note.

Preserve at any cost.

She set the map down again on Matron's desk.

Nisha moved to the Council library, a large, rectangular room lined with shelves holding piles of rice-paper scrolls, scrolls that held the history of the Empire. She dusted them and checked the pages for decay.

Her mind wandered while her hands cleaned. Half-formed plans, slices of memory, and bits of conversation flowed past like grain falling out of a sack. She thought about Devan while she cleaned, imagined when she'd see him again, what he'd say, then turned to the jostling crowd of cats. A smile tugged at her lips as she remembered the first time she'd ever fed them. She had been in the City only a short time, a lonely little girl who still cried for her parents. Watching the cats had made her smile. Her first smile since her father had left her at the gates.

She'd smiled even more when a kitten broke from the group and waddled toward her. And her smile had turned to wide-eyed wonder when the kitten had fixed her with his golden eyes and spoken straight into her mind.

My name is Jerrit. What's yours?

Nisha had never cried alone again.

The thought of tears turned her mind to Zann, crying by herself in the maze. What had she been asked to do that made her so sad? Zann was bound to the House of Jade now, trapped in the

City for life as a bond slave, banned from the House of Music and from what she loved.

The familiar ache of guilt started again, and Nisha's mind flew back to the day Zann had asked for a favor. . . .

Nisha was ten years old and was as lonely as she had ever been her first days in the City. Sashi had begun her more rigorous training as a Jade healer and no longer had time to talk and play in the maze after tea. Tanaya, who had always made time to speak to Nisha, had just been chosen for the High Prince. She could talk of nothing else, and it made Nisha feel young and out of place. Nisha had always known that she wasn't going to have a secure future like her friends, but seeing their excitement only made her feel more like an outsider.

So when Zann, the brilliant musician whom Vinian had been crowing about for months, asked if it was true that Nisha had access every place on the estate, Nisha had said yes. It made her feel important, telling Zann that she could go anywhere in the City. It made her feel like she mattered.

When Zann had asked her if she could get to the records of the girls who had been spoken for, Nisha had said yes again.

And when Zann asked her to sneak into Matron's study and see if anyone had expressed interest in speaking for her, Nisha– flattered by all the attention–had said yes to that, too.

It was a mistake. Zann, who was dreaming of a musical apprenticeship in the capital, was devastated to learn that she was to be married instead, and to a man old enough to be her father. She had flown into a rage, slamming her door in Nisha's face.

The next day Matron had called Nisha into her study. Kalia was waiting there, a cold smile on her face and a whip-thin rod in her hand. The burning pain of the rod whipping across her back, the overwhelming shame—Nisha still remembered them vividly enough to make her shudder.

But it was the guilt over Zann's punishment that had overwhelmed Nisha, driving her to the one thing she'd never dared to do.

Run away.

Nisha swallowed and set down the dusting rag, remembering.

It had been difficult to slip past the guards who had stood at the gates then, but somehow Nisha had managed it. She had sneaked out of the City and made it deep inside the forest. She was running and looking over her shoulder and she never saw the body.

The man had been a Wind caste outlaw, a thief caught by the Emperor's soldiers days before. The soldiers had wounded him and tied him to a tree for the wolves. It was the death sentence usually given to men like that. The law said they weren't worth the cost of execution, so common outlaws were simply left to die. Leaving the body far into the woods kept the wolves away from the main roads.

Nisha had tripped right over his legs, slipping on his exposed intestines and covering herself with his blood.

But the worst part hadn't been the body. It had been the howls and barks of the wolves nearby. To a little girl, they were hungry, vicious noises that spoke of sharp teeth and red, wet mouths, torn flesh. Panicked, Nisha had run back to the City.

She hadn't ventured more than a few steps into the forest since. Not even with Devan.

As if her dark thoughts had conjured them, Nisha suddenly felt unfriendly eyes watching her. Goose bumps rose on her arms. She raised her head and saw Zann in the library doorway.

15

ZANN HELD a basket full of stoppered jars, the kind the healers used for storing medicines. Her hair fell in messy strands over her forehead. Her bronze wrist cuffs were crusted with dirt.

"You saw her yesterday, didn't you?" she said, staring at Nisha. "The dead girl, Jina, you saw her."

Nisha wondered what Zann was asking. "I was there."

"Did it look like she died in any pain?" Zann asked. A worry line creased between her eyes. Her hands gripped the basket so hard that her fingers turned white. "Or was it just like she died in her sleep? Did she look peaceful?"

"She looked dead, Zann," Nisha said, wishing the other girl would just go away. Her head was throbbing. "I don't want to talk about it."

Zann opened her mouth as if to say something, then pressed

her lips together. "I– Never mind," she snapped. "I should have known you wouldn't be any help."

She stalked away as Nisha stared after her. Zann's behavior was growing odder. Maybe it was the strain of seeing another Redeeming come and go without her. Or maybe she was–

Nisha's musings were interrupted by a thud behind her.

Whirling around, she scanned the room, her every sense alert. Low bookshelves marched in orderly rows down the middle of the library. Behind one of them, something was moving. In a low crouch, she crept closer.

There was a rustle of paper, the swish of fabric on the rug. Nisha peered over the top and saw Chandra, Kalia's assistant, huddled behind the shelves. She was absorbed in a scroll spread out on her asar.

"What are you doing?" Nisha asked, forgetting to be quiet.

Chandra jerked her head up, her wide eyes meeting Nisha's. Terror poured off her in an almost visible wave. Then Chandra scuttled backward like a pond-crab until she hit the next bookshelf. She flung her arms up over her head and closed her eyes.

"It's all right," Nisha said. "Chandra? I'm not going to hurt you."

Chandra didn't open her eyes or respond, just curled in on herself like a dried leaf.

Nisha tried to move closer, but Chandra whimpered in fear. That whimper, along with the girl's helpless, huddled body, made Nisha sick with pity.

Chandra was clearly doing something she wasn't supposed to,

and she was obviously terrified at being caught.

Nisha didn't want to leave her here, but how could she get Chandra out of the library? If she touched her, the girl might scream. And if Chandra screamed, she'd be discovered, and if she was discovered, Kalia would punish her.

Punish them both.

The thought sent a jolt of fear through Nisha, and she almost turned around.

Nisha? Esmer sent, her voice dim with distance. *Did something happen? We're outside, and we felt your fear.*

I'm fine, Nisha sent. *But I do have a problem.* Quickly she sent Esmer a picture of the cowering girl.

Esmer's normally sharp voice softened. *Poor child. Stay with her; I'm on my way. We'll have to sneak in.*

All right, Nisha sent. *Don't get caught.*

When Esmer arrived, she was not alone. A female named Rashi, her spots almost lost in her deep brown fur, padded close behind. Behind them came Brill, a sleek tom with beige streaks on his sides, and a tiny gray-brown female with rust-colored spots who answered to the oversized name of Valeriana.

The four cats gathered in a loose circle around Chandra. Nisha looked at Esmer, whose coat shone like a freshly polished sword.

What is this? Nisha asked. *Why all the cats?*

We will sing away the fear, Esmer sent. *This child has been terrified for long enough. We will give her some of our strength and help her find her own.*

Jerrit padded in and sat next to Nisha. *I've heard about this* ceremony. It's used only under the most extreme circumstances. I've never seen it before.

There was a smile in Esmer's voice when she sent, *Well then, both of you, watch and see.*

As if they'd rehearsed it in advance, Brill and Rashi curled up on either side of Chandra. Esmer draped herself over the girl's feet, while Valeriana wriggled into the hollow of her curled-up body.

Esmer's tail flicked once, and the cats' voices rose in a soft harmony. The low purrs and warm mews merged into an intricate melody, filling the room. *Safe*, they sang. *Safe, warm, loved.*

Chandra cracked her eyes open. Her arms, which had been stiff with terror, relaxed, and she uncurled the defensive huddle of her body.

The cats did not stop singing. *You are strong like the forest*, they purred. *Resilient as the river. Nothing can twist you, nothing can break you. You will survive.*

Without looking at Nisha, Chandra picked up Valeriana. She held the tiny cat to her cheek, and the loneliness on her face tore Nisha to the bone. It reminded her so much of who she had been without the cats.

"Chandra," Nisha said.

Chandra gathered the cats closer, holding them as a shield. Then she lifted her head to meet Nisha's eyes.

"Chandra," Nisha repeated as gently as she could. "I'm sorry I frightened you."

Chandra nodded.

"Are you supposed to be in the library?" Nisha asked.

The girl shrank a little but answered. "No," she said, her voice barely above a rustle.

"I won't tell Kalia," Nisha said.

Chandra picked up a rice-paper scroll covered with delicate watercolor drawings. Tensing as if expecting a blow, she handed it to Nisha.

"A botany scroll?" Nisha said.

"I like plants," Chandra said. "Plants don't care what House you are or what caste you'll be." Her voice grew stronger with every word. "They give their beauty to everyone, and all they ask is to be cared for. Kalia won't let me go to the greenhouse because she thinks it a waste of time. So sometimes, when Kalia doesn't need me, I come in here to look at the pictures, learn the names." She went pale. "If Kalia finds out I'm here–"

"I won't tell," Nisha repeated, knowing Chandra needed to hear it again. "I promise."

Chandra looked unconvinced. The slump of her shoulders sent a pang of sympathy through Nisha.

"Is there . . ." Nisha hesitated. "Is there anything I can do to help you?"

"No." Hopelessness twisted Chandra's mouth. Her lips were rough and chapped, as if she were drying up like an old riverbed. "No one can help me."

Nisha, Esmer sent. *The Council members are starting to stir and come down to breakfast. If you leave, we can help Chandra sneak out. She'll follow us.*

Nisha rose, obeying the clear order in Esmer's tone.

"Good-bye for now, Chandra," she said.

Chandra looked up. Shadows, like the echoes of a nightmare, filled her eyes. "Stay away from Kalia, Nisha. Don't trust her." Then, as if those words of warning had taken all her strength, she dropped her eyes.

Go, Esmer prodded. *We'll take care of her.*

Nisha slipped out the library door, Jerrit following close behind.

There was a tawny spotted tom stretched across the doorway, guarding it. Nisha couldn't remember his name, but she smiled at him as she stepped carefully over his long body. She was rewarded with a slow blink of thanks.

Jerrit leaped over with a careless twitch of his tail, and the tom growled but didn't move.

Are you going to the armory? Jerrit sent.

Nisha glanced down. *How did you know?*

You're touching your tiger mark again, Jerrit sent. *That's how I know you're upset. And when you're really upset, you go to the House of Combat and ruin Josei's practice dummies by beating them with your staff.*

Not even Chandra's warning echoing in Nisha's ears could keep her from smiling at that. *I suppose I do take my frustrations out on them,* she sent. *And it sounds like a wonderful idea.*

Of course it is. And Josei can help you figure out what to do next.

I hope so, Nisha sent, going into her room to pull on her Combat tunic. *I really hope so.*

When she reached the armory, Josei was nowhere in sight. Her new assistant was sitting at a table, polishing a curved sword with a wicked edge. He looked up as she came in and Nisha reddened, remembering the wink he'd given her. But this time the young man simply gave her a nod and went back to cleaning the sword.

Feeling a little snubbed, Nisha turned to the wall of weapons. Fighting sticks, daggers, short swords, spears, and long-handled maces all hung with military precision. Low storage chests along each wall held padded leather armor, along with cleaning and mending supplies.

Nisha fingered a *lati* stick of polished bamboo. The wood felt cool and comforting under her hands.

Josei's assistant rose and hung the sword on its proper hook. He looked at the *lati* stick Nisha was holding and grinned. With surprising grace, he pulled a shorter fighting stick of dense ebony off the wall and held it one-handed, twirling it slowly. He raised one eyebrow at Nisha, a clear challenge.

Nisha knew she should refuse. The City allowed few men within its walls, and the girls were forbidden to socialize with them.

But she was tired. Tired and angry and scared down to her bones. And today she didn't care about the City or its rules. The idea of fighting someone who wasn't testing her sounded even better than beating the stuffing out of a practice dummy.

So instead of shaking her head and walking away, Nisha put

down her long staff and picked up a matching fighting stick. She moved to the center of the open floor, muscles ready and knees bent.

Come and get me. I'm not afraid of you.

The attendant's grin widened, and he attacked.

He was good, Nisha thought, blocking him as he lunged at her, but it was all natural talent. He moved like someone who hadn't been fighting long, his form sloppy but effective.

He was *fast* though. It was all Nisha could do to keep pace with him, and every time she thought she had him pressed against the wall, he would spin away. They fought one-handed, which meant a longer reach than Nisha's usual two-handed style. But it also meant sometimes they got very, very close.

Once Nisha struck at him, and he deflected her stick up. Her momentum brought her close enough to see the gold flecks in his brown eyes. For a moment they froze. Then Nisha gave him a wicked grin and hooked her foot behind his, shoving against his hard chest with her free hand.

The assistant fell. But instead of sprawling on the floor, he tucked his body in, executed a perfect roll, and came up on his feet. He grinned at Nisha, who found herself laughing.

"At least you can fall properly," she said. "More?"

The attendant tossed his stick from one hand to the other. His hair had fallen over his forehead, and his eyes were full of silent laughter. He nodded, and they started again.

Soon the fight fell into a rhythm so perfect that Nisha could almost hear the beat of drums underlying every step. Sweat dampened the back of her tunic, and her hair was coming loose from its tie and she didn't care. For a few wonderful moments there was no past, no future, nothing but her and him and the clack and rattle of sticks.

16

SOMEONE COUGHED. NISHA froze, body half extended in a strike. The assistant straightened up and held his fighting stick straight up and down at his side. Nisha turned her head to see Josei watching them.

Heat flushed Nisha's cheeks, followed by a wave of anger. Why shouldn't she practice with whoever she pleased? She folded her arms, waiting for Josei to scold her.

But the House Mistress wasn't looking at her. Her disapproving gaze was on her assistant. "I don't believe sparring is part of your job description, Tac."

The young man put his stick down and gave her a defiant scowl.

Josei sighed. "We'll talk about it later. Will you go give the bows a proper waxing? The novices have been complaining of brittle strings."

The attendant's merry, brown-gold eyes met Nisha's. Placing one hand on his chest, he bowed to her. It was a ritual end-of-match bow, the kind exchanged between two warriors of equal skill. Nisha returned it, the corners of her mouth twitching.

Tac bowed to Josei and left. Nisha watched him go before turning back to Josei. Josei raised an eyebrow. "Having fun?"

"Yes," Nisha said, meeting Josei's eyes straight on. "Are you going to punish me?"

The fox-woman snorted. "Why? I always thought you girls would be better off if we allowed you to interact with more men before sending you out into the world. The Council has always been afraid it would lead to problems, but that doesn't mean they can tell me how to handle my own novices." She showed her teeth in a fierce grin. "I'd like to see them try."

Nisha felt a rush of gratitude, followed by a twinge of envy. If only she could defy the Council like that. She thought of how free she had felt, fighting with Tac. Nisha wanted more of that freedom, wanted it so badly she could taste it like a sharp, green fruit on her tongue.

"Besides," Josei said, "if I was going to be angry at anyone, which I'm not, I'd be angry at Tac. He knows better."

"He doesn't say much, does he?" Nisha ventured.

Josei smiled. "No, he doesn't talk. But he's strong and helpful, if a little reckless." She picked up the sword Tac had been polishing and inspected the curved edge. "You, on the other hand, fight like someone who's trying to forget."

The sweat on the back of Nisha's neck was turning cold in the chilly air, and she shivered. "I'm in trouble, Josei," she said. "If I can't find a good reason for Matron to keep me until after the Redeeming, the Council is going to sell me. Orders of the new Council Head."

Josei growled deep in her throat. "That man smells like tree rot," she said. "He's bad to his core, cares about no one but himself and his own power."

"But what can I do?" Nisha said. "There's nothing I'm doing for Matron that any other servant can't do."

Josei whirled the sword in a circle, the steel blade flashing. "I wouldn't say that," she said. "Did you know the Council has forbidden Matron to ask for an official investigation into Jina's death?"

"What?" Nisha stopped in the middle of hanging up her staff. "Why?"

"They're afraid," Josei said. "Afraid that it could be a girl from the Houses. The City of a Thousand Dolls was founded under the Second Lotus Emperor because families from every caste were abandoning their unwanted children, especially girls. The City's reputation allows our Emperor to continue to justify the limiting of a family's size, which keeps the Empire's population down and makes us easier to control. If the City of a Thousand Dolls ever fell, it would make people question the Empire's way of sustaining itself inside the Barrier.

"If the Emperor determines that the Council isn't managing the City properly, he could replace them all. Remember, the Lotus family rose to power by channeling the people's fear and anger to overthrow the Old Emperor. They know if it happened once, it could happen again."

When Nisha realized she was pacing, she forced herself to stand still. "But that's even more reason for the Council to let Matron investigate!" she cried. "They can't just tie her hands like that."

"They can," Josei said grimly. "The Council has been trying to get rid of Matron since Akash tar'Vey was named Council Head. He wants her power for someone from his own family, and the other Council members are following his lead. They know the tar'Vey family is rising in the court, and they don't want him as an enemy. Some of them they think Akash will increase the City's wealth and importance, which will in turn benefit them all."

Nisha looked down at her feet. "Like scavengers following a predator in hope of scraps."

"Exactly." Josei went on, "The official story now is that Jina's death was an accident, like Atiy's."

"I don't believe that, and neither will anyone else," Nisha said. "How do you accidentally poison yourself?"

"But no one will argue with it." Josei whirled the sword in her hands faster and faster. "The House Mistresses want to keep their positions, and none of the girls are going to make trouble this close to the Redeeming. Matron will try to investigate discreetly. But without someone who can move among the Houses freely without raising suspicions, it's difficult."

The blade flashed down, embedding itself in the table with a *thunk*.

Josei pulled it out, testing the edge. "None of the other servants have as much experience working with all the Houses as you do, and you have a . . . history of providing Matron with information. You might be able to turn that to your advantage." She glanced at a nearby water clock. "I have to teach an archery class." She patted Nisha on the shoulder and headed for the door. "Good luck."

"Thank you," Nisha said. But she wasn't really paying attention. She stood still, her fingers drumming gently her staff.

Jerrit poked his head around the doorpost. *You're looking very thoughtful.*

"I think–I think Josei just told me how I can buy some time from the Council."

Jerrit sighed. *I'm not going to like this, am I?*

Nisha put the staff up and grabbed her overrobe. "Probably not. I'll tell you on the way."

Where?

Jerrit trotted after her, but Nisha did not slow. "To see Matron."

The two walked in silence down the path toward the Council House. They passed a sitting garden, where a group of Music novices practiced a folk song. The lively tune made Nisha's step a little lighter. Matron might not agree to her plan, but at least she was doing *something*.

As she approached the Council House, Nisha could see Pavilion Field and a bright cluster of colors. The tents were up and now the decorating could begin: The House Mistresses and novices would fill the tents with books and pillows and low tea tables, burn incense, and cover the ground with soft carpets. The longer a client stayed in the tent, the more likely he was to find a girl from that House that he wanted to speak for.

"Matron," Nisha said, catching up to Matron outside her study. "Is there a way for you to take a message to the Council for me?"

Matron gave her a long look, then pushed open the door to her study. Heart thudding in her ears, Nisha followed.

"You have something to say to the Council?" Matron asked.

"Well," Nisha said, smoothing the fabric of her Combat tunic. "I was thinking about what you said, about trying to convince the Council to hold off from selling me, and I have something to offer them."

"Really?" Matron gave her a sharp, surprised look. "What would that be?"

Nisha's throat felt dry and scratchy. She reached out mentally for Jerrit. *I can't do this.*

You can, Jerrit whispered in her mind. *I know you can.*

Nisha swallowed. "I can help you figure out what happened to Jina."

Matron said nothing, but Nisha struggled forward. "I know the Council won't let you ask for official help. I can ask those questions for you."

Matron paced the room, her silver asar glimmering. "I was hoping you'd offer something like this, Nisha. We really should be looking into Jina's death. And if it's only you investigating, we won't have to risk anyone outside the City of a Thousand Dolls finding out."

"And if I fail," Nisha said, "the Council can always sell me after the Redeeming."

The silence stretched out like a thin rope. Matron tapped her fingers on her arm. "You might have found the one thing that could convince the Council to wait. They want to have this . . . issue solved without scandal. If word gets out that girls are dying here, the City is finished. I can at least ask."

Matron seated herself. She picked up some papers on her desk and set them down again. "Nisha, has it occurred to you that this might be dangerous?"

Nisha thought about Jina's hair drifting in the water, her hands smudged black with charcoal and twisted in death. But life in the Houses could be dangerous in all kinds of ways.

"I'll risk it," she said. "I don't have much choice."

Matron nodded. "No, you don't." Something that might have been compassion touched her eyes; then she bent her head. "I'll speak to the Council this afternoon. Good luck, Nisha."

Nisha bowed and left Matron's study. *I'm going to need it,* she thought.

Jerrit joined Nisha in her room as she changed back into her gray asar. *I can't believe she agreed to that. But what about Atiy?* he sent.

Nisha paused. She had resisted connecting the deaths, too busy reassuring herself that Atiy's death wasn't her fault even if it was suicide. That there was no way she could have stopped it. The idea that it might have been murder made a chill ripple over her skin.

I don't want to start there, she sent. She tried to keep the fear out of her words, make it sound like a rational decision. *Let's rule out Jina killing herself first.*

All right, Jerrit sent. *How?*

Nisha frowned. *Well, we want to know what poison she took. The best people to ask about poisons are the healers at the House of Jade.*

17

THE HOUSE OF Jade was the quietest place on the estate.
With the warm greenhouse on one side and an immaculate meditation garden on the other, and always smelling of herbs, ink,
and old scrolls, the House of Jade exuded tranquility. The novices
moved quietly, trying to imitate their teachers. No one ever raised
her voice. Here Nisha was always treated with detached courtesy.

Jade's perfect rows of miniature trees in the meditation garden
were beautiful, but unsatisfying, making Nisha long for tangled
vines and wild spaces. Her favorite place in the House of Jade was
the rehabilitation courtyard around the back, where the healers
taught their craft by tending injured animals.

Sashi was in the back courtyard, kneeling beside a red deer with
a broken leg. The doe lay on her side, panting softly, her pupils
dilating and shrinking. Three of the other novices held the deer

still, and one of the healers stood to the side.

Nisha paused in the archway. She watched as Sashi's sure fingers set the slender bone. The deer trembled and jerked with every adjustment, but Sashi's touch was gentle, and she seemed to make no mistakes. Once she had set and splinted the deer's leg, she rose.

"Let her up," Sashi said. "Let's see if she can stand."

The novices let the doe go and the animal struggled to her feet, holding the bandaged leg off the ground.

The healer walked around the deer, her calm eyes missing nothing. "Excellent work, Sashi," she said. "Once we have found you an assistant to help you with sighted tasks, you will be a credit to your teachers."

"Thank you, healer," Sashi said. "I appreciate the confidence."

The healer patted Sashi on the shoulder. "You will repay it; I have no doubt." She turned to Nisha, acknowledging her with a nod of the head. "Be welcome, Nisha."

"Nisha?" Sashi turned. Her face was flushed with pleasure, her unfocused eyes warmer than they had been the last time Nisha had seen her. "How long have you been standing there?"

Nisha was so proud of her friend she couldn't help herself. She ran forward and threw her arms around Sashi, hugging her tightly. "Long enough to watch the best healer-in-training I know. That was wonderful."

"It was routine," Sashi said, looking suddenly uncomfortable. She fidgeted. "Just a broken leg. But surely you didn't come here just to tell me that."

"I don't think you need me to tell you," Nisha said. She lowered her voice. "But I did have some questions for you, if you have the time."

Sashi turned her face in the healer's direction. The woman's mouth tightened. She gestured to the watching novices.

"Sashi, I will see you later," the healer said, inclining her head. "Good day to you, Nisha." She walked away, trailed by the novices.

A servant in a pale-green tunic touched Sashi's arm, then put a wet towel in her hands. Sashi turned away from Nisha, wiping the blood off her fingers. "What do you need?"

Sashi always responded better when she felt like people were being honest with her. And Jina *had* been a Jade novice.

"It's about Jina," Nisha said directly.

Sashi bent her head, her dark hair falling over her face. "It was a sad event," she said. "But grief is another emotion we must clear from our minds if we are to be free. Why are you asking about her?"

"I knew her. And I want to understand what happened. What kind of poison killed her? Where did she get it?"

"The healers don't know where she got it," Sashi said. "But we do know what it was. *Gunia* seeds. There were a few mixed in with the seed mixture she was eating when she died. One seed alone can kill you. More than one–it would have been fast. Painful, but very quick."

"Is that . . . is that a common choice for suicides?"

Sashi looked up, her forehead creased in thought. "Not that

I know of. The herbal books say most people use an overdose of sleeproot or ladydeath. Those make you drowsy, send you to sleep, and you just never wake up. Besides, the *gunia* seeds are locked up, like all our poisons. Only the full healers have the key."

Nisha shuddered at the words *all our poisons*. "So if Jina had wanted to kill herself, she'd have had to break into the poison cupboard?"

Sashi nodded. "And no one broke the lock. The healers checked. The cupboard hasn't been opened since we mixed up a batch of red paint a couple of days ago for the girls at the House of Beauty."

"You make poison paint?" Nisha asked.

Sashi's studied calm cracked, and she smiled grimly. "Not exactly. Ground up, *gunia* seeds are a bright, vibrant red. We add some clay and herbs to neutralize the poison before mixing the paint. You wouldn't want to drink it, but you won't die if you get it on your skin."

Nisha scratched her forehead. If Jina had killed herself, she would have researched the poison first. Why would she have chosen this one?

"Thank you, Sashi," she said. "Can we keep this between us? I don't want Matron to know I'm asking questions outside of my regular duties."

"Of course." Sashi eyebrows flashed up in surprise. "I'm surprised you have to ask."

It was true—no one could pry a secret out of Sashi. Why had Nisha felt like she had to ask Sashi to keep quiet? Her mind spun with the new information she'd learned—she wasn't thinking clearly.

The healer appeared in the doorway of the main building. "Sashi, it's time for your study period."

Sashi gave Nisha a forced smile. "I have to go. I'll talk to you later—over tea, perhaps?"

The servant took Sashi's elbow, guiding her over the small step. The healer stared at Nisha for a moment, then followed Sashi inside.

Nisha went and sat down heavily on a bench in the meditation garden. Unlike the other garden spaces in the City, there were no riots of flowers, no sheltering trees. Instead it was a calm, open space, dotted with stretches of sand that rippled like a river. Benches sat on pools of moss, and the miniature trees were carefully and precisely trimmed. It was the perfect place to consider what she'd learned.

Jina hadn't killed herself. Nisha knew it in her gut the way she knew hunger and sleep and danger. The girl with the clear-eyed smile, the girl who had to know everything, wouldn't have chosen to spend her last minutes in that kind of pain. Someone had scattered those deadly seeds into her food on purpose. Someone had murdered her.

The last time anyone had access to the cupboard was when the healers made the paint—but Nisha couldn't believe a Jade healer could have killed one of her own. Besides, someone with a healer's knowledge could kill in subtler ways. They wouldn't use a clumsy poison like *gunia* seeds and make Jina's death a spectacle in the center of the City.

Could a few whole *gunia* seeds have accidentally been mixed in with the paint before going to the House of Beauty? But that didn't make sense either. The House of Beauty and the House of Jade hardly ever overlapped. The House of Jade considered the worship of physical beauty to be a shallow and unworthy pursuit, even if they did make kohl and who knew what other concoctions for the Beauty girls. And Nisha had heard the Beauty girls dismiss the House of Jade as being boring and cold. But dislike was not a reason to kill.

Nisha watched a tiny black spider crawl across the soft sand near her foot. The more she found out, the more confusing everything became.

Nisha spent the rest of the day crossing items off the list Rajni had given her. She easily found kohl for the girls' eyes and the ribbons. But not all the girls had extra hairpins to share, and those who did were willing to give up only a few. Each time she got a handful, Nisha delivered them to the House of Beauty and tried to talk to one of the girls in private. But Beauty girls—more than any of the other girls in the City—hated to be alone. They slept in groups, ate in groups, and moved in crowds like herd animals. Once Nisha learned from one young novice at exactly what time the red paint had been delivered to the House of Beauty, she started trying to figure out where the girls were at the time.

It wasn't difficult to get the girls to talk. They were all buzzing about the upcoming masquerade, and most of them were spending all their time getting ready. All Nisha had to do was fix them with wide eyes and ask questions.

I've never been to the Redeeming before. It must be so exciting. How do you even prepare?

Oh there's so much to do. Yesterday I had to spend the whole morning giving myself a lemon-and-cucumber mask, because I woke up with a pimple. And then I had to go a dance lesson, and finish painting my display teacup and—

But every girl Nisha talked to had been attending a lesson or had been with two or three others who could vouch for her. She wandered into the art room and picked up a bottle of fresh red paint. She peered through the cloudy glass. There was no sign that any stray *gunia* seeds had gotten into the bottle, and the seal was still unbroken. The seeds couldn't have come from this paint.

Nisha was tired and discouraged, and a headache tugged just above her eyes. She wanted nothing more than to go back to her room, but instead she grabbed a quick lunch and went back to the House of Jade.

The Jade girls seemed glad to finally talk about their dead friend. Nisha didn't even have to ask questions. She only offered sympathy.

I'm sorry about Jina. I wish I had known her better.

Those words opened the floodgates, even from the most disciplined Jade novices.

She was so kind.

Not an enemy in the world.

Everybody loved her.

It made Nisha wish she really had known Jina better. The thought filled her with a peculiar sense of loss, as if she were mourning something that never had a chance to be. When she felt tears gather in her eyes, she knew it was time to leave.

On her way out, she sat down on the steps of the House of Jade and took several deep breaths. Everyone agreed that Jina had no enemies and no rivals, so her death probably wasn't personal. She'd been killed from a distance, like someone would poison a pest.

But why?

Nisha remembered Jina's mischievous grin. *There's a shelf of restricted scrolls in our Mistress's private study. . . . Maybe the Shadow-walkers got her.*

An ice-cold chill skittered down Nisha's spine. Jina had been convinced the Shadow-walkers were real. Had she seen something in those scrolls she wasn't supposed to see? Was someone willing to kill to protect her secrets?

Matron was reading a scroll but looked up when Nisha walked into her study.

"Nisha, hello. I took your message to the Council, and they agreed to hold off on selling you for now. Akash was surprisingly open to the idea, though he made it clear the buyer is very impatient."

Matron's voice was dry with suspicion, but Nisha didn't care. She had bought herself time. And with time, anything was possible. Maybe Devan would speak for her after all. The Council would never dare to turn down a nobleman's son. If Devan could convince his parents before Akash or Kalia found out . . . Or maybe, if she had to, she could find the courage to escape.

Matron interrupted Nisha's thoughts. "So what have you learned?"

Nisha sighed. "The poison that killed Jina came from Jade." She repeated what Sashi had told her "But Sashi also said that only the people who made the paint had any access to the *gunia* seeds. I want to find out more about what Jina was working on. She said she was researching love poetry, but I'm not sure if that was all. I have a suspicion . . . that she might have been killed because she knew something she wasn't supposed to."

"Jina was known for her curious mind. I'm sure it never occurred to her that there could be something in the world that you're not supposed to know," Matron said with a wry smile. "It's certainly a point worth pursuing." She paused. "Do you think she found out about anything in particular?"

Nisha hesitated. If Jina was uncovering secrets in the Houses, one of the people who could have stood to gain by her death was Matron. Matron could have arranged for Jina's death easily, could have agreed to let Nisha to investigate just to throw suspicion off herself.

But Matron was the only thing standing between her and life as a bond slave, and Nisha had to trust her. She did trust her.

"Jina told me something interesting the day before she died," Nisha said. "She hinted that she'd sneaked into the House Mistress's study and read the restricted scrolls there."

Matron's eyes widened. "Those scrolls are forbidden to novices. They're for the House Mistress's private use only."

"But why?" Nisha leaned forward. "The whole point of being a scholar at the House of Jade is to learn the truth."

"Knowledge isn't a game of dice, Nisha," Matron said, her words as sharp as the point of a knife. "You don't win by finding out more than everyone else. Knowledge is dangerous. Certain . . . aspects of the Empire are dangerous. Girls might learn those secrets too, in time, but they will learn them under the tutelage of scholars who can guide them."

Nisha considered this. "What if Jina found something in the scrolls that someone was willing to kill for? She mentioned the Shadow-walkers—"

Matron set her scroll down with a snap. "Please, Nisha. The Shadow-walkers are a legend, a tale the servants use to scare young children." Her eyes slid away from Nisha's. "You'll have to do better than silly rumors if you want the Council to believe that you can solve this."

Rubbing the back of her neck, Matron picked up another scroll, her voice steady. "If that's all, I have a lot of work to do. You're dismissed."

Nisha stared at Matron, her mouth open.

Matron was lying to her. The way she'd shut down the conversation, the way she'd glanced away, all of it reeked of a lie. Matron could be evasive, even manipulative, but to Nisha's knowledge she had never outright lied to her before. It was unexpectedly painful.

Matron looked up. "Is that everything, Nisha? I said you're dismissed."

It was a clear command, and Nisha obeyed it. She walked out of the study, her heart thumping with the betrayal.

Matron had lied to her, had tried to throw her off course. Nisha knew it down to her core. And if Matron was lying, that meant that some part of the rumors had to be true.

Nisha quickened her steps. Somewhere on the estate there might be a House that trained assassins, a shadow House that no one knew about. A House that could be connected to Jina's death.

And Nisha had to find it.

To some eyes, Aarya's death looks like a simple training accident. But the Mistress of Shadows is convinced that the novice Aarya stepped into the path of that dagger on purpose. Aarya had become increasingly restless and distraught over her future, begging to be transferred to another House, calling herself a monster.

I and no other bear the guilt for her death, but what could I do? Aarya was raised in the ways of the Black Lotus. It would have been too dangerous to put her with the other girls. My concern is the City as a whole. If the novices knew all the things we trained girls for, knew the dark requests we are sometimes called upon to fill . . .

There was no other choice. But I do not think I will sleep well for some time.

From the scrolls of the Matron of the Houses

18

NISHA CLOSED HER eyes and saw the City of a Thousand Dolls as if she were looking at a builder's plans. There were the six Houses: the House of Flowers, the House of Beauty, the House of Pleasure, the House of Combat, the House of Jade, and the House of Music. There was the Council House, the bathhouse, the cremation field, the gardens, the stables, the forest—

Her eyes flew open. The forest, the one behind the House of Combat. Nisha had been to every corner of the estate, but she had never bothered to go deep into the small forest inside the walls. The trees were too thick, reminding her of the woods outside the City.

But if I were hiding a House full of assassins, that's exactly where I'd put it, Nisha thought. *That's where I have to go next.*

Getting into the forest was easy. Combat novices practiced

scouting in the fringes all the time, so all Nisha had to do was put on her Combat tunic and trousers, and she blended right in.

It was *finding* the House that proved difficult.

After creeping past all the Combat girls on the outskirts of the forest, watching, listening, and searching for what felt like hours, Nisha was hot and discouraged. There were no paths through the forest, and the trees grew close together. Her tunic caught on branches, bushes, and thorns. As the trees thickened and the light dimmed, she could barely see her own feet.

What in the name of the Long-Tailed Cat are you doing out here? The voice was low and tinged with amusement. Esmer appeared like a ghost near Nisha's feet. Her dark-gray spots were black in the fading light.

Are you looking for what I think you're looking for? Esmer sent.

"That depends," Nisha said, folding her arms. "Are you following me?"

Of course, Esmer sent, without shame. *You didn't think we'd let you go hunting by yourself, did you? Besides, this forest is my favorite spot to catch breakfast.*

Nisha almost bit her tongue in frustration. The cats hunted all over the estate. Of course they would know if there was a secret House somewhere. Nisha was starting to get the feeling that the cats knew a lot more than she did about this place.

I need to find the House that trains assassins, she sent. *It's important.*

Esmer flicked her slender tail. *Why?*

"Because people are dying," Nisha snapped. "And I need to find out why."

Esmer shook herself. *I suppose I can't blame you for that*, she sent. *The House you're looking for is called the House of Shadows, but they have nothing to do with any of this.*

Nisha pushed past a wild rosebush, scratching her hand in the process. "How could you possibly know that?" she asked, holding up her hand. "Never mind. I have to talk to them myself. If I can ever find them, that is."

Well, you've been going in circles for about twenty minutes.

Nisha stopped. She had passed this way before.

Esmer sat in one of the few beams of soft light and washed her ears.

Nisha waited. All her years with the cats had taught her patience. Esmer yawned and began to lick her shoulder clean.

The cat curled up and closed her eyes.

Nisha gave up. "Esmer!"

The cat blinked. *What?*

"Do you know where the House of Shadows is?"

Maybe. Esmer started to wash her tail.

"Will you tell me how to get there? Please?" Nisha forced the "please" through clenched teeth. She knew better than to be rude to a cat when she needed a favor.

Esmer sat straight, her playful manner gone. *On one condition. You take me with you. You need someone at your back.*

Nisha bent down and petted the cat's sleek fur. She had a point. If Esmer was wrong, and the Shadow-walkers did have something to do with Jina's death, walking in there alone would be the height of stupidity. Nisha would still do it, but it would be stupid nonetheless.

"All right, you can come," she said. "Will they talk to me?"

Esmer gave a purr that shook her body like a laugh would a human's. *You might be surprised.*

The way to the House of Shadows was a deer trail, so narrow that it was almost invisible. Thick, thorny trees grabbed at Nisha's legs. Esmer led the way, a pale flicker in the still gloom.

Finally they stepped out of the trees and into a natural clearing. A small brick building occupied one corner. Like the Houses she knew, it was copper trimmed and flat roofed. A greenish-black blanket of heavy vines smothered half the structure. Ropes, some smooth and slender, others thick and knotted, hung down the sides. Shadows blurred the roof.

Fascinated, Nisha stepped forward, ignoring Esmer's warning hiss.

Nisha! Don't!

Something leaped onto Nisha from a nearby tree, slamming her into the ground. Blinding pain shot through her cheek. Someone forced a gag into her mouth, a silk cloth that tasted like black pepper and burned her tongue and lips. Slender cords that cut like wire bound her wrists and ankles. There was a jabbing pressure between her shoulder blades that felt very much like a knee. Through watery eyes, Nisha saw a black leather boot step into her field of vision.

"Adequate, Mayanti, quite adequate." The voice was like velvet over ice, soft and freezing to the touch. "You snapped a twig before you leaped, though. If this intruder had not been staring like a frightened goat, she would have heard you, perhaps pulled a knife, like this."

There was a flicker of motion just above her, and the weight on Nisha's back grew very still. A warm drop of liquid dripped onto Nisha's cheek, and it wasn't until it ran down and touched the corner of her mouth, all copper and bitter and sweet, that she realized it was blood.

"Tell me the price of carelessness, Mayanti," the velvety voice commanded.

"Death, Shadow Mistress." The girl sounded neither terrified nor hurt, just calm and wary.

"And the price of hesitation?" More hot blood dribbled into Nisha's hair and trickled into her ear. She fought to keep from struggling.

"Death, Shadow Mistress," the girl said.

The Shadow Mistress's voice dropped to a purring whisper. "And the price of failure?"

The girl shifted, sending a twisting pain through Nisha's spine.

"Death," she said. "The Black Lotus has never failed. The Black Lotus will never fail. We are the shadow in the alley, the arrow in the dark. We are—"

"*Death*," the woman finished, a tinge of amusement warming the words. "You have performed to expectation, Mayanti. You may go."

The pressure melted off Nisha's back, and the cords were whisked away as though they had never been there. Nisha scrambled to her feet and tore off the gag. She wiped the blood from her cheek and ear; then, her mouth still burning, she turned to meet the Mistress of the House of Shadows.

She was the thinnest woman Nisha had ever seen. The House Mistress's hair was cropped close to her head, and her eyes were so dark brown they looked black.

"What do you want at the House of Shadows?" the woman asked in her cold, soft voice. Her hollow eyes, and the sticklike thinness of the woman's arms and legs, gave Nisha the uneasy impression that she was talking to a skeleton. "How did you find us? Why have you come?" Her long, thin fingers twirled, the flash of knives glittering in her hands.

Esmer wound herself between Nisha's ankles. *Pick me up*, she sent.

Why? Nisha sent.

Trust me, Nisha. Pick me up.

Without taking her eyes off the motionless woman, Nisha bent down and gathered the spotted cat into her arms.

As she straightened up, she caught a flash of recognition in the Shadow Mistress's eyes. But all the woman said was "Follow me."

Nisha put Esmer down and followed the Shadow Mistress across the clearing and through the heavy front door, the spotted cat trailing behind. The House Mistress wore a tunic and trousers of mottled brown and gray, like the flickering shadows in the forest. In the dark, narrow hallway, she almost disappeared.

The Shadow Mistress directed Nisha to a tiny side study, empty but for two chairs and a wall of cabinets made from the same dark wood as the front door. Nisha sat on a hard chair and forced herself not to look all around her.

The Shadow Mistress stared at her for a long time, and Nisha felt as if the woman's eyes were taking in every detail. "Nisha Arvi," she said finally. "You've grown since I last saw you."

Nisha gaped at her. "How do you know me?" she asked.

"You don't remember?" The Shadow Mistress studied Nisha's face as if looking for something she'd lost. "I was the one who brought you into the City."

What? Nisha looked down at Esmer, who stared back impassively. Nisha closed her eyes, thinking back to the memory she'd played a thousand times. The hard stone against her back, watching her father walk into the woods, and then . . .

And then—like a scroll unrolling—the memory stretched a little further. Nisha remembered a lean woman with wiry muscles and short black hair coming out of the gate. A hand held out, a voice tinged with pity but underlined with steel.

Come inside, Nisha.

Nisha opened her eyes. "You've changed," she said.

For a moment, she was afraid the Shadow Mistress would be offended, but the woman gave a barely discernable shrug. "My profession is not an easy one. And ten years is a long time."

"How did you know I'd been left there?" Nisha asked.

The Shadow Mistress turned away. "That is not what you came here to ask. There is another question in the set of your mouth, one important enough to brave my woods and my novices. State it, and be on your way."

All of Nisha's half-formed plans dissolved like smoke on a hot day. The Shadow Mistress's eyes stared through her, and Nisha knew—without knowing how—that those eyes had seen more lies than any one person could tell in a lifetime. This woman would accept only the complete and utter truth.

Esmer jumped up into Nisha's lap.

She took a deep breath and told the Shadow Mistress about the two deaths and everything that had happened since she had come upon Atiy's dead body two days before. When she was finished, the woman sat unmoving for a long time.

"You suspect my daughters?" The ice in her voice was so thick and hard that Nisha felt bruised by it. She hesitated, opened her mouth—

"Do not think to engage me in a dance of words, girl," the Shadow Mistress said. "I have played the game of intrigue for longer than you have been alive, and I tire of it. Answer me true. Do you suspect my daughters killed these girls?"

"No!" Nisha almost shouted, louder than she'd intended. Quieter, she said, frustrated, "I mean, that wasn't the only reason I came. I hadn't thought that far yet." She swallowed and hugged Esmer closer. "But they could have. I mean . . . you do train assassins, don't you?"

To her amazement, the Shadow Mistress let out a barking laugh.

"The Black Lotus is more than an assassins' guild," she said. "It is a way of life that requires focus and stern discipline. All day yesterday I had my daughters in meditation and balance exercises.

They were all in the same room with me from Firstlight to Darkfall. We did not even stop to eat. While I cannot say where they were this morning or two days ago, I can tell you none of them were gone yesterday."

The Shadow Mistress's voice turned as flat and cold as a frosted pane of glass. "I tell you the truth, Nisha, I ordered no such killing. If one of my daughters ever took a life without permission, *I* would deal with it."

Nisha remembered the novice's blood trickling over her cheek and shuddered. The Shadow Mistress's way of dealing with disobedience would no doubt be very painful and very final.

But Nisha still had to ask the question she'd come here to ask. "This House is a secret," she said. "One that Jina had somehow uncovered. Who would kill to protect that secret?"

Something very close to a smile crossed the Shadow Mistress's face, and she rose. "There is more than one kind of secret, Nisha."

Crossing with soundless steps to the cabinets, she opened a cupboard door. "There is the secret that no one may know, the kind one kills to protect. And then there is the secret that everyone may know, but no one will admit to knowing. This House is the second kind of secret."

The woman pulled out a red silk scarf, thinner than paper but so richly red and vivid that it lit the room as if it were made of fire. "Then there is the secret that everyone knows, except the person the secret is about."

Turning, she put the scarf into Nisha's hands. "Think about this, Nisha. There are more secrets in the City than you can possibly know. Which ones do you really care about?"

Esmer hissed, a sharp sound that made Nisha jump. The Shadow Mistress raised one eyebrow.

"It is time," she said. For a moment, Nisha wasn't sure if the Shadow Mistress was addressing her or the cat. "I have debts to pay, and so do you. And now I must take my leave."

The Shadow Mistress turned to Nisha, who sat with her mouth open and the unexpected gift held gingerly in her hands. "I trust you can find your way out? You should not be harmed, but if I were you, I would not linger. My daughters will practice their archery soon, and their arrows are tipped with steel."

With that she left, and the door creaked slowly shut.

Nisha stared down at the scarf. The embroidered silk caressed her hands. The pattern was familiar, and her gut gave a visceral lurch. Her fingers crept to the collar of her tunic, touching the tiger mark under her collarbone, a tiger identical to the ones woven into the scarf.

"Esmer–" She looked up in time to see Esmer's tail vanish through the closing door. Nisha was alone in the room with just the faint brush of vines against the windows, and the mysterious scarf.

Nisha stumbled out of the House of Shadows into the dim light of the woods. Her fingers played with the scarf, the thin, soft fabric, the slight stiffness of gold threads. The lines of the embroidered tigers burned under her fingers.

Long-forgotten memories–so foggy they felt like they couldn't be hers, bits and pieces of a life that had belonged to someone else so long ago–assaulted her.

A mother's gentle hands. Her father's beard, rough, scratchy, and scented with sandalwood.

A cart creaking, the smells of spices and dried meat and drink, the laughter of other children.

Her father haggling with someone while her mother watched the cart, one hand on her belt knife.

Were her parents merchants? No. Merchants didn't give marks like hers to their children. And they weren't nobles, either. Once, Nisha had pretended that her parents were wealthy and powerful people who had been forced to hide her from enemies. They would one day come to claim her and sweep her away to a life of ease, free from worry. But noble children were marked at birth with the Flower tattoo, not strange animals. Nisha had soon given up that dream.

The thin silk weighed down Nisha's hand like a stone, and the Shadow Mistress's voice followed her as she tried to trace her steps through the forest.

There are more secrets in the City than you can possibly know.

There is the secret that everyone knows, except the person the secret is about.

Now that she knew where the trail was, Nisha made it through the woods easily. By habit, she soon found herself in the hedge maze. Each dead end she turned down seemed to mock her, like the scarf in her hand. She wandered for what felt like hours, always turning around when she approached the fountain, until it was dark and she was so tired she couldn't walk or think anymore.

She went back to her favorite corner and lay down, pulling her cloak around her. It was a little cold to be outdoors, but the open air made Nisha feel calmer, and she couldn't go inside yet.

She put the scarf against her cheek, and a big, dizzying hope swirled up in her chest. Maybe she didn't need to put herself in danger to chase clues about a killer she couldn't stop, just for the Council to approve of her. Maybe she didn't need to ask Devan to speak for her when she wasn't ready yet. Maybe she didn't need Matron's protection.

If the scarf was a link to her parents, maybe she could find them and find out who she was. And if she did that, she wouldn't need the City anymore at all.

She'd have a family again.

·19·

A SOFT TOUCH on her nose pulled Nisha out of the weight-less drift of sleep. She grunted in protest.

Nisha, came Jerrit's voice. *Nisha, wake up.*

The ground was hard and soaking wet. Nisha cracked her eyes open to see Jerrit's face inches from hers.

Get up, Nisha. You've been out all night. You need to get up and get warm or you'll sicken.

"Don't be such a mother hen," Nisha muttered. "I'm fine . . . Ouch!" She sat up as sharp claws dug into her arm. Thick pale mist flowed over and around her. Nisha glared at Jerrit, who glared right back.

"That's cheating," she said. "Claws aren't allowed."

Neither is sleeping outside after the White Mist starts, Jerrit sent. *You know Esmer's rules. If she catches you, you'll get worse than a scratch.*

The cold hit Nisha for the first time, and she shivered. Maybe a warm bath *would* be a good idea. "Fine. I'll go to the bathhouse. Happy?"

Jerrit sauntered in a circle around her. Nisha stood up and shook the scarf at him. "Did you know about this?" she asked, the words coming out wounded and small.

Jerrit held his head low and his ears down.

Yes.

"How could you?" Nisha said, hurt burning in her chest. "What does this symbol mean, Jerrit? Tell me what's going on."

He can't tell you anything, Esmer sent, slipping through a thick hedge to stand between Nisha and Jerrit. *Don't be angry with him, Nisha. It's not his fault. We were sworn to secrecy long ago. We swore it by the Long-Tailed Cat.*

"The Long-Tailed Cat?" Nisha asked. "I've heard you say that name before. . . ."

Esmer shook her head as if shaking off a fly. *The Long-Tailed Cat is sacred to the cat tribes. Her tail encircles all of time, and the present rests between her paws. Those who break the oath of the Long-Tailed Cat are rejected by all the spotted cat tribes, doomed to wander, homeless and honorless.*

Nisha gathered Jerrit into her arms. She buried her face in his fur and tried to breathe deeply. Jerrit licked her chin. His silent sympathy helped more than any words could.

"I just don't understand how you could keep this from me."

Esmer let out her breath in a long sigh. *It wasn't supposed to be this way,* she sent. *You were supposed to go to the Redeeming and evaluate all the options, and then we were to tell you everything before you made a choice. You were going to have a choice. . . .*

Nisha understood. Things were different now. Had it really only been a few days ago that she was making her own plans for the Redeeming? Back when her only worries had been how to ask Devan to speak for her, and not belonging to anyone in the City but herself and the cats? The deaths and fear of the last days seemed like an awful dream.

Esmer crept closer and touched Nisha's foot with her paw. *I'm sorry, Nisha. I wish there was more I could say right now.*

Nisha wanted to tell her it was all right, but it wasn't. Everywhere she turned, there were secrets and lies.

I know.

Nisha set Jerrit down and started walking toward the bath-house, through the maze. The maze was always quiet in the morning, and she didn't feel like talking to anyone. Jerritt followed her silently.

I'm not mad at you, Nisha sent at last. The hem of her asar was soaked from the mist, and she shivered again as icy water dripped onto her sandaled feet.

Doesn't matter, Jerrit sent. *You're unhappy, and so I'm unhappy. You know that we wouldn't keep something this important from you if we didn't have to.*

Nisha wasn't sure if she knew that. She didn't feel it. *I just–I hate feeling like this, like there's so much I don't know. It's like I'm putting together a mosaic and missing half the tiles.*

They approached the fountain, which Nisha had been avoiding when she was alone. She sat on the rim and clutched her knees. "Tanaya's snapping. Sashi's starting to act more like a master healer than a friend, and Matron is worried and not telling me anything. It's like everything is falling apart."

So what do we do next? Jerrit sent.

Nisha dragged her hand across the fountain's textured stone. What she wanted to do was to go back to Matron and Esmer and shake them until they told her the truth about who she was.

But her past wouldn't matter if she couldn't save her future.

"I need to go to the House of Pleasure and talk to Camini," she said finally. "If the Shadow Mistress is telling the truth, Jina's death doesn't have anything to do with the House of Shadows. But maybe it is connected with Atiy's." Nisha winced as the words left her mouth. She knew she'd been avoiding the idea all along. And if the deaths were connected, then her situation was more serious than she had thought. And much more dangerous.

She was running out of choices and running out of time. "Jina knew something. If I can figure out how Atiy died, it could be the most important clue we could possibly have about who killed Jina."

I've been smelling hints of ash and smoke all morning, Jerrit sent. *I think Camini's attending to Atiy's cremation.*

Nisha shuddered. She hated the ovens and the cremation fields. "That could take all day. I don't like the idea of interrupting her . . . but we can't wait."

Jerrit growled, and Nisha laughed. "After I change into a dry asar first, of course," she said.

And warm up, Jerrit said.

Nisha picked up the cat, running her fingers through his sleek fur. "Of course," she agreed.

After a hot bath, Nisha walked through the too-still fields to the cremation fires. Only the nobles of the Flower caste were allowed to keep their bodies in death. Everyone else was burned, their ashes scattered. The builders of the City had set apart a small, swampy area in this far corner of the estate to absorb the ashes.

Nisha looked up at the gnarled gray branches as she passed underneath the frost flame trees that surrounded the swamp. All the leaves had fallen, a sign of the coming Earthsleep, and the bent branches looked old and tired. But once the frost came, they would bloom with fiery orange-and-red flowers, bright spots in a cold, white world.

The cremation oven itself was guarded by tall *arjin* trees, whose needles stayed green all year long. The spiny trees hid the fires and the smoke from the girls and caretakers who lived in the City.

Camini, a lone figure in red, stood staring at the flames. The huge clay oven rose in the middle of a large circle of flat stones, ringed with statues of the Ancestors. Smoke rose into the air in a black, swirling pillar. The smell was indescribable, like burned deer, only worse. Nisha forced herself close enough to call out to Camini.

"May I talk to you?" she asked, waving her hands.

Camini didn't try to shout over the roar of the fire, only beckoned Nisha over.

Nisha's stomach demanded that she not take another step into that horrific smell, but she pinched her nose shut and forced her feet to move. Jerrit made a pained mewling sound. Up close, Nisha could see something dark and slimy smeared across Camini's upper lip. Turning back to the roaring oven, the House Mistress passed Nisha a clay pot with a brown salve inside.

The salve had a pungent, bitter smell. Nisha sagged in relief when it overpowered the odor of burning bone. She bent down and wiped some on Jerrit's nose.

Camini continued to stare at the oven. Despite its heat and the protection of her heavy brocade asar, the House Mistress stood with her arms wrapped around her body as if she were cold. She wore no kohl around her red-rimmed eyes, and there were traces of tears on her cheeks.

"Mistress, I ask you to forgive me," Nisha said, feeling a sudden stab of guilt. She turned to go, but Camini held out a hand.

"No, stay. It is not always good to be alone, even if it's what you think you want." She smiled and looked Nisha up and down.

"You've turned into a woman, haven't you? And a lovely one too. With the Redeeming so soon, you might want a lesson or two at my House."

Nisha felt herself turning a dark red, and Camini gave her a gentler smile. "I'm only teasing you, Nisha," she said. "I know that what the House of Pleasure teaches isn't for everyone."

Nisha took her courage in both hands and tried to steer the conversation toward Atiy. "Don't you ever have to train unwilling girls?" she asked.

The House Mistress gave an emphatic shake of her head. "Never. A truly unhappy or unwilling girl is no use to me. I cannot force, I can only train and guide."

Nisha's thoughts rebelled, and she spoke too quickly. "But what about Atiy?"

At her feet, Jerrit hissed. *Nisha!*

Nisha stopped and felt herself turning red again. What was wrong with her? She needed to be more careful than this. Anxiety twitched her fingers, and she laced them together. "Forgive me, House Mistress."

Camini crossed her arms. "I know what you're thinking, Nisha. But Atiy did not jump off that roof."

"I'm sorry," Nisha said. "I didn't mean to offend."

"I know you didn't." Camini rubbed her hands over her face, leaving a streak of ash behind. "I can see why you think Atiy could be unhappy. But you didn't know her. You didn't know what being selected as a secret mistress meant to her."

She stared into the flames of the clay oven. "I called her my little rock dove. And she was: beautiful, soft, and so timid that she fled at the sound of any stranger. Atiy became tongue-tied when asked to speak to people she didn't know well, and she was only truly comfortable with me and her teachers. Even the other girls frightened her."

Nisha fought the urge to look into the fire. She didn't want to see the charred remains of a timid girl who had only wanted to be alone. A girl who had been content with her life.

"I choose my girls very carefully for their positions," Camini went on. "To be tucked away in a private world, to be cared for and provided for and to never have to talk to strangers, not everyone is made for such a life. But Atiy should have been happy. She *was* happy."

The pain and conviction in Camini's voice touched Nisha in a way no words could. As far as Camini knew, Atiy had been happy.

Then why was she dead? "So being a secret mistress was an honor. . . ."

The House Mistress shook her head. "It's not about honor or dishonor, Nisha. It's about fitting the girl to the position. Most of my novices are performers by nature, bold and outgoing. None of them would have wanted to be in Atiy's place."

Camini turned back to the fire, and a tear slipped silently down her face.

The hot, smoky air pressed in on Nisha, suffocating her. She looked at Jerrit, and by common consent they walked away, leaving the House Mistress to keep faith with the dead.

As soon as they were out of the smoke of the cremation field, Nisha scrubbed at her upper lip, trying to get the bitter smell of Camini's salve off. Her eyes stung from the smoke. Behind her Jerrit scraped his nose against the grass.

"I don't like this," Nisha said. "What was Atiy doing on the roof? Was she meeting someone there?"

Jerrit sent, *But who? If she was so shy, she wouldn't be sneaking away to meet someone. It doesn't make sense. . . .*

The cat trailed off, his ears pricking up.

"What is it?" Nisha asked.

Jerrit started running. *I don't know. It's Esmer . . . something's happened.*

Nisha ran after him.

20

SOMEONE HAD BEEN in Nisha's bedroom.

When Nisha and Jerrit burst through the door, Esmer was sitting in the center of the room on the worn rug. A red-brown pool spread over the floor. The near wall was streaked with the same dark stain. Two painted words stood out clearly:

STAY AWAY

Nisha forced words past her throat. "Is that blood?"

Esmer wrinkled her nose, and her gray fur, standing on end, seemed to shudder. *I don't think so*, she sent. *Whoever did this had a pocketful of clovermint. I can't smell Jerrit right now, not that I'd want to.*

I'd smell like clovermint, Jerrit sent. *Just like everything else in this room.* He sniffed the pool; then, with a quick flick of his pink tongue, he tasted it.

Blech. He sat back. *It's ink.*

"Ink, not blood." But Nisha couldn't stop staring at the red-brown words. STAY AWAY.

Fear wrapped cold fingers around her heart. Jina's and Atiy's deaths hadn't been accidents or suicides or any of the explanations Nisha had been secretly hoping for. Someone was afraid of Nisha's investigations. Someone wanted to scare her off.

The two cats circled the room, sniffing for more clues as Nisha sank down on her bedroll. Without thinking, she put her hand under her pillow, where she'd hidden the red silk scarf the Shadow Mistress had given her. Her questing fingers met nothing but her bedroll.

The scarf wasn't under the pillow. It wasn't under the bedroll or in the clothes chest. Nisha even lifted the rug, careful not to disturb the seeping ink, but the tiger scarf was nowhere to be found.

What's wrong? Jerrit sent.

"The scarf is gone," Nisha said. "The scarf the Shadow Mistress gave me." Her voice came out flat and dull, like old paper.

Oh, Nisha . . . , Esmer sent, nuzzling her foot. *I'm sorry.*

"I didn't even know what it meant," Nisha said, hugging herself against the pain of the words. "I didn't know what it meant, and now it's gone. Why would the killer steal it? It didn't mean anything to anyone else."

The cats said nothing. There was nothing to say.

Nisha was suddenly tired all the way down to her bones. She wanted nothing more than to sleep, to make it all go away: her friends changing, the murders, the Council, and the stolen scarf, the only link she'd had to her parents and her past. Not caring that she still had chores to do, she crawled onto her bedroll and closed her eyes.

Stay with her, Jerrit, Esmer sent. *I'm going to talk to the tribe.* Giving Nisha another nuzzle, she padded out of the small quarters.

Nisha crawled off her bedroll to reach into the clothes chest. She pulled an old carving of a spotted cat out of the bottom and ran her fingers over the smooth wood. It was the last thing her father had given her. She held it tightly and curled into a ball.

Jerrit was pacing, double-checking every corner of the room. *Nisha, this is getting too dangerous. If someone's scared enough to leave you a warning . . . I don't think you should keep poking into these deaths.*

Nisha fingered the toy cat, taking comfort in its familiar shape. "I don't have much of a choice," she said. "I know I can't stay here as things are. If the Council decides to sell me, I won't even get to the Redeeming. But I'll be careful, Jerrit, I promise."

Careful may not be enough, Jerrit sent. His tail lashed. *If the killer can get into your bedroom, whoever it is can get to you anywhere. It isn't safe.*

"I haven't been safe since Akash decided to get rid of me," Nisha said, sitting up. "I don't like this any more than you do, but I have to find out the truth. And not just for me–for Atiy and Jina. They didn't deserve to die."

Swear to me that you won't go anywhere alone, Jerrit sent, anxiety in every line of his lithe but muscular body. *I know you. You go off on your own too much. Promise you won't do that. Swear it by the Long-Tailed Cat.*

Nisha hesitated, but the pleading note in Jerrit's voice undid her. He sounded so worried. "All right, I swear," she said. "By the Long-Tailed Cat. I won't go anywhere alone."

Jerrit relaxed. *Thank you. If anything happened to you, Nisha, I don't know what I'd do.*

He leaped onto the bed. Nisha put the wooden cat down and clung to Jerrit as if he were the only solid thing in the world.

"Don't leave me," she whispered.

Never, Jerrit replied. *I promise.*

Nisha stared at the dark ink spattering her wall. Despite his promise, Jerrit's voice seemed thin and far away, and she felt more alone than ever.

Something was tickling Nisha's nose, pulling her out of sleep. She rubbed her face and forced her eyes open.

Jerrit was standing over her. *Wake up, Nisha. Wake up. Something's wrong.*

"Wrong?" Nisha's mouth was dry and sour. "What's wrong? How long did I sleep?"

Jerrit jumped to the floor. *It's just after first light. And your yellow Music asar is missing. I've checked three times. It's gone.*

Nisha frowned, her mind still fuzzy from sleep. "You're not supposed to be in the clothes chest," she said.

You left it open, Jerrit pointed out. *I just wanted a look. Your asars are so soft . . . That's not the point. One is missing.*

Nisha came fully awake as the meaning of Jerrit's words hit her like the flat of a sword.

"The killer has a Music asar now," she said. She looked at Jerrit, who bristled with understanding. There were so many girls taking lessons in the House of Music, it would be easy for someone to sneak in.

Nisha flung her feet out of bed. "Come on. We have to do something."

The House of Music was quiet in the early-morning light. Only a few notes from a long flute drifted from an open window.

No one here smells any tenser than usual, Jerrit sent, pacing beside Nisha.

"That just means nothing has happened yet," Nisha murmured, quickening her steps. "Keep your eyes open."

And my nose, Jerrit agreed. *What are you going to tell Vinian? So many girls from Beauty and Flowers are taking lessons here now. She won't turn girls away so close to the Redeeming, and there's no way to watch everyone.*

"Don't remind me," Nisha said. "I'll think of something."

They found Vinian in the kitchen, eating a breakfast of wild apples and baked rice cake. The spicy scent of her morning chai filled the room, and the sleepy chatter of the Music girls floated through the door that connected the kitchen to the dining room.

"Nisha!" Vinian said, blinking with surprise as Nisha burst in the back door. "What are you doing here so early?"

Nisha tried to sound casual and not as though she'd run all the way from the Council House. "I'm sorry, Vinian, I do know it's early. But I need your help."

"About the Redeeming?" Vinian asked, setting down her chai with a clink. "Have you not been able to find anyone else to endorse you?"

I wish that was my only problem, Nisha thought. She sat down and pulled Jerrit into her lap. "Nothing so drastic. It's just that someone broke into my room. Now my Music asar is missing."

"Goodness," Vinian said. "Have you reported it? And why would anyone steal a Music asar?"

Nisha chose her words carefully. "I thought it might be a prank. Maybe someone was dared to do it. I don't want to get anyone into trouble."

"Well, I can get you a new asar by tomorrow. But I don't like the idea of a prankster running around my House." Vinian picked up a slice of apple and chewed it thoughtfully. "I'll talk to the older girls. Each of them has a 'little sister' who she's tutoring, and they could be the ones to notice if any new novices showed up." Vinian set her food down. "Nisha, is there any chance it might be Zann?"

Guilt twisted in Nisha's stomach like spoiled milk. "I don't know," she managed, holding Jerrit tighter.

"I know it's not a pleasant subject," Vinian said. "But Zann *was* a novice—"

"Before I made her rebel," Nisha finished.

"No!" Vinian hit the table with her open hand, making Nisha jump. "You were a child; there was *no* way you could have known."

Nisha stared at the table. "If I hadn't agreed to help her, none of it would have happened," she said, voicing her shame. "You must be angry with me for depriving you of your most gifted student."

"I was angry with myself for a long time," Vinian said. "I should have fought harder to keep her, despite the bad example. I should have found a way."

"What do you think happened to her?" Nisha asked, her shame receding enough so she could look at Vinian again. "I couldn't understand why she took everything out on what she loved. . . ."

Vinian sighed. "Zann came to me in tears, wanting to know if she really had to marry an old man. I tried to explain, to tell her that he was a respected and honorable widower who loved music as much as she did. All he wanted was a companion, someone who could play for him."

She shook her head. "If she had listened, I could have calmed her down. She was scheduled to start the next phase of her training soon. We would have hired an older man as a special teacher and built him up as a mentor until she relied on him for approval and security."

Nisha pressed her lips together and leaned back, folding her arms. She hated this part: the manipulation, the deceit.

"You don't understand," Vinian said, looking closely at Nisha. "You've never been formally trained, so you see us only from the outside. We work for specific results: contentment, happiness, girls who can contribute to society wherever they're placed. That's why we kept Zann's Spoken a secret. Zann's only true passion was music; she loved it more than anything else. She would have been redeemed as a fully trained musician. Her emotional attachment would have transferred easily from her teacher to the man who redeemed her. She would have had as much time to devote to music as she could ever have wished.

"But she hated the idea that we would ask her to be anything but a professional musician, hated the thought of marrying a man old enough to be her father. She screamed at me and ran out, then ran to the practice rooms and began to destroy instruments. You know the rest."

Nisha could not imagine the girl who Zann had been—the passionate, dedicated musician—destroying the very things she loved.

"She destroyed a third of the House instruments before we stopped her," Vinian said, her slender hands tightening around her cup. "Including all her personal instruments. The destruction was incredible. Sitt-harps with their strings sliced, tab drums with huge holes in them, bells dented and twisted. We couldn't save anything."

The Music Mistress spread her hands. "I tried to plead for her. She was so young. And I did convince them to keep her on here so she wouldn't starve. But the Council insisted on making her into a bond slave until she earned back the cost of the things she broke. She never forgave us."

Or me, Nisha thought. Somewhere along the way, Zann had decided that her disgrace was all Nisha's fault. As if Nisha didn't already blame herself enough.

Vinian reached over and touched her hand. "It wasn't your fault, Nisha. You were only a child, and we should have explained everything to you properly. But we never thought–" She pressed her lips together. "What's done is done," she said in a gentle tone. "You cannot change it."

People keep telling me that, Nisha sent to Jerrit.

Perhaps you should listen, the cat sent back.

Nisha's smile felt thin and brittle. "Thank you, Vinian. I'll come back tomorrow and pick up a new asar."

"Do that," Vinian said, picking up her chai again. "I'll let you know if anyone shows up in your old one."

See, she didn't blame you, Jerrit sent as they left the House of Music.

Nisha shook her head. She felt empty and a little nauseous. "I still blame me," she said. "If I hadn't done what Zann wanted, everything might have been different."

If you figure out a way to fold back time and change the past, let me know, Jerrit sent with rare sarcasm. *I have some hunts I'd like to try again. In the meantime, instead of wallowing, you should race me to the main gate.*

He took off, a golden-brown streak against the grass.

"Dirty cheater," Nisha muttered, then pounded after him.

Jerrit followed the outside curve of the hedge maze, and Nisha ran hard to catch up with him. Her feet felt light. As long as she had the cats and she could run, things couldn't be that bad.

She put on a burst of speed and slammed into a figure coming out of the maze.

Something hard and rough struck her in the chest, and she fell. Her flailing hands met loose fabric as she hit the ground with her shoulder. Something jabbed into her hip. She heard Jerrit yowl with pain. Then a heavy weight landed on top of her. An elbow pushed into her windpipe, cutting off her air.

Fear gave Nisha strength, and she struck out blindly. Her closed fist hit skin and bone with a satisfying *crack*, and the weight rolled off her.

Gasping, she tried to sit up and brace herself for another attack, only to realize she'd barreled into Zann.

21

ZANN WAS ON the ground, surrounded by the wood she must have been carrying. Blood poured from her nose. Her face was streaked with dirt and sap. She stared at Nisha with blank, uncomprehending eyes.

"Zann," Nisha said, stretching out a hand. "I'm sorry, I thought–"

Zann tried to wipe the blood from her face, but all it did was smear. She looked down at her bloody hand and gave a low moan.

Then, before Nisha could stand, Zann struggled to her feet and ran off, still bleeding.

"Zann!" Nisha called after her. "Wait!"

She tried to lever herself up, but a stab of pain in her left hand stopped her. She was lying on several pieces of wood and had scraped her hand on one of them when she fell. Angry red scratches punctuated with dark slivers of wood crisscrossed her palm. Blood oozed from the scratches and down her wrist.

Nisha! Esmer ran out of the maze. *What happened? I heard Jerrit yell . . . Look at you!* She climbed into Nisha's lap and licked her forehead with a rough tongue.

"I ran into Zann," Nisha said. Her head hurt, and her shoulder and hand throbbed. "I think I punched her in the nose."

Esmer hissed, kneading her claws into Nisha's thighs. *I don't blame you.*

Nisha thought of Zann's face, covered in blood.

"I didn't mean to," she said, feeling the utter uselessness of her defense. "It was an accident. I thought I was being attacked."

Esmer went back to licking Nisha as if Nisha were a dirty kitten. *Of course you did,* she sent. *All this running around after murderers has got all of us worked up. And it shouldn't even be necessary.* She shook her head.

"Is Jerrit all right?" Nisha asked. "I think he got stepped on."

He ran off, Esmer said. *It's just a flight instinct. He'll be fine, if a bit embarrassed.* She sniffed at a patch of bloody grass. *That's odd.*

"What is it?" Nisha asked. "What do you smell?"

Guilt, Esmer sent with surprise. *Acidic, soul-eating guilt.* She shook herself as if she were wet. *Strange. It's rare for human emotions to smell this strongly. Fear does, of course, but not the others. This has soaked all the way through. . . .*

It was strange, Nisha thought as she staggered to her feet. Zann had always made it very clear she blamed everyone else. What could she be feeling guilty about now?

Nisha was still pondering the mystery of Zann's behavior when she turned around and started walking. The greenhouse was on the other side of the hedge maze, and she needed to go and get her hand bandaged. Esmer trailed her like a speckled gray shadow.

Inside the greenhouse, the damp heat embraced Nisha like a friend. She breathed, savoring the smells of tangy herbs, sweet blossoms, and thick green growth.

"Sashi?" she called.

Only humid silence answered her. Nisha thought briefly of trying to find a healer, then dismissed the idea. A healer would want an explanation, and Nisha wasn't sure she had one. She could mix up the poultice herself.

Nisha gathered pieces of the herbs she needed along the way to her space on the workbench. She put the leaves onto her flat grinding tablet, then reached for her rollstone. It wasn't there.

Nisha glanced around. She thought she had left the stone right next to the grinding tablet. Then she spotted the rollstone on Sashi's part of the table. She must have borrowed it and forgotten to return it.

Nisha picked up the rollstone, a slender cylinder of satiny white marble. She was about to go back to her herbs when she caught a whiff of something.

The smell was gone too quickly to identify, but it made Nisha pause. A faint alarm bell clanged in the recesses of her mind.

She leaned closer to the bench and sniffed delicately. At first she smelled nothing. Sashi was a fanatic about keeping her bench clear and washed. Nisha sniffed along the length of the rollstone.

There was a hint of herbs, but not enough for her to recognize the smell.

Ignoring her throbbing hand, Nisha looked over the workbench one more time, running her fingers over the wood of the table. This time she caught a flash of green, a tiny leaf caught in a crack.

Nisha pulled the leaf from its hiding place and rolled it in her fingers. The smell was as sharp and clean as the taste of frost on her tongue.

Clovermint.

Nisha remembered Sashi's hand breaking pieces of lavender as she talked about Atiy's death. Sashi, who worked regularly with poisons, who had could have gotten the key to the poison cupboard easily. Sashi had been rolling clovermint.

Confused and sick, Nisha rolled her herbs and mixed a poultice for her hand. Grabbing some bandages, she stumbled out of the greenhouse.

Was Sashi there? Esmer sent.

"No," Nisha said, swallowing. There was only one person left in the City she could trust to help her and not ask questions. "Maybe Tanaya can help me get these splinters out."

Nisha walked blindly around the maze to the House of Flowers, her thoughts knotted in an endless tangle. Sashi needed a guide whenever she left the House of Jade. How could she have been involved in Atiy's death? Unless the deaths weren't connected after all. Could Sashi have sneaked the seeds into Jina's snack bowl while the girl was asleep? But why? Was there a rivalry that Nisha didn't know about?

No. It couldn't be . . .

Nisha clutched at the bandages, feeling as if the world were tilting on her. How much of Sashi's peaceful air was real, and how much was a mask? Could her friend really be a part of this?

Tanaya was kneeling on the floor of her room, painting an exquisitely detailed figurine of a dancer in midleap. She looked up when Nisha staggered in, and her smile of welcome shaded into concern.

"Nisha, what's happened?" Tanaya sprang up and helped Nisha to her reclining couch.

Nisha sat, berating herself for jumping to the most obvious conclusion. Sashi was studying to be a healer. She wouldn't kill. She used clovermint in her medicines all the time.

"Goodness," Tanaya said. "What happened to your hand?"

"I fell," Nisha said, pulling her thoughts back to the present. "I fell and scraped it badly. Sorry to interrupt, but I couldn't bandage it by myself."

"Don't apologize, Nisha," Tanaya said. "I've been stuck in this room all day. Of course I'll help. Just tell me what to do."

Nisha gave her careful instructions as Tanaya pulled out the slivers, then wrapped her hand with the poultice and clean bandages Nisha had brought. By the time she was done, the throb in Nisha's hand had dimmed to an ache. It still hurt, but the pain was bearable.

"You poor thing," Tanaya said as she finished tying the bandages. "You lie here for a minute and relax." She leaned over Nisha to adjust a pillow. The ruby necklace at her throat glistened, and her sleek black-and-gray asar smelled of lavender.

"That's a new scent for you," Nisha mumbled.

"Do you like it? The girls from the House of Jade brought us some lavender today. I've never tried it before, but I was getting bored with the night-queen scent. Now you rest. I'll tell Matron you're helping me if anyone asks."

"Thank you, Tanaya," Nisha said. She was starting to feel the effects of her early awakening. Maybe if she just took a short nap, she could think more clearly.

Nisha closed her eyes, trying to push out the image of Sashi's hands snapping the lavender twigs.

How long she dozed, she didn't know. But a staccato knock at the door jerked her awake. Nisha sat up, trying to clear her fuzzy sleep thoughts.

Tanaya had changed into a gray-and-red asar and sat putting her hair up. "Enter," she called around the hairpins in her mouth.

One of the Council House servants burst into the room.

"Matron sent me to find Nisha," she cried. "Something terrible has happened!"

Nisha jumped up, forgetting the pain in her hand. "What is it?" she asked, a sick certainty in her gut.

"Another death," the girl said, white-faced. "I've been looking for you all over. Matron said to bring you to–"

"The House of Music," Nisha said, ignoring Tanaya's puzzled gasp.

The girl shook her head and gave Nisha a confused look. "No," she said. "Not the House of Music. It was the House of Beauty."

Leaving Tanaya in her room, Nisha followed the servant girl out of the House of Flowers and down the short stone path that led to the House of Beauty. Confusion blurred her mind. She'd been so sure that the killer was going to the House of Music. Had the stolen asar been just to throw Nisha off the scent?

Nisha barely noticed the spotted shadows that darted after her as she stumbled along. Esmer had to yell to get her attention.

Nisha, slow down!

Are you all right? Jerrit sent, shame coloring his voice. *I'm sorry I ran away. I felt your distress all the way across the estate.*

There's been another killing, Nisha sent in a tense burst of thought. *At the House of Beauty.*

Both cats reacted with stunned silence.

There was no way you could have seen this coming, Esmer sent. *We did everything we could.*

It wasn't enough! Nisha snapped back, surprised by the quickness of her own anger. Leaving the cats to wait outside, she walked in through the front doors of the House of Beauty. The foyer was smaller than that of the House of Flowers, and more comfortable, filled with padded benches and paintings in soft colors. The air smelled of jasmine and lavender. And unlike the broad main stairs of the House of Flowers, the House of Beauty stairs were a graceful spiral, hung with lilies. Nisha climbed them, following the servant to an upstairs room.

A crumpled figure lay on the bedroom floor, a wide black stain stretching across the carpet underneath her. Nisha bit her lip.

It *wasn't* enough. It wasn't anywhere close to enough.

22

"NISHA, WHAT ARE you doing here?" Rajni, the Mistress of the House of Beauty, was standing behind her. Her slender hands were clenched hard, turning them the color of the White Mist.

"Matron sent for me," Nisha said. "To help." She gestured at the body.

"Indeed I did," said Matron, appearing beside the trembling Rajni, looking pointedly at Nisha. "I wanted you and Josei to examine her first. Josei should be here soon."

Confusion wrinkled Rajni's smooth forehead. When Matron didn't explain, the House Mistress turned to the servant.

"News of this . . . accident doesn't leave the room," Rajni said to the servant, her voice ragged with anxiety. "If I hear one whisper, one rumor about this, I will revoke your work permit and turn you out of the estate."

Nisha cleared her throat. "I was with Tanaya in the House of Flowers when I heard," she said. "Someone should probably tell her not to talk about it, too."

Rajni frowned. "See to it," she ordered the servant.

"Yes, House Mistress," the servant girl said with a bow, perfectly submissive. "It will be as you say."

"Yes, it will," Rajni said, dismissing the girl with a wave. "This is terrible," she said to no one in particular. "Nothing like this has ever happened in my House before."

Nisha walked around the body, careful to touch nothing. The dead girl was huddled in on herself, little more than a heap of blue muslin and a tangle of dark-gold hair. Nisha's nose twitched at the dry, metallic smell that soaked the room. The deep-purple carpet underneath the body was stiff and dark with blood.

A flash of white caught her eye. She reached out a hand, careful not to disturb the body, and drew a small folded piece of rough paper out from under the tangled hair.

There, on the front in black block letters, was her name: NISHA.

Rajni was talking to Matron, and neither of them was looking at Nisha. Nisha slipped the note into an inner pocket.

A hand touched her shoulder, and she jumped.

"She was stabbed," Josei said. She had come into the room so quietly that Nisha hadn't heard her. She sniffed, her sharp nose subtly tasting the air. "Smells like a stomach wound. She must have been stabbed in the gut."

Nisha copied Josei, taking a deep whiff of the room. There

was a foul, decaying tang underneath the blood smell, one that she hadn't noticed before. She held her breath until the nausea passed.

Josei didn't seem to notice. The Combat Mistress was feeling carefully under the body. "Is there a weapon here, I wonder? Ah, there it is."

Josei reached under the girl's hip and slid out a thin metal object as long as her hand. The tip of the object was shaped like a butterfly and set with deep-blue sapphires; it sparkled deep blue in the light from the window. The sharp, slender point was crusted with blood.

"That's her hair ornament," Rajni said, her voice thick with shock.

Josei raised one dark eyebrow. "It's a dagger," she corrected. "You arm your girls?"

"It's more than a dagger," Rajni said. "It's a symbol. The girls here are not just beautiful, they are creators of beauty. They draw and sculpt, arrange flowers, paint. Beauty is the only skill, the only dowry they have. And beauty is not only to attract or impress. It's also a medicine, a tool . . . and a weapon."

Rajni tugged her curls. "The girls are given the hair ornaments the year they are ready to be spoken for, on their sixteenth birthdays. It's a reminder to them of beauty's power and danger."

"Beauty is serious business," Nisha murmured.

"Exactly," Rajni said. "The House of Combat is not the only House that teaches its girls to survive."

Josei twisted the hair ornament, watching it flash in the light.

"So this belonged to the dead girl? That will make things more difficult."

Nisha noticed a sapphire sandal peeking out from the soft blue fabric. The stones matched the hair ornament exactly. Nisha imagined the dead girl's graceful feet dancing about the room, the sapphires glowing as she moved.

"What was her name?" Nisha asked.

Rajni's liquid brown eyes filled with tears. "Lashar," she whispered. "Her name was Lashar."

"Lashar," Nisha repeated. She knelt beside the tangle of hair, brushing it away from the cold, still face. The girl's light, clear eyes were wide and glazed over in death.

"The killer did it face-to-face this time," Nisha said. "She looked into Lashar's eyes and slashed her open."

Josei muttered a curse. "This is no long-distance poisoning. This death was personal. Was this girl already spoken for?"

"Yes," Rajni said. "She was to be an estate wife. She and the client had met a handful of times. He's the son of a minor lord and wanted a good bedmate when he was home."

Nisha grimaced. Wives without political power or connections were known as estate wives. They were kept in style at luxury country houses, entertained their husbands' friends with lavish parties, and gave birth to heirs. Estate wives did not often visit the Imperial Court, leaving the husband free to gain power and status through carefully chosen flirtations and affairs.

With so many plots and intrigues around, no wonder the House of Beauty gave its girls daggers.

Something clicked in Nisha's mind, falling into place with an almost audible snap. "Did you just say the client wanted a good bedmate?"

Rajni nodded, a puzzled frown creasing her golden skin.

Matron's eyebrows went up in a flash of understanding. "Rajni, did Lashar ever receive training from the House of Pleasure?"

"Yes," said Rajni. "She never went there–but one of the trainers came here."

"Three girls dead, all connected to the House of Pleasure," Josei said. "How interesting."

Nisha rubbed the back of her neck, feeling the tension in her muscles. What possible reason could anyone at the House of Pleasure have to kill so many girls? She felt as if there was a thread here that she wasn't seeing, a connection that would make all the pieces fit.

Maybe there was a clue in the note.

Nisha fingered the note in her pocket and peered around. The others were deep in conversation. No one was looking at her. Carefully, so as not to make noise, she unfolded the note. The edges of the thin paper were torn, and shaky black letters streamed across the page like drunken footprints. Nisha forgot about the paper–her eyes were drawn to the words.

You're looking for me, but you'll never find me. Come to the old quarry that lies to the south at Darkfall tomorrow. If you don't show up, or if you tell anyone, I will kill again.
And I've set a trap for your friend in the House of Flowers. If you find it first, you might save her life.

Nisha crumpled the note, her mouth dry with fear.

Tanaya was in danger.

Nisha bolted past the House Mistresses, ignoring their startled looks. She raced down the stairs and straight out of the House of Beauty. Her heart was pounding, and the faces of the dead girls followed her.

Not Tanaya. Not her.

She was darting up the front steps of the House of Flowers when she heard the scream.

No.

Nisha flew up the wide main stairs and into Tanaya's room. Tanaya stood on her couch, her eyes wide, one hand at her throat. On the carpet was a coiled reddish shape banded with white.

Nisha skidded to a stop. It was a blood krait, the most poisonous snake in the Empire. And Nisha was much too close to it.

Sensing movement, the snake turned its unblinking eyes on her. Its forked tongue flicked in and out, tasting the air for the new arrival. Then it hissed.

A whimper caught in Nisha's throat. Blood kraits moved quicker than the eye could follow. There was no way she could get away in time.

Blunt head moving back and forth in a hypnotizing dance, the snake slid toward her. It was the length of her arm, and its scales slipped over the carpet with an obscene caressing sound. The slitted golden eyes pinned Nisha in place.

She couldn't move. Couldn't breathe. She could only watch her death slither closer–

A tawny-colored streak shot past her feet. With a cry of rage,

Jerrit placed himself between Nisha and the snake.

"No!" Nisha jerked out of her trance. "Jerrit, don't!"

The snake reared up with a vicious hiss. Long fangs like curved blades jutted from its open mouth. Jerrit hissed back, a sharp sound of pure fury. His back arched as he circled the snake. The snake lashed out and Jerrit danced away, dodging the lethal bite.

"Jerrit, no!" Nisha looked around for a weapon. Something. Anything. But Tanaya's room was all soft pillows and heavy furniture.

Jerrit and the snake circled each other. Jerrit slashed at the snake with his claws, drawing a wound down the long slithery body. The snake's hiss intensified, a deep, evil sound. Its head darted back and forth.

Then it struck.

The two rolled over in a blur of fur and scales. The snake's fangs gleamed as it hissed and writhed. Jerrit twisted his body away, burying his teeth into the snake's neck.

"Jerrit!" Nisha circled the hissing, yowling tangle. This couldn't be happening.

Someone seized her wrist, and with surprising strength, Tanaya pulled Nisha up onto the couch.

"You can't help him," Tanaya yelled. "They're too close!"

"Do you have your daggers?" Nisha asked. Tanaya shook her head.

With an effort, Jerrit tore the snake's head from its neck and–as quickly as it had started–the battle was over. The cat stood over the twitching body of the snake. Blood matted his golden fur, and his legs trembled.

Nisha jumped off the couch. "Jerrit?"

Nisha. The sending was ragged with pain. *Nisha, I have to tell you—*

"No," Nisha whispered, running her hands over his heaving sides. "Just rest, Jerrit. Don't try to talk. You'll be all right if you just rest." Her hands came away streaked with red, and a sob built in her throat.

Nisha, you need to know . . . Jerrit's voice was growing weaker, fading from Nisha's mind. Then he collapsed.

Nisha wanted to throw her head back and howl, but she couldn't get the sound past her throat. "No," she choked out. "No."

"Oh, Nisha," Tanaya whispered. "I'm so sorry."

A dark rage like the heart of a flame flared up in Nisha's chest. "Don't be sorry! Because Jerrit isn't going to die! Do you hear me?" she shouted, scooping up Jerrit's barely breathing body. "I'm not letting you die!"

Cradling him, she ran out of the room and down the stairs.

A crowd of the spotted cats had gathered at the base of the steps. Nisha ran past. *Esmer, find a healer,* she sent. *We'll be in the greenhouse.* She sensed wordless assent and worry as the cats saw the limp body in her arms and took off in all directions.

Nisha ran as carefully as she could. Jerrit's body felt far too light in her hands, and his heartbeat tripped and dimmed with every step she took.

"Please," she breathed like a prayer. "Please, please, please."

Nisha stumbled into the greenhouse and almost burst into

tears when she saw Sashi already standing there. The girl's unseeing brown eyes were wide with shock, and a handful of growling cats led by Esmer guarded her front and back.

Nisha staggered up to her, shoving Jerrit's still form into her hands.

"A snake bit him, a blood krait," she gasped. "He needs help." Her knees nearly buckled. "Please," she whispered.

The shock left Sashi's face, replaced by a look of intense concentration. She laid Jerrit on the workspace, her nimble fingers exploring his fur.

"No paralysis yet," she murmured. "But his heartbeat is slowing." She looked down, her face cold and set. "Nisha, stop sniveling. If you want me to save him, I need help. The poison's working slowly. He only got scratched by the fangs. But he *will* die if we don't hurry!"

Nisha scrambled to her feet. "What do you need?"

"Starflowers," Sashi said, her hands still moving over Jerrit. "North corner, by the wall. We have to keep his heart going. Then I'll need some water and some white willow bark–"

Sashi worked steadily, always calm. She poured a potion down Jerrit's throat, then spread a green poultice over his wounds. Nisha could see several long gashes from the krait's fangs, but no direct bites.

Time blurred, the hours feeling like minutes. Nisha ground herbs until her hands ached. She held Jerrit's mouth open for the medicines and cradled him when he convulsed, each jerky movement stabbing through her like a knife. A few times he stopped breathing, and Sashi had to force air into his lungs, cupping her hand over his nose. Nisha's eyes were blurry and hot, and every breath she took was a prayer to any ancestor or god who would listen. *Save him. Please help me save him.*

Finally, just before Darkfall, Jerrit's breathing eased. Sashi raised her head, her face worn but triumphant. "The poison's working its way out."

Nisha felt herself go weak and leaned against the workbench. She put her face down on Jerrit's damp fur, savoring the quiet pitch and heave of his breath.

"Thank you," she said, but there was no answer. Sashi had already gone to a washbasin to rinse the blood and medicine off her hands.

I'll let the others know, Esmer sent, her words jagged with relief. The gray cat stopped pacing in the shadows and slipped outside.

Nisha ran a hand down Jerrit's side. His heartbeat flickered against her palm, an echo of the blood pounding in her own ears. She'd almost lost him.

No more, Nisha vowed to herself. *This ends now.* She would go to meet the killer, but she would go early. Wait. Hide. Watch. Maybe she could identify the killer, or even capture her.

But she *would* stop this.

23

NISHA LAID JERRIT in a soft bed of blankets in the warmest corner of the greenhouse, then went to get a clean robe. It wasn't until she stepped behind the changing screen that she remembered.

Devan. In all the chaos of the day, she had forgotten to meet Devan.

Worry curled in Nisha's chest. She'd never failed to meet him before. Would he be angry? The last thing she'd said to him was that she was scared, that being with him frightened her. What if he thought she didn't care about him anymore?

Nisha swallowed the thought. If she just told him what had happened, Devan would understand. He knew how much the cats meant to her. All she had to do was explain.

If she ever got the chance.

As Nisha was reaching for one of the folded Jade asars, she noticed something odd. A crumpled green asar had fallen into one corner. Nisha picked it up. Spotting the front of the asar were dried dark streaks.

Esmer, Nisha sent. *Come back inside and look at this.*

After a moment, the older cat slipped around the screen. *What is it?* She sniffed the asar. *Nisha, that's blood.*

Are you sure? Nisha asked. *I thought it might be ink.*

No, this time it's definitely blood. The stains are too dry to know whose, but it's human. Nothing else smells like that.

Human blood. Nisha thought of the stain under Lashar's dead body, and her hands started to shake. She almost threw the asar back into the corner.

It must be from healer training, Nisha sent, but even as the words formed in her mind, she knew there were always servants on hand during healing procedures to take used asars away and wash them. The House of Jade was fanatical about cleanliness. Nisha had never seen a soiled asar abandoned in the corner like this. Someone must have thrown it there outside of supervised training.

But it didn't mean that it was Sashi's asar. There were other healer trainees here who used the greenhouse, even if none of them loved it the way Sashi did.

There was one way to know if the asar was Sashi's or not, but Nisha needed to be cautious about it. Holding the asar away from her body, she walked over to the washbowl.

"Sashi, I found a dirty asar over here," she said. "What would you like me to do with it?"

Sashi turned from the washbowl, her forehead furrowing in confusion. "A dirty asar? What's on it? I can't see what you're pointing at, you know."

Nisha forced her breathing not to change. "Looks like a bit of blood. Do you have a basket or something for these?"

"Blood?" Sashi stiffened, and swallowed hard. "Oh." Her voice sounded forced, and she dried her hands with quick, hard swipes. "I'm afraid that asar is mine. I cut myself trimming some fever-bush. I'll take care of it."

"Cut yourself? Here, let me see." Nisha reached for Sashi's hands, but the girl pulled back abruptly.

"I'm fine now. It was just a small cut."

"There's no such thing when you work with poisons. You should really let me have a look."

"No!" Sashi put her hands behind her back. Nisha could see the pulse in her throat beating wildly, like a fluttering moth. "I mean . . . I don't need your help. I can take care of myself."

"I never said you couldn't," Nisha said. "But I don't think you cut yourself, Sashi."

The other girl took a deep breath. "All right, I lied. It's my asar, but it's not my blood. But I can't tell you whose it is."

"Why not?" Nisha asked. "Sashi, this is important."

Sashi walked back to her bench and began to chop herbs. "I don't understand why you're pushing this, Nisha. It's just a little blood. Let it go."

Nisha wanted to let the subject drop, but fear—and the memory of Lashar's wide, dead eyes—drove her on. Lashar was gone,

Tanaya's life had been threatened with that snake, and Jerrit had almost died. If Sashi knew anything, Nisha needed to know it too. "There are things happening that you don't understand, Sashi. I'm trying to help."

The brown hand holding the cutting knife trembled. "There *is* a lot going on that I don't understand. Like how I could be standing here, cutting up roots, when suddenly I'm surrounded by snarling, growling animals. They wouldn't let me take even one step away from the bench. I had no idea what was happening. Do you have any idea how terrifying that was?"

"They *snarled* at you?" Nisha looked at Esmer, who stared back without blinking.

We needed her. We were frightened too.

"I'm sorry the cats scared you, Sashi," Nisha said. "But they wouldn't have hurt you."

"How do you know that?" Sashi whirled around, the knife still in her hand. "Don't tell me you can talk to them."

Nisha swallowed and didn't answer.

Sashi snorted. "Well, you keep your secrets, Nisha, and I'll keep mine. I can't tell you about the blood." Sorrow and guilt twisted her features. "You'll just have to trust me."

Nisha grabbed Sashi's arm. "Sashi, a girl was killed today, stabbed. You have to tell me how you got blood on your asar. Please."

Sashi pulled her arm out of Nisha's hand. "You think I stabbed someone?" she said. "You think I could *kill*?"

Nisha hesitated.

The hurt in Sashi's face was like a blow. "Nisha, we were friends."

Nisha crumpled like a paper kite. "We are friends." Her protest sounded weak to her own ears.

"It doesn't feel like that to me," Sashi said, her voice raw. "The healers were right. Putting so much trust in friendships *is* unwise! Emotional attachments only hurt you and get in the way." Sashi set the knife down on the table with a sharp *click*. "I should have listened."

"Sashi–" Nisha said, holding out her hand. "Wait."

But Sashi had already walked through the greenhouse door.

Nisha stared after her. For a moment, she considered running after her, but the anger in Sashi's voice had cut deep. Nisha didn't want to get tangled in another argument before she could give Sashi a solid reason to trust her.

She had to think.

After checking on Jerrit, Nisha lit a clay lamp and made her way back through the heavy black of Darkfall toward the Council House and her bedroom. Her shoulder and hand still hurt from the run-in with Zann, and her mind churned and frothed with questions.

How had Sashi gotten blood on her asar? Why wouldn't she talk about it?

And what was she going to tell Matron?

Because she had to tell Matron something–Nisha had no doubt of that. She had to tell her enough to make her protect Tanaya. The killer had seriously threatened Tanaya once, and there was

nothing stopping her from trying again.
was might move unseen and unnoticed in
itself.

If she told Matron about the note, N
to go to the quarry tomorrow. Or, wo
to apprehend the killer. And if the ki
would be in danger. Nisha couldn't let that happen.

Nisha thought of Sashi working over Jerrit. She didn't believe
that her friend could have hurt anyone. It wasn't just that she
liked Sashi and didn't want to believe the girl was a murderer.
The idea went against every instinct she had. But more than
that, it just didn't fit. There was the connection to the House of
Pleasure, for one thing. Sashi had no reason to visit that House.
And there was no reason for her to be up on that roof with Atiy.

If only I could be sure.

And that was the problem—Nisha couldn't be sure. Not without knowing what Sashi was hiding. *What do you think?* she asked
Esmer. *Should I tell Matron about Sashi?*

I don't know, Nisha. Esmer's mind-voice was as uncertain as
Nisha had ever heard it. *I have never in my life bit the hand that fed
me, but—*

But what if another girl dies? Nisha finished. She felt as if someone was twisting her insides. *Sashi just saved Jerrit. I don't want to
turn her in on a suspicion. But I can't let someone else die.*

I know, Esmer sent.

The side door was locked. Nisha hit the thick wood of the door
with her palm, feeling it sting with the force.

e to go in the front.

ouncil House was lit by long-burning torches on either
of the front steps. Nisha ran up the steps and pushed her
way in. Still thinking about Sashi's odd behavior, she walked
quickly down the hall, forgetting to be quiet.

"Nisha." Matron peered into the hallway, running a hand
through her hair. "What's wrong?"

Nisha scooped Esmer up in her arms, holding her as if she
were a shield. She didn't want to talk to Matron right now, not
when she was tired, heartsick, and so confused she wanted to
scream.

"Nothing happened. Someone locked the side door early. I'm
sorry I disturbed you, Matron. I'll be more quiet."

Matron narrowed her eyes. "I'm afraid that's not good enough.
You've been neglecting your chores, which leads me to believe
you're pursuing an angle you haven't told me about. Then you ran
out of the House of Beauty without any explanation. Now you're
sneaking back in and you look like you've been in a fistfight."

Nisha looked down at her gray asar, rumpled and streaked with
Jerrit's blood. "I . . . There was a medical emergency in the House
of Jade, and they needed some extra hands. I was . . . passing by
and they called me in. That's all. Everything's fine."

"You're lying, Nisha. And not very well." Matron reached out
and grabbed Nisha's arm, her knobby fingers pressing her skin
painfully. "I want the truth. I won't let you go until you tell me."

Nisha's mind went blank.

She had to protect Sashi. She had to protect Tanaya. She had to speak. She had to stay silent.

"I . . . it's nothing . . ."

Matron's grip tightened.

Nisha hunched her shoulders, feeling defeated. "Not here," she whispered, stalling for time.

Matron followed Nisha down the hall to the library. Flickering light from the fireplace played over the long shelves of scrolls. Matron shut the heavy oak door behind them. "Well?" she asked, folding her arms.

Nisha tightened her grip on Esmer. She could tell Matron about the attack on Tanaya.

"I found—I had a bad feeling," she lied. "I was looking at Lashar's body, and she looked so much like Tanaya. . . . I just had this horrible fear that Tanaya was in danger too. And she was."

"She was?" Matron went pale around the mouth. "Is she all right? What happened?"

"She's unhurt," Nisha hastened to reassure her. "Someone put a blood krait in her rooms, but she's fine."

"I must put a guard on her," Matron muttered. "I must increase security. How did she get away? How did *you* get away?"

A lump clogged Nisha's throat. "Jerrit—Jerrit—one of the cats attacked the snake. He killed it, but he was wounded. That's where this blood came from. I took him to the House of Jade."

Lines of fear etched Matron's face. "What is happening to my City, Nisha?"

"I don't know," Nisha whispered. She thought of Sashi's shaking hands and the pulse beating in her own throat.

Matron gave her a sharp glance. "Is there something you're not telling me, Nisha?"

Nisha squirmed. "No," she said, trying desperately to make her voice calm and convincing. "Nothing else happened."

Matron reached out and grabbed Nisha's wrist. Her face was harder than Nisha had ever seen it. "Don't push me, Nisha. If Tanaya is in danger, then the stakes have just gone up more than you can possibly imagine, and I *will* do anything I have to in order to protect this City. Hold back on me, and I will sell you myself."

The betrayal of her old protector's words made Nisha feel as if someone had punched her in the stomach. It would be that easy for Matron to hand her over, for her life to be gone. How could Nisha take care of her friends if no one would take care of her?

A dam somewhere within Nisha broke. She felt the words flow out: She told Matron about Sashi saving Jerrit in the greenhouse, about the blood on Sashi's asar. "It doesn't necessarily have anything to do with the murders," she finished dumbly. "One of the servants could have cut themselves, or Sashi could have brushed against a bloody asar without realizing it. She could be protecting someone else who was careless."

"It's possible." Matron frowned. "And I would not have considered Sashi–" She shook herself. "Say nothing of this to anyone, Nisha. I must decide how best to use this information." Her words were a dismissal, but Nisha didn't move.

"I don't think you should take action yet," Nisha argued. "We don't *know* anything. Give me time to figure this out. Please."

She swallowed down her desperation, aiming for a persuasive tone instead. "The House of Pleasure connection, for example. That can't be a coincidence." She forced herself to look Matron straight in the eyes, as if they were equals. "It will look bad if we accuse the wrong person, even worse if the killer turns out not to be a House girl at all."

"True," Matron said. "I will do what I can." She turned to go, then looked back, her mouth hard. "But let me be very clear, Nisha. If it would save the City of a Thousand Dolls, I would sacrifice any girl here. Even you."

Nisha was too tired to push anymore. "I understand," she said. "Good night."

As soon as Matron left, Nisha sank down on one of the low padded benches that dotted the library. Esmer snuggled against her, and Nisha closed her eyes.

Did we do the right thing? Nisha asked the gray cat.

Esmer did not answer.

24

THE SOUND OF rustling paper brought Nisha out of her restless sleep. There was no warm cat next to her, and as she blinked awake, she realized it was day.

Something moved in front of the long window, a dark smudge against the gray light.

Nisha blinked. The smudge resolved itself into a girl seated cross-legged on the floor, her hands holding a scroll. The girl was wrapped in a black overrobe, the hood pushed down. The light turned her bent head to burnished gold.

"Tani?" Nisha propped herself up on one elbow. A hectic flush stained Tanaya's smooth cheeks, and faint lines accented her perfect mouth. The light from the window threw her cheekbones into sharp relief.

"You look terrible," Nisha blurted before she could stop herself.

A flash of fear crossed Tanaya's face. She put down the scroll and picked up the fan lying next to her.

"It's the strain of the Redeeming coming so soon," she said. "I've been getting so pale and puffy lately."

"No–" Nisha started, but Tanaya cut her off with an imperious wave of her fan.

"I appreciate your concern, Nisha, but please stop." Her voice was heavy with an arrogance that Nisha had never heard before. At least, not directed at her.

Nisha pushed down a stab of hurt. Tanaya *was* under a tremendous strain. She probably didn't realize how she sounded.

"What are you doing here, Tanaya? You have music lessons in the morning."

"It's not morning," Tanaya said, a smile lifting her face. "It's well after lunch. I asked Matron to let you sleep. It was the least I could do after last night." She shuddered. "That snake gave me nightmares. How is your cat?"

Nisha smiled. The relief of Jerrit's recovery was like a warm blanket she hugged to herself. "He'll be all right. Where did that horrible thing come from?"

Tanaya started playing with her fan, opening and closing it aimlessly. "I have no idea. I opened my chest to change my asar, and there it was, staring at me."

"It's a good thing it hadn't slithered farther down into the chest," Nisha said. "If you had reached in without seeing it–"

Tanaya wrinkled her nose. "Let's not think of that."

But Nisha could not stop thinking of it. She knew why the

snake hadn't been placed in the bottom of the chest. It had been a warning, not a true attempt on Tanaya's life. Nisha and the killer were playing a game now, one that she wasn't at all sure she could win. She knew the only way she could keep the killer from striking again was to go to the quarry. Tonight. Before anyone else got hurt.

Nisha went to Tanaya and hugged her hard, feeling the knife-like shoulder blades under her black overrobe.

"It's over now," she said.

"Really?" Tanaya asked, with unexpected vulnerability.

"Really," Nisha said, looking her friend in the eye. Tanaya had protected her when Nisha was a child. Now Nisha was going to protect her. "Trust me."

Tanaya smiled.

The door to the library flew open with a bang. Matron looked both calm and deeply displeased as she strode into the room, filling it with her presence.

"Tanaya, where have you been? House Mistress Indrani is looking for you. You are taking dinner with High Prince Sudev's representative today–have you forgotten?"

Tanaya's smile drained away, and the fan in her hand snapped open and shut in a dance of irritation. "I am speaking to Nisha," she said. "And I intend to go on speaking with her. I will have plenty of time to prepare for dinner."

"Indrani is looking for you," Matron repeated. "To choose the asar you will wear to dinner. No more of these somber colors. And for the love of heaven, girl, eat something this time. You're growing too thin as it is, and we don't want the prince to think you're getting sick."

Tanaya drew herself up until she was as narrow and tight as a well rope. "*I* choose my wardrobe," she said. "Not you, and not Indrani. I will wear exactly what I choose to wear. I will eat exactly what I choose to eat. Nothing more."

"Girl, you are forgetting yourself." Matron's quiet tone sent shivers down Nisha's spine.

"But Matron, I am never allowed to forget." Tanaya made a gesture with her fan that Nisha couldn't identify. "I would remind you that you need me more than I need you. I owe you *nothing*. Do you hear? Nothing!"

She touched her ruby-and-gold necklace with trembling fingers. It seemed to calm her, and the tense, angry lines on her face smoothed themselves out. "I will go find Indrani, as you *request*." She swept out of the room, leaving Matron looking after her with narrowed eyes.

Nisha looked after Tanaya, her mind slow with shock. "Why is she so angry?"

"I don't know," Matron said, and her tone was so positive that Nisha knew she must be lying again. "Indrani claims that Tanaya has been irritable and erratic lately. And she appears to have stopped eating." Matron paused. "She talks to you, Nisha. Has she told you anything?"

"Only that she's nervous about the Redeeming," Nisha said. "That's what she meant when she said you needed her more than she needed you. . . ."

Matron looked down awkwardly. "Yes. The reputation of the City is now tied to this union. If Tanaya becomes defiant or shows herself in any way to be unsuitable–"

"Why would she do that?" Nisha asked. "It wouldn't be worth it. She'd be thrown out, casteless."

Matron's mouth pinched as if tasting something bitter. "Tanaya would survive well enough. The demand for beautiful and intelligent courtesans is great enough that the employers would look the other way–and Tanaya doesn't have her caste mark yet. She could vanish easily. If you are smart enough and ruthless enough, there is always a way."

"Tani would never lower herself to that," Nisha protested.

"Tanaya won't have to lower herself to anything," Matron said. "She is the most important novice we have ever trained, and the first to marry into the Emperor's family. The Council will bend over backward to protect her and keep her happy. And Tanaya is perfectly capable of ruthlessness. It was part of her training."

"You're wrong," Nisha said. "Tanaya isn't ruthless. She's anxious and scared."

Matron's eyes rested on Nisha with something close to pity. "Sometimes, Nisha," she said, "people are not who you expect them to be."

"Matron." Kalia appeared in the doorway. Her eyes narrowed when she saw the two of them together, and Nisha had to force herself not to step behind Matron. "I need to talk to you."

"I'm busy, Kalia," Matron said, clipping her words. "Can't it wait?"

A flush passed over Kalia's face. "Well, if you're too important to be bothered, perhaps I should talk to Akash instead," she snapped. She turned to go.

"Kalia." The word was softly spoken, but it stopped the Mistress of Order in her tracks.

"Remember, you report to me, not Akash," Matron said. "And as long as I am Matron, the appointment–and dismissal–of House Mistressses is up to me. That includes you."

Kalia straightened her white asar and tilted her chin up. "Akash is my cousin. Surely you wouldn't deny me permission to speak to my own family?"

Matron gave her a level stare, meeting Kalia's eyes until the other woman looked away.

"Of course I will obey you, Matron," Kalia said, her words poisonous-sweet. "For as long as you are in charge." Kalia's eyes flicked to Nisha, who stared at her feet.

Matron rubbed the bridge of her nose. "Nisha, you may go."

"Oh, let her stay," Kalia said. "We don't spend nearly enough time together, do we Nisha?"

"Nisha." Matron's voice held no room for argument. "You are dismissed."

Nisha obeyed, forcing herself not to run. She walked casually until she was out of Kalia's eyesight, then broke into a quick trot. Time was running out, dribbling through her hands like water, and she was no closer to a solution than she had been five days ago. Sashi was furious with her, Tanaya was unraveling, and girls were still dying.

It had to stop.

Once in her room, Nisha pulled on her House of Combat tunic and a pair of loose trousers. The cotton fabric was a little thin for creeping through the woods, but it was the sturdiest thing she had. There was an old practice staff in the corner, not as well made as the ones in the armory, but she didn't have anything else.

Nisha tied the staff to her back and grabbed a clay lamp. If she hurried, she could get to the quarry well before the light failed, but she'd need the lamp to help her find her way back. Especially without a cat's help.

She felt a twist of guilt as she remembered her promise to Jerrit not go off alone. But if she told *any* of the cats where she was going, Jerrit might hear about it. That stubborn cat was perfectly capable of dragging himself to the quarry if he thought she was putting herself in danger. And then he would injure himself again, or get sick.

She'd almost lost Jerrit once. She couldn't risk losing him again.

And she couldn't do nothing. The killer had taken three girls, three happy, innocent girls full of dreams and plans and life. Their deaths had ripped open the fabric of the City, spreading sorrow and grief and risking all the girls' futures. And now Tanaya was being threatened.

Nisha had to stop it, not just for Tanaya, but for all the other novices in the City. The City had been a safe place for girls, a shelter in a world that didn't want them. Now it was a sad, dangerous place.

I will make it safe again, Nisha promised herself. *I will*.

The always-gray sky was just starting to darken as she left the Council House. She hurried to the main gate, pushing down a niggling feeling that she'd forgotten something. Jerrit would understand. She was protecting everyone by going alone. It was better this way. Stupid, but better.

Just outside the main wall, Nisha stopped. The trees rose in front of her, shadowy and full of danger. At the thought of walking into the forest, the old panic tightened her chest. Nisha forced herself to take one step, then another. The tightness squeezed the breath from her lungs, and her hands were cold and clammy.

She took another step. Even if the fear killed her, she was going to that quarry.

A flash of purple caught Nisha's eye. Nestled under a bush by her feet was a lavender orchid, a pale slip of paper tied to its stem. Nisha scooped it up.

> *Solid, steady earth*
> *Under your graceful slippers*
> *Is the love I offer*

The ink was a little smudged and the paper damp, but the elaborate *D* was unmistakable.

Devan.

Nisha couldn't stop the smile of relief from spreading across her face. She put the orchid to her face, breathing in the heady scent. The feel of the soft petals gave her new courage. She could be brave. She could do what she had to do to protect Tanaya and the other girls.

She could do this.

The pale trunks of the trees, instead of threatening Nisha, beckoned her. Remembering the Kildi man she'd seen before and Devan's remark that that more Kildi were camping nearby, she studied the line of trees carefully. But there was no sign of any other human. She was alone.

Taking a deep breath, she moved her feet, one after the other, until she was deep in the forest.

The broad teak leaves were edged with brown, and a few already graced the carpet of wiry grass. Nisha avoided them. Even mist-damp leaves would rustle under her feet, sending word of her presence to anyone who might be lurking in the woods. Nisha's footsteps grew sure as she walked, and her breathing eased as she headed in the direction of the quarry.

The quarry was a legend in the City. It was supposed to be haunted by the spirits of builders who had died digging stone for the City walls.

The legend was nonsense, of course. No one had ever died in the quarry, and there were no deaths connected to the building of the City in any of the history scrolls she'd read. Nisha suspected the House Mistresses invented tales like that to keep curious girls out of the woods. It made a good story to tell the younger children on cold nights. Nisha almost laughed, thinking how little she'd needed stories to keep her out of the woods. She'd had her own reasons.

Even though she didn't believe in the ghost stories, Nisha expected to feel lost and frightened. It was her first real journey into the woods since her attempt at running away six years ago. But a strange thing happened. She slipped into the rhythm of the forest like she was born to it. Even in the dim light, the life of the woods vibrated around her: the rich scent of teak leaves and grass, the sleepy trills of the tiny parrots huddled in the branches. She hiked toward the quarry at an easy lope. Soon she was deeper into the woods then she'd ever been, and the deeper she went, the more comfortable she felt.

Josei was right. I'm not a child anymore. The knot of terror in her chest–the one that had been there since Matron had first told her she was to be sold–loosened. If she had to, she could escape. Jerrit and Esmer would come with her, maybe more of the cats too, and she would survive.

But she didn't have to go, not yet. She had to make sure her friends were safe and see Devan again–to ask him to speak for her, or to say good-bye. Nisha held the orchid to her face again and smiled.

No, she wouldn't leave just yet.

Still, the knowledge that she could warmed her like a tiny flame in the back of her mind. Nisha no longer felt like a parakeet in a cage, flapping her wings at the bars. Now the door was open, and possibilities stretched out before her. She could find the school that Matron had told her about. Or she could work in a village or join a Wind caste caravan. Josei thought she would make a good guard. She was young, healthy, and strong and could hold her own in a fight. She could build a place for herself somewhere.

Even the idea of slavers and bandits didn't frighten her anymore. As long as she wasn't trapped, Nisha knew she wouldn't be too frightened to fight back. Not even against the killer she was about to meet.

Just on the edge of the quarry, she stopped to catch her breath and listen. No footsteps, no startled birds, nothing out of place. The slate-gray sky was turning the color of charred wood. Nisha's fingers curled around Devan's orchid.

Something chittered behind her.

Nisha spun, her heart jerking in her chest. A monkey with a black face moved out of the shadows and onto a low branch. It seemed neither startled nor afraid but regarded Nisha with an expression of benevolent curiosity.

"Hello," Nisha said, not sure what else to do.

The monkey chittered back, inching closer along the branch. Its narrow tail twitched, and its dark eyes were fixed on the orchid in Nisha's hand.

"You want this?" she said, holding it out. The monkey bobbed its head and leaned closer to the flower. Thin bones moved under fluffy silver-tipped fur. Nisha held the flower closer.

"Go on," she said on an impulse. "You can have it."

A dark paw flashed out, and then both monkey and orchid were gone. Nisha watched the long-limbed form of the monkey pulling itself up into the tree until it was out of sight. Then she turned away, the cool air like a silk coverlet on her empty hands.

The old quarry was a narrow valley of hard gray stone, cut

and tumbled in massive boulders. A shallow lake glistened in the center.

Nisha scanned the rocks, a jumble of indistinct shapes. Pale mist was beginning to pool around the stones. There wasn't a breath or a sound.

Pulling out her staff, she began to pick her way toward the lake. The trees around the rim of the quarry were thin and didn't offer enough cover to hide in. She knew she would feel safer with her back to the water. She would conceal herself among the large rocks and wait for the killer.

The rocks were slick with moisture from the mist, and Nisha had to be careful not to slide into the cracks and crevices between them. That was good. It would be hard for anyone to get all the way down to the lake without her spotting them.

She was just about to climb over the last mound of rocks between her and the water when she spotted a flash of color off to her right. Nisha scrambled in that direction, skirting a boulder as large as herself in the process. There! A spark of red in a stew of gray and white.

It was her scarf.

Nisha sniffed the mist-scented air and listened, but nothing moved. There was no sign of another person. Hints of frost still stuck to the edges of the fabric. The scarf must have been here overnight. A crushed, dead butterfly also edged with frost lay on the stone next to it.

The killer had been here, maybe even right after breaking into Nisha's room. The scarf could be a tease, or bait.

But Nisha was still early. She was alone. And she couldn't bring herself to walk away and leave the only link to her parents behind.

One end of the scarf was caught in a deep crack between two boulders, and she had to lie on her stomach and reach her arm in up to the shoulder to pull it free. She had just worked the end loose when she saw a thin, dark shadow out of the corner of her eye.

Nisha tried to scramble to her feet on the slick rock, her every instinct screaming danger.

But it was too late.

There was the harsh grate of stone on stone. Nisha caught the scent of clovermint just before the boulder crashed down on her legs.

Searing white agony, then nothing.

Flowers for the noble born in palaces of stone

Jade is for the learned ones studying alone

Bamboo merchants buy and trade ivory, gems, and wood

A Hearth for those who work the land, to bring up what is good

But beware the Wind caste, who claim no house or town

Always running, always moving, till they all fall down!

Bhinian children's rhyme

25

CONSCIOUSNESS TEASED NISHA in fuzzy impressions. A hard, damp surface underneath her cheek. Chill eddies of air on her skin. The pulse of blood flowing through her veins.

Bright sparks of pain danced behind her eyes, and she forced them open.

Her first thought was that she was lying on something cold and uncomfortable. Her second was that she hurt. Everywhere.

Her head throbbed with a dull ache that only now began to separate itself from the rest of her pain. She must have hit it when she fell. She could feel her fingers and move them without pain. One hand gripped a sodden wisp of fabric. Her body was sore and battered, but she could breathe without effort.

Her legs. Something was wrong with her legs.

Nisha took a deep breath and focused on her left leg. The leg wouldn't move, it was true, but it felt as though it was caught between rocks, and though it ached with a bone-deep pain, it was the pain of bruises and sprains. Nothing too serious.

She wriggled the toes of her left foot and tried to shift it, but it was caught fast. And there was a sudden ferocious pain in her right foot that discouraged any more movement.

She couldn't feel the toes on her right foot. She couldn't feel her foot at all, just pressure and pain.

Nisha's mind snapped back to clarity with the force of a bow-string. The killer. She had come early to meet the killer, but the killer had come early too. Nisha had been set up, outmaneuvered.

Stupid girl. You walked right into that.

Nisha cursed silently. If she'd only told someone where she was going, they would be looking for her by now. She could have taken the time to find a cat, or send a message to Esmer, but instead she had gone off alone, breaking her promise to Jerrit. She had tried to lay a trap, but the killer had been waiting for her.

And it wasn't Sashi.

There was no way that Sashi could have picked her way over those jagged, uneven rocks without being able to see them. And even if she had, she certainly wouldn't have been able to disappear so quickly. Nisha knew her friend was innocent. Even in the middle of her pain, the thought was as welcome as a drink of cool water.

Nisha tried to call for the cats but heard only silence. Her mind-strength was too weak, or the distance was too great. Or they were no longer listening.

The thought hit her with as much force as the boulder. Now, when it was far too late, she remembered what she had forgotten. Esmer's serious voice echoed through her memory.

Those who break the oath of the Long-Tailed Cat are rejected by all the spotted cat tribes, doomed to wander, homeless and honorless.

Nisha had broken the oath.

No one would come to help her now.

She gave an involuntary jerk of her feet. She heard the bones in her right foot grind together, and a blaze of pain came and took everything away.

When she woke again it was dark, and she knew she was going to die. She knew it because of the pain in her leg. She couldn't even pull herself up to look at it without seeing white. And a wound as severe as this would become septic very soon. She knew death was near because of the way her teeth chattered and her body shivered, exposed to the damp cold of the White Mist. But most of all, she knew she was going to die because she was thirsty.

In the quiet of Darkfall, Nisha could hear the muddy little lake lap its shores. The sound of all that water—only a few steps from where she lay—made her breath come faster.

It felt like she had swallowed a ball of wool, and her lips stuck together in painful dry patches. She tried to remember how long a person could survive without water. One day? Two? Not that it mattered. Either the thirst would kill her, or it would weaken her enough so the cold would finish her off.

A broken, animal whimper rose from Nisha's throat. Black

spots fogged her vision, and hot tears slid from her eyes. Her last thought was that no one would ever find her body.

No one knew where she was.

Jumbled voices.
  Jarring pain.
  Cool hands.
  No more hurt.
  Darkness.

Nisha swam through the black. Pain was returning, and light. She tossed her head and moaned in protest, wanting to sink back into the dark. Something warm and wet touched her cheek.

She forced her heavy eyelids open. Pale blue glowed above her. Fabric. And something was licking her cheek.

She turned her head and met the curious eyes of a droopy-eared goat.

A squeak came from her dry throat. The goat cocked his head. Then it started chewing on a piece of Nisha's hair.

She was in a narrow tent made of blue cotton. Stacks of brightly colored blankets and bulging sacks lined the inside walls. One sack was partly open, spilling grain on the floor. Another knock-kneed goat was munching on the grain, his stubby tail swishing happily.

A soft cashmere blanket covered Nisha's legs, and as she woke further, she realized there was a heavy cast on her foot. The bandages around her hand were gone, and someone had tied the red scarf the Shadow Mistress had given her around her wrist.

A girl of about ten with dark skin and an abundance of curly black hair ran into the tent and began scolding the goats. The goats shook their horns and *maa*ed in protest. But the girl's waving hands had the desired effect, and the goats were pushed out of the tent.

As she followed them, the girl saw Nisha awake for the first time. The child's mouth dropped open, and with a swish of her light gray skirt she was gone. Nisha heard her shouting outside.

Nisha bit her lip. She was in a Kildi tent.

Everything she'd ever heard about the mysterious nomadic people ran through her mind. Kildi were Wind caste, traveling from place to place in large family groups. Some said they worshiped the old gods, gods from before the Empire was cut off. Others said they were the remnants of a noble family doomed to wander as a punishment for ancient sins; many people thought they were just a collection of thieves and beggars.

As Nisha struggled to sit up, a tiny old woman with a wrinkled-nut face came bustling through the door. When she saw Nisha, she made several *tsk* noises and set down her burden, a copper pot with steam coming out of the top. Then she pushed Nisha gently but firmly back onto the bed.

"Where am I?" Nisha asked. "Why did you save me?"

The old woman smiled at her, her bronze face folding into wrinkles. "When our children take the goats to drink and find an injured girl, why should we not help her?" she asked. She ladled some of the pot's contents into a clay cup and held it to Nisha's lips.

Nisha closed her mouth and shook her head. She wanted

answers, not sleeping potions.

The old woman tilted her head. "You should drink this. It is for the pain; there will be no harm."

Nisha tried to sit up–to say that she felt no pain–when a deep throb in her foot stopped her. Looking down at the shapeless, stiff form of the cast under the cashmere blanket, she remembered the scrape of bone on bone. She winced at the memory, then gasped as another thump of pain shook her leg.

The woman offered the cup again.

"No," Nisha said through dry lips. "I don't–" She stumbled over her words. "I don't want to sleep."

The confusion on the woman's face cleared. "No. It will help the pain but not cause sleep. Drink." She put the clay cup to Nisha's mouth again, and Nisha gave in. She was thirsty.

The liquid was a spice tea flavored with barley and herbs. It felt like warm silk on her parched tongue, and Nisha drank it all in quick, greedy sips.

She handed the clay cup back to the old woman. "Thank you. Please, I need to go home. Back to the City of a Thousand Dolls, where I came from."

"Back to the City?" The old woman gave her a gap-toothed smile. "Why? We will take care of you here."

"But I don't belong here. I must get back." Nisha clutched the blanket and tried to speak calmly. The woman was only trying to help. "I know I'm hurt. But if you send word to the Matron, she will come for me."

"No, you must rest," the woman said, a stubborn set to her

mouth. "Rest, until the *Kys* comes. He will explain everything."

"Who is the *Kys*?" Nisha asked. "Will he take me home?"

The old woman looked at her with pity. Then she turned and left the tent.

"Wait!" Nisha called. She had to get out of here and back to the City of a Thousand Dolls. She had to apologize to Jerrit and tell Matron that Sashi was innocent and make sure Tanaya was safe and see Devan again.

Maybe it was Nisha's brush with death, or the memory of Devan's orchid and the strength it had given her to walk into the forest, but Nisha felt something now that she hadn't known before: She did love Devan. She wanted him to speak for her not because she wanted to escape, but because she cared about *him*. She loved the way he smiled, loved the sound of his voice when he talked about the places he'd been. Devan didn't care that she was casteless. He made her feel beautiful and special.

Nisha closed her eyes, remembering the warmth of Devan's hands on her skin, the scent of the orchid, words of love written on a scrap of paper. Her chest felt full to bursting with the words she wanted to say to him. She wanted to tell him everything she hadn't been able to tell him: the Council Head, his own relative, threatening to sell her as a bond slave; the danger she'd taken on to protect the City and to expose the real murderer; the way that she felt about him. But first she had to get out of here.

Nisha looked down and saw she wasn't wearing her Combat tunic. Someone had dressed her in a loose white tunic and a red cotton skirt the same shade as the scarf around her hand.

Nervousness trembled in her stomach. The City of a Thousand Dolls was the only human settlement for many miles. The Kildi knew she came from there, but they hadn't returned her. Why?

Whatever the reason, Nisha didn't trust them to take her back just because she asked. She had to find out where she was first.

Nisha slid her legs off the bed. The pain from her injured foot flared, making the edges of her vision go white, and she bit back a cry. Half hopping, half falling, she stumbled to the tent flap. The pain in her foot increased with each step until she could barely see. Blinking away tears, Nisha reached for the flap and pushed it open.

She caught a glimpse of bright colors, of people moving in all directions, and then the dizziness hit her again, a wave of gray that made everything go dim.

Concerned voices swarmed around her, and she felt strong hands hold her up. Her foot throbbed until all she could feel was the pain.

When it eased, Nisha found herself back in the bed with the old woman standing over her.

The woman shook her graying head. "That was very stupid," she said. "You will not get well that way."

"You can't keep me here!" Nisha said, trying to sit up again.

The woman shook her head again and pulled her scarf tighter around her thin shoulders. A faded yellow scarf with a border of stylized tigers.

Nisha felt her breath freeze in her chest. Carefully she reached out trembling fingers to touch the edge of the shawl. "Where did you get that?"

The woman smiled. "It is the sign of the Arvi," she said. Her bent hands pulled down the collar of her robe, and Nisha saw a dim, tiger-shaped mark under the old woman's collarbone.

The air seemed to thicken around Nisha, holding her in place. She could only watch as the old woman reached over and touched the tiger engraved into Nisha's own skin. Her fingers were dry and papery.

"See? You are family."

"And you are home," said a deep voice. A man with skin the color of weathered bronze stood in the doorway of the tent. He wore pale-brown trousers, an open-necked tunic, and a bright-red silk kerchief knotted around his throat. It was the man she'd seen in the woods.

"Welcome back, Nisha Arvi," he said. "Daughter of my brother."

26

NISHA COULDN'T MOVE. The words *daughter of my brother* hung in the air, taking on a life of their own, washing out everything she thought she knew.

A Kildi? I'm one of the Kildi?

The man saw her blank stare and winced as if in pain. "The Horned God take you, brother," he muttered. "Your own child does not know us."

Hands out, as if approaching a wild animal, the man stepped closer. His eyes were the light brown of almonds. Three parallel slashes, like claw marks, scarred his cheek. "You are Nisha Arvi. Daughter of my brother, Emil Arvi, and one of the Kildi."

Nisha felt as if a giant hand were squeezing her chest. In all her dreams about finding her family, she had never imagined this. And on the heels of her shock, she remembered the Shadow Mistress's strange words.

Then there is the secret that everyone knows, except the person the secret is about.

Everyone knew. That was why Josei had hinted that Nisha should run away. Matron surely knew as well, and the cats, too. This was the secret they had been sworn to, the one that they couldn't tell.

Everyone had known who Nisha was. And no one had told her.

She didn't realize she was crying until a tear splashed onto her scarf, soaking into the thin red fabric. Nisha blinked rapidly, willing her eyes to dry. She didn't want to cry in front of these strangers.

The man stood watching her, while the old woman bustled around the tent, preparing a pot of thick, smoky stew. She handed a bowl to Nisha and gave her a wide smile.

Nisha took the rough clay bowl and breathed in the spicy steam. "Please. What is your name?"

The skin around the woman's eyes crinkled in amusement. "Aishe," she said. "I am the Rememberer."

"Rememberer?" Nisha asked.

"Rememberer of the Ancient Lands," the woman said. "What we call the *Arothan*. When great lights ruled the sky and the Kildi were warriors and kings. Before the Ending and the Corruption."

"The Ending?" Nisha asked. "You mean when the Empire was cut off from the outside world?"

The woman nodded, her eyes dark and sharp. "The Kildi are the descendants of those who were cast down, the only ones who remember what used to be."

Forgetting her own problems, Nisha leaned forward. "The

rulers of the Old Empire, the ones who were overthrown after all the magicians died, they were the Kildi?"

Aishe nodded. "We ruled under an open sky. Now we wander a land no longer our own until the magic returns again."

"Returns?" Nisha stared at her. Magic had been burned out of the Empire entirely, dying with the magicians. Everyone knew that.

"Aishe, don't confuse her." At the sound of the man's voice, Nisha forgot about history, magic, and the ancient legends. All that mattered was her own past, and the questions that crowded her mind.

Finally she could speak the question she'd waited ten years to ask. "Where are my parents?"

The lines of pain on the man's face deepened. "Dead. Soon after they sent you to that horrible place."

Nisha's face grew hot. "No. They were supposed to be here."

Finding her family had always meant finding her parents. They were supposed to be alive somewhere, waiting to explain, to tell her why they'd abandoned her. "How do I know that what you tell me is true?"

The man took a deep, heavy breath. He strode to Nisha's side. Tugging the red scarf from his neck, he draped it over her wrist, touching the scarf the Shadow Mistress had given her. The two fabrics were identical. And Nisha could see it on the uncovered skin–he had a tiger mark to match her own.

"I swear by the Horned God and the Sacrificed Bull that I am your uncle. Your father was my brother and my friend. Please, let me carry you outside. Aishe says you need air. And I will try to explain."

Nisha still wanted to know about her parents and her past, and there were no answers in the tent. "All right . . . but what is your name?"

The man bent and gathered Nisha into his arms. "I am called Stefan. I am *Kys* of the Arvi clan."

"You're the *Kys*?" Nisha asked. "Does that mean you're the leader?"

"In a way." Stefan's arms were strong, and he carried Nisha gently, tucking the bright, soft blanket around her. This close, she could smell a trace of sandalwood. It was so like her vague memories of her father that the tears threatened to come back. She'd wondered if the memories were real. Sometimes it felt like they were stories that she'd told herself during lonely nights, fanciful tales with no basis in reality. Now she knew they were true, and she clung to Stefan as he pushed his way out of the tent.

The first thing Nisha noticed was the noise. The camp was full of clattering pots, shrieking children, the ringing of hammer blows, and the barks, squeals, bleats, and lowing of more animals than she had ever seen in one place before.

A tiny girl dashed past with a smaller boy hard on her heels. "Da!" she squealed, followed by something that sounded very much like "Save me!" Nisha could feel the laugh in Stefan's chest.

"My children," he said to Nisha with obvious pride. "Sonja is always tormenting her brother and then trying to get me to save her."

Nisha watched the children with interest as they tussled. Little boys especially were unfamiliar to her. Nisha rarely saw men in the City except visitors or temporary hires like Josei's assistant Tac. And there were no younger boys at all.

Boys were more valuable than girls, as they carried on the family name and inherited property. Orphaned boys would find a welcome anywhere, because they made good laborers and good apprentices. Some childless couples would even search for orphaned boys to adopt. There was no need for a City of boys.

The children were full-out wrestling now, and it was impossible to tell who was winning. Their giggles reminded Nisha of chasing Tanaya through the hedges, tickling Sashi with a grass stem as her friend tried to meditate, taking her first clumsy dance steps as Vinian looked on. Those days seemed far away now.

"Will he hurt her?" Nisha asked.

"Maret?" Stefan smiled. "No. Sonja may be small, but she can fight. Would you like to meet your cousins?"

The idea of having cousins was so strange to Nisha that it was a moment before she could manage a smile. "Let them play. It's been a long time since I heard laughter like that."

Her uncle's arms tightened. "Did they hurt you in the City?" he asked. "Did they mistreat you or try to change you in any way?"

"No," Nisha said, feeling an unexpected shame. The City hadn't wanted her, her parents hadn't wanted her. Where did she belong?

"Good," he growled. "People who would twist a child should be beaten. I never should have let my brother leave you in that madhouse. But that's fixed now. You're here, and that's all that matters."

There was a long, uncomfortable pause.

"The healer is gathering herbs in the forest," Stefan said. "I'll carry you to the edge of camp, and we can wait there for her."

The camp was a rambling gathering of wagons and tents, as active as a honeycomb full of bees. The air smelled of leather and animals, and the steam from the various cooking pots added a hint of ginger to the air. The spindly-legged goats were everywhere, outnumbered only by children, who played various games, fetched water and wood for the adults, and tried to keep the goats from eating everything in sight.

"Those goats are our main livelihood," Stefan explained as he carried Nisha past a group of old women carding piles of fluffy goat hair. "The Arvi are the best spinners in all the clans of the Kildi, and we make the finest cashmere in the Empire."

The women nodded and smiled at them.

"Are *all* these people from the same family?" Nisha asked, a bit dizzy from the noise.

Stefan nodded. "We are all Arvi. These are your father's aunts, uncles, and cousins."

Nisha watched the Kildi go about their business, each one with a blood tie more binding than rope. "It must be nice, belonging somewhere like this." The wistfulness of her own voice surprised her, and Stefan's voice softened in reply.

"A Kildi without clan is like a crane without a flock. But those days are over. You're not alone anymore."

Nisha wanted to believe him. But too many questions were still unanswered.

"If you are my uncle, why did you leave me in the City for so long? Why didn't you come and get me?"

"I tried," Stefan said, his brows furrowing in anger. "Right after your parents died. I went to the harridan who runs the place and begged to get you back. She said it wasn't safe for you to leave yet. Safe! As if you were safe there with those unnatural people, bending you into whatever they thought they could sell you for!"

Stefan's anger blended into shame, and he looked away. "I was still reeling from my brother's death, you understand, and I was furious that he had taken you to the City without telling me first. So when she told me to get out . . . I left."

Stefan carried Nisha past a row of flat wagons heavy with supplies. A handful of small donkeys with limpid eyes grazed nearby. One donkey wandered over to them, ears alert. Nisha put her hand to the soft muzzle and received a wet snuffle in return.

"Left?" she asked. "What do you mean?"

Stefan let out a breath. "I mean we all left. I packed the camp and took us to the wild places in the east."

Nisha stared at him. "I was there for ten years! You never once came back to make sure I was all right, that I hadn't been turned out or sold?"

"I lost my temper."

"For *ten years*?"

Stefan didn't answer. Instead he carried Nisha to the edge of the camp. Here the forest spilled into the clearing, and the noise of the camp was surrounded and overcome by the silence of the trees.

Stefan lowered her to the base of a tree. Nisha hissed as the movement sent another wave of pain through her leg.

Her uncle rubbed his hand over his face.

"Nisha, the City of a Thousand Dolls represents everything that's wrong with the Empire. The way they groom girls to accept the fates chosen for them, the way they give them no choice and then sell them . . . we would rather send our children to other clans or to be raised by the elderly than give them up to that. I was furious with my brother for leaving you there. And then he died."

Nisha was unable to hold back the question anymore. "How did they die? And *why* did they leave me at the City?"

Stefan sat next to her, cross-legged. "To explain that, I have to tell you who your parents were. Your father was the Master Trader of our clan. He had a smile that made you trust him at once, and a silver tongue that could sell you anything. He was in charge of all the buying and selling, including the trade we did with the City of a Thousand Dolls."

Disgust wrinkled Stefan's face. "I confess, I was more than happy to let him handle that. That place has always made my skin crawl. Your mother usually went with him. She wasn't Kildi. Emil had fallen in love with her on a trip to Kamal and brought her home."

"Tell me about her," Nisha whispered. *Am I like her? Did she love me?*

Stefan smiled and put a hand on her head. "Your mother was strong and graceful, and she moved like the wind over the river. She had been some kind of warrior, but she never talked to anyone but your father about her past. I saw her fight a few times, and she was as deadly as she was beautiful. Your father called her Shar, which means tiger-cat in the old tongue. And since it seemed fitting–the tiger is the symbol of the Arvi clan–that's what we all called her. She worked hard and made my brother happy, so to us, she was family."

The earth under Nisha was cold and hard, and she pulled the cashmere blanket tighter, ignoring her aching leg. "What happened to them?"

Stefan shook his head. "I'm not sure," he said. "We camped here, as we did every year at that time. Your parents went on a routine trading trip to one of the fishing villages, somewhere they'd been a thousand times before. You had a touch of fever, so they left you here. They were gone a long time–much, much longer than they should have been. When they did return, your father's eyes were like those of a hunted thing. They said they had broken a cart axle, but I knew they were lying. They didn't leave the camp much after that, and they grew quieter and quieter, always looking over their shoulders."

Nisha's throat felt tight. What could have terrified her parents so much?

Stefan continued, "One morning the children found a dead grouse, lying on its back with wings spread out in the middle of camp. I assumed it had been killed by a wolf or a fox, but I was standing next to your mother when she saw it, and her face–Before or since, I've never seen anyone so frightened. The next day your father disappeared into the woods with you. When he came back, you weren't with him. When I pressed him . . ."

The man's grim tone suggested he'd done more than pressed.

"When I pressed him, he said he'd left you at the City of a Thousand Dolls, that it was the safest place for you now. I couldn't believe it. I demanded he go and get you back, but he refused. He said you would be safe, that he and your mother had made sure of that, and that if anything happened to them, I was to leave you there for at least one year. The next day your parents were gone. Their bodies were found on the road to Kamal."

There was silence as vast as the forest beside them. Nisha felt empty, as if the story had hollowed her out. Her parents were dead, and she couldn't even tell them how much she hated them for leaving her. Or how much she had missed them and wanted them back.

"How could they just leave me there?" The words splashed out of her like spilled tea.

Stefan started to pace. "Your parents loved you," he said. "I don't want you to doubt that."

Too late, Nisha thought. "They might have been trying to protect me. But they abandoned me instead. I didn't even know who I was."

"I'm sorry," Stefan said. "When that woman slammed the door in my face, I snapped. I was angry at my brother and angry at the City, and it was childish and stupid. But this year, you would be sixteen. You would be old enough to leave the City. I wanted to see if you were still safe. So we came back. And when I saw you outside the walls that day . . . looking so much like your father, and moving with your mother's grace . . . I knew then that I was wrong. That you belong here with us, and you always have."

Nisha looked out at the woods, at the pale trunks crowding close together, a wall as high and intimidating as any she'd ever seen.

"What about my friends?" she asked. But the words came out so quietly that Stefan didn't hear her. And before she could ask again, they were interrupted by a voice from the woods.

"There's my new patient. I'm glad to see you awake again, Nisha."

A woman with a guarded smile stepped from the woods. She was sleek and dark, her hair black as a cormorant's wing. She wore a muted brown-and-green tunic, different from the ordinary Kildi clothing Nisha had seen so far. Nisha saw no obvious Kildi mark on her skin.

The woman quickened her step and knelt down to feel the heavy cast on Nisha's leg. "My name is Isita, camp healer. How is the pain?"

"Bearable," Nisha said honestly. "Aishe gave me something for it. How long will it take to heal?"

The healer raised her head to Stefan's in surprise. "You did not tell her?" she asked.

The Kildi man shifted. "She didn't ask. I thought it might be better explained by you."

"I don't understand." Nisha looked from the healer to her uncle and back again. "Is it broken?"

Isita sat back on her heels and sighed. "Nisha, the boulder that fell on you landed right on your feet. Another stone protected your left foot, and it's merely bruised. But your right foot is a different tale." She shook her head. "You can thank the Ancestors that your foot wasn't crushed. As it is, your right ankle and your right heel are both broken. I set the ankle and stopped the infection, but I couldn't completely set your heel."

Nisha stared at the healer for so long that her eyes stung. She'd spent enough time at the House of Jade to know that even the best healers couldn't do much for a broken heel. She wouldn't be able to put weight on her foot for at least a season. No more running or dancing or fighting. Even when it healed, she might have a limp for the rest of her life.

No one would want her now. Not as an apprentice, not as an assistant.

Maybe not as a wife. The thought of losing Devan when she'd only just recognized her feelings for him sent a pain through Nisha deeper than the one in her foot.

Isita touched her shoulder. Stefan had slipped away, leaving Nisha and the healer alone. Her smile had faded a little, and in her eyes was a sadness that Nisha didn't understand.

"I knew your parents. They did me a great service once." She touched Nisha's leg just above the cast. "I would give much to be able to mend this, but I can't. I can relieve your pain, though."

The woman's fingers were light on Nisha's skin.

Nisha's ankle throbbed once, then grew hot. The pain faded. She watched. It looked like magic, but that was impossible.

The healer saw Nisha's puzzled expression. "Pressure points," she explained. "Your foot will hurt horribly. But if you stay well rested, the pain should be minimal." She smiled and nodded encouragingly, but Nisha thought she looked uneasy.

The woman rose with a limber grace. "I must go. There is a birthing I must attend on the other side of camp. I'll tell Stefan to come for you." She vanished into the tents and wagons.

Nisha watched her go. Her thoughts flew to her foot, to the bleak, uncertain future stretched out ahead of her. Her head pounded.

It was true, she'd felt like a nobody before. Now she was worthless in the eyes of anyone with sense. There would be no more dancing, sparring, or running down stone paths.

One stupid choice, one promise broken, and she was lost.

Nisha dropped her head into her hands.

27

A BRISK VOICE broke into Nisha's dark thoughts. "That's enough. No student of mine will sit around and feel sorry for herself."

Josei settled down under the tree. Nisha gaped at her.

Josei gave her a feral grin. "You know, with your mouth open like that, you look like a carp."

"Wha–what?" Nisha sputtered. "What are you doing here? How did you find me?"

Josei shrugged. "When you disappeared, Matron sent me to find you. It took me an hour to track you to the quarry and two days of searching the rim to locate your trail back out. The Kildi always cover their tracks well, to protect their home camp from outsiders."

"But if they hate to be found . . ." Nisha looked toward the camp. "Do they know you're here?

"Oh, yes," Josei said. "Fortunately, I've . . . dealt with the Arvi before. They weren't happy that I demanded to see you, but as you can see, I was allowed."

"Wait," Nisha said, the meaning of Josei's words sinking in. "It took you two days to find me? But I just left the City last night. . . ." She trailed off.

How long had she been unconscious?

The fox-woman shook her head. "You were gone for three days."

"Three days?" Nisha's thoughts were in a whirl. Had Jerrit healed? Had there been another death? And if it had been three days, that meant . . .

"The Redeeming is tomorrow!"

"Yes," Josei said. Her face was a careful blank. "Nisha," she said, "you don't have to come back with me. I could say I never found you, and you could stay here. The Kildi would take you in. They are your family."

Nisha paused. It was true. She had felt trapped in the City of a Thousand Dolls. Now she was free, free from the danger of being sold, free from the constant fear of death.

Nisha waited for a feeling of relief or happiness, but instead she thought of Jerrit's heartbeat under her hand, like the pulse of her own blood. She remembered Devan's kisses, the sound of Sashi's not unkind laughter when they made fun of the Beauty girls.

Sashi. Even if she didn't go back for good, she had to help Sashi.

"Josei," Nisha said, "Sashi can't be the killer. Someone pushed a boulder on me at the quarry. There's no way Sashi could have done it."

Josei listened to Nisha in silence, a troubled expression in her brown-gold eyes. "I wish I had found you sooner," she said.

Nisha's hands went cold. "What do you mean?"

"Nisha, when you vanished, the Council placed Sashi under house arrest, confining her to her room. Akash has convinced the Council to charge her with all three deaths."

"But she didn't do it!" Nisha dug her fingers into the hard dirt. "You have to tell them!"

"I will try. But the Council, the whole City, is frightened, and frightened people often cling to the easy answer. My word won't be enough."

Nisha knew her word wasn't more important than Josei's, but she had to try. "Then I'll have to go with you," she said, sitting up straighter. "I'll make them listen!"

Josei looked hard at Nisha, forcing her to meet her fierce eyes. "Nisha, you have no proof. And if you go back now, you will not get another chance to leave of your own free will. Is an attempt to clear your friend's name worth risking your freedom?" She paused. "You can't do this just to absolve your guilt for implicating Sashi."

Nisha had made a mistake suspecting Sashi. Her dangerous conclusion, once said out loud, had set in motion events she had never intended. She had to fix it. But that wasn't all.

There were other people she needed to see. The pull of her love for them tugged her back, making the dangers seem insignificant.

The decision came to her as easily as her next breath.

"I'm going. Will you help?"

A satisfied smile of approval flitted across Josei's face. "I've already asked the healer if you could travel. You shouldn't try the journey until tomorrow. That gives us the rest of the day." She clapped Nisha on the back.

"To do what?" Nisha asked, stunned.

Josei reached into her asar and pulled out two daggers with wrist sheaths. "To teach you how to use these. They are for you until you are healed enough to fight with a staff. I'll not have it said that I sent any student of mine into the world defenseless."

"Fight with a staff?" she asked, a faint hope whispering in her. "Like this?"

"Why not?" Josei snapped. "The best stick fighter I ever knew was a deaf old man with no toes on his left foot. You are still my student, and you will do as I say."

"Yes, House Mistress," Nisha said.

"Good." Josei's fierce smile made her look even more like a fox. "Let's get started."

At first Nisha was clumsy with the unfamiliar daggers. She was used to *lati* staffs and fighting sticks, weapons you controlled with your arms and your shoulders, weapons you held on to for the entire fight. She'd never been interested in learning how to use weapons that you just stood still and threw.

Her first attempt landed within an arm's reach of Josei. The House Mistress handed the dagger back to her.

"Sit up straighter" was her only comment. Then, "Try again."

Nisha sat up as straight as she could and put more force into the throw. This time the dagger flew farther, but in a slightly different direction than she was aiming for. Again Josei retrieved it, telling her to add more follow-through.

Over and over again, Nisha threw the dagger, with Josei correcting her hand position, the angle of her shoulders, the timing of her release. Nisha saw that they were drawing a crowd. A group of children, including Stefan's children, Maret and Sonja, were sitting nearby, faces alight with interest. Nisha gave them a shy smile and was thrilled when they smiled and waved back.

"Eyes on your target, Nisha." But Josei was smiling too.

By midday, the cluster of children had grown to include men and women. When Nisha and Josei took a break to eat, a skinny boy with laughing dark eyes brought them roasted chicken and coarse, spiced rice. Several old men came to eat with them, patting Nisha's shoulder and whispering encouragement and advice.

By the time Nisha could hit each tree she aimed at, the group of Kildi watching them had taken on the air of a festival. They cheered whenever she hit anywhere close to the target, bringing a blush of pleasure to her face.

As she let the last dagger fly, she heard an approving chuckle behind her.

Stefan's broad, bearded face stretched in a wide grin. "It is good not to lie down and be swallowed by the wolves of fate. You are as determined as your father."

Not even her sore arm could stop the grin that spread across

Nisha's face. "I would like to come back someday," she said. "May I?"

Stefan laughed. "Come back? Why would you even need to leave? You don't belong to that place anymore. You belong to us."

Her uncle's expectations pulled on Nisha like thin, strong wire. He thought she was here to stay. How could she explain to him that he was wrong? That there were people she loved in the City, people she had to try to save?

"Thank you," Nisha said carefully. "I can't tell you how much it means to me that you want me here. But I have to go back. There is something I have to do."

"There is nothing in that cursed place important enough to risk yourself," Stefan said, his eyes darkening. "I can't allow it."

"But there is," Nisha said. "You don't understand. But I'll come back, I promise."

Stefan's eyes narrowed, and something hardened in his face. "Is this about that nobleman I saw you with?"

"What?" Nisha stared at him. Had Stefan been *spying* on her?

"I told you, I saw you outside the walls. I was making sure you were safe," Stefan said. "So I hid and watched, and you came. I almost killed that boy for putting his hands on you. But I thought you might be pretending, trying to gain a protector. That was good. Don't tell me you actually care for that soppy wretch."

"And what if I do?" Nisha answered, her temper kindling. "What if I love him?"

Beside her, she felt Josei draw a breath, but the fox-woman stayed silent.

"Love?" Her uncle spit out the word. "Do you even know what

the word means? Those Flower people—" he said the words with disgust. "They displaced us and condemned us to wander for five hundred years. And they claim privileges they should not have because they 'saved' the Empire. From us! I should have stuck my dagger into him when I had the chance."

Nisha felt dizzy and sick. It seemed the Kildi had rules as unyielding as the ones that governed the City of a Thousand Dolls. She took a deep breath and tried to speak calmly.

"I know the nobles overthrew you. I understand why you would hate them. But Devan . . . he's not like that. He has nothing to do with why I'm really going back. I have to go back to help a friend who's in trouble."

"You can't help," Stefan said evenly. "Those people twist children the way a spinner twists thread. Everything they touch rots. No girl who lives there could be uncorrupted."

Hurt sliced through Nisha, as sharp and as unexpected as a thin blade in her back. "Not even me?" she asked, her voice quiet. "I was there for ten years."

Her eyes met her uncle's, and he flinched. His broad shoulders slumped. "Don't you want to stay?" he asked.

Nisha swallowed. "Yes." And she did. But she couldn't sacrifice the people she cared about just to keep herself safe. She tried to explain—after all, her uncle clearly believed in loyalty too—but her tongue was heavy and slow, and the words would not come.

"I'm sorry," she said finally, lifting her eyes to Stefan's angry stare. "I can't. Not right now."

Stefan's hands clenched into fists. "Fine. Go back to your friends and your noble lover and your precious City. Forget your family and your blood. But know this: No true child of the Kildi would go back." He paused, turning from her. "Your father would be ashamed of you."

Stefan stomped away. The crowd of Kildi who had been watching with silent faces melted back into the camp.

Nisha watched them go, feeling numb. She was unbearably tired, wrung out like a discarded dishrag.

Josei touched her shoulder. "I brought Tac with me. He will carry you back to your tent."

The Combat Mistress turned to the crowding trees and gave a low whistle, the liquid call of a bird. One of the shadows solidified into the light-haired young man she'd last seen in the armory.

He'd been smiling then, eyes sparkling with mischief and effort, hair hanging in his eyes and mussed from their staff fight. Now his smile was gone and he looked . . . older.

He moved to Nisha's side, lifting her without effort. Once she was in his arms, he looked at her intently, as if he were memorizing her face.

Nisha squirmed under Tac's gaze. What must he think of her after all the things Stefan had said? Because it was true—she *was* turning her back on the only real family she had in the world. Nisha knew she had no choice, but would Tac understand that? Did he think her stupid for going back?

But there was no sign of condemnation on Tac's face, and his grip was gentle. Nisha found herself relaxing into his strong arms and leaned her head against his chest.

Maybe tomorrow she could try to talk to her uncle again. Tomorrow.

Tac's heartbeat pulsed evenly against her ear, a soothing sound that sent Nisha drifting into a soft, uneasy sleep.

When Nisha woke, the light behind the blue cotton of her tent was the dim, cold light of morning. Aishe, a grim set to her mouth, was bustling around the enclosed space, one eye on a pot of steaming soup. The old woman's bent back was stiff, and she muttered as she wrestled with a bulging sack.

At Nisha's first movement, Aishe straightened. "You are leaving us?" Her dark eyes were troubled.

"Yes," Nisha said, regretting the words as they left her lips. Part of her still wanted to stay, to belong to these people who had loved her parents. "I have to."

"I am sorry to hear this. But loyalty to one's friends is a trait all Kildi value. I wish Stefan remembered that." Her voice grew thick with frustration. "He sees only his hurt. My daughter, his heart-wife, could have helped you. But she went Beyond several years ago." She tied off the top of the sack with several hard yanks.

"He has decreed that as soon as you leave, we are to break camp."

Nisha swallowed the lump that rose in her throat. So her uncle was planning to leave again. "Does he always do this when he's mad?" she asked, hurt turning to disbelief.

Aishe rolled her eyes. "He is a spoiled boy now, with no brother or wife to advise him. He runs from his hurt and pulls the rest of us with him." She pushed the sack toward Nisha. "This is for you. Blankets and fabric. You are Kildi, and Aishe will not see you go with empty hands."

"You don't have to do that," Nisha started, but something in Aishe's even gaze held the words in her throat.

"You will take this," the old woman said, in a tone so final that Nisha's half-formed arguments died away. "It is your inheritance."

At that moment Tac pulled back the tent flap and walked in on silent feet. His eyes, warm with sympathy, found hers. He smiled, and Nisha found herself smiling back.

Josei followed him.

"Is my uncle coming to say good-bye?" Nisha asked her. Maybe if he did, she could try to end things better, for now. Aishe understood her. Why couldn't Stefan?

Josei shook her head. "They are already tearing down the tents," she said. "Stefan expects the Kildi to be gone by Darkfall."

How could it be so painful to be exiled from a place you'd never really known?

Tac brushed the hair from Nisha's face, his fingers giving gentle comfort, then picked her up as if she were made of spun glass.

Josei gave her a pat on the shoulder, and Nisha remembered that Josei's mother had left her when she was young too.

Their silent sympathy helped, but the sharp pain in Nisha's chest remained. And as they started the walk back to the City, Nisha was aware of only two things: the steady pace of Tac's gait, and the silent tears that slipped from her eyelids and soaked the fabric of his shirt.

28

THE KILDI HAD camped in the woods on the far side of the quarry, as far as they could get while staying close enough to water. Tac couldn't walk quickly with Nisha in his arms, so they moved through the forest at a gentle pace. Josei walked beside them, carrying the bag that the old Kildi woman had given Nisha.

While they walked, Josei told Nisha what had happened since she'd gone missing. Tanaya was safe, but Akash tar'Vey had stopped any investigation into the murders after Sashi had been arrested, and he had kept Matron far too busy to do anything about it.

Josei's information confirmed what Nisha suspected. If no one came and spoke on Sashi's behalf, her friend was doomed. And if Matron couldn't do speak for Sashi, Nisha would.

Finally the stone walls of the City came into sight. As they neared the main gate, Nisha heard a familiar whinny. Her heart jerked. There was Devan's mare grazing just outside. And behind the horse, as handsome as ever, wearing a gold-embroidered tunic, stood Devan.

A burst of wild, absurd happiness blurred Nisha's eyes. She'd missed him.

Devan caught sight of them. "Nisha!"

Tac's arms tensed, and Josei put a hand to her sword. Nisha hastened to reassure them. "It's all right," she said. "He's a friend."

Josei adjusted the bag on her shoulder and gave Tac an unreadable look. "I'll put this in your room, Nisha. I'll find Matron." Then she vanished through the gate.

"Devan," Nisha said, more conscious than ever of Tac's arms supporting her. "What are you doing here so early? Are you here for the masquerade?"

Devan eyed Tac, who stared back at him without expression. "Of course. With the High Prince attending, every young noble in the Imperial Court is coming. Most of them are still on their way, or occupied making ridiculous demands at the inn down the road." He paused. "Do we have to have the servant?"

"He's not a servant," Nisha said. "And yes, we have to have him, unless you want to carry me in by yourself."

"Don't think I wouldn't," Devan said, concern in his dark eyes. "Do you trust him?"

"Of course," Nisha said, surprising herself with her own certainty. "Besides, he doesn't talk."

"I could use a few servants like that," Devan said, then dropped his eyes and his flippant manner. "I was so worried about you. The servant picking up scrolls in your place wouldn't tell me anything. It was like you vanished."

"I'm sorry," she said, warmed by his words. "I didn't mean to worry you. If I could have sent you a message, I would have." Tac set her down, her back against the wall.

Devan knelt next to her and ran his hand down her cheek. He spoke quietly. "I was just about to go to Matron and demand to know where you were, and damn the consequences. I was afraid you'd gotten into trouble because of us."

He touched her cast. "Looks like you got into trouble of a different kind. What happened?"

Nisha opened her mouth to tell him everything, but something held her back. Devan would be angry with her that she had gone poking around the questions surrounding Atiy's, Jina's, and Lashar's deaths herself. He probably didn't even know about them. She knew he couldn't understand.

"I fell," she said. "I was exploring the old stone quarry, and I slipped and a rock fell on me. I've been in a Kildi camp all week."

"The Kildi? They're notorious thieves. They took care of you?" Devan snorted. "I'm surprised you still have all your teeth."

"They're not thieves!" Nisha said, stung. "They were very kind people, and they set my foot. They keep goats and weave cashmere."

Devan laughed. "Well, it would be impolite of me to mock your rescuers. Still, I don't trust people who can't stay in one place. Did they have a good healer there, or should I bring you mine?"

"They had a very good healer," Nisha said. She reached out and took his hand, feeling their fingers intertwine. The story bubbled up in her throat: the Council's threat, the danger she was in. She needed to trust him. "Devan, I have to tell you something–"

Devan leaned forward and touched her cheek. "You can't imagine what I thought when someone else came for the mail. I thought you'd disappeared for good, and there were so many things I hadn't gotten the chance to say."

"I know," Nisha said. "And I need to tell you what's been happening."

"Nisha, wait. There's something I want to say." Devan took a deep breath. "I want to speak for you."

Nisha's eyes blurred. "Really?" she whispered. "You do?"

Devan traced the line of her jaw. "I want to marry you, Nisha. I want to spend the rest of my life with you."

"But what about your family?" Nisha asked.

Devan smiled, a smile that wrapped her up like a cashmere blanket, soft and warm. "I'm a second son, Nisha. As long as I marry a girl who won't embarrass my family, my father won't care that you're not trained for the court. I mean, isn't that what this place is for?" He waved a hand at the City gate. "To make it all right for men to marry outside their caste? Isn't that why High Prince Sudev is marrying a girl from here?"

Nisha felt a burst of gratitude toward Tanaya. She was doing so much for the rest of the girls. Because of her, Nisha, an abandoned girl with no future, could be with Devan, a nobleman's son.

Devan settled against the wall and put one arm around her. "So," he said with a playful lilt to his voice. "How long will your foot take to heal? I want to be able to dance with you at our wedding."

"Well, that might be difficult," she said, resting her head on Devan's chest. "I broke my ankle and my heel." She said the words with a laugh, inviting him to share the joke. But he was silent.

Nisha wanted to close her eyes, wanted to enjoy the wonderful, bright moment, but instead, Devan pushed her back gently by the shoulders. His eyes searched hers with an intensity she didn't understand.

"But it will heal, right? You'll be able to walk normally again?"

A cold fear touched Nisha's heart. "I'll be able to walk again, if the foot heals right. But I might have a bit of a limp."

Devan's hands were cold on her skin. The light in his eyes faded, replaced by blank understanding. "A limp," he repeated tonelessly.

"Does it matter?" Nisha asked. The bright happiness faded, and she felt something dark and painful hover over her, waiting.

Devan laughed, the sound breaking into brittle shards like glass. He pushed himself to his feet. Nisha watched him pace, his sharp footsteps the only sound.

"Does it matter?" he repeated, giving the words a hollow, ugly sound. "Does it *matter*? Nisha."

He dropped to his knees before her, like a criminal begging for mercy. "No one is physically imperfect in the Imperial Court. No one. It is the worst sign of weakness."

No, Nisha thought, as if she could stop Devan's flood of words with just her frantic thoughts. *Please, please don't do this.*

Devan's eyes burned into her. "Nisha, my family . . . we have powerful enemies. Enemies who want my father's place on the Court of Lesser Princes. Any whisper of weakness could destroy us. I can't let that happen, Nisha. I can't let my family down like this."

A dark, painful thing had come and hit her with the force of the boulder. Nisha felt flattened, smothered, and broken all at the same time. She wanted to scream, to cry, to break something.

"There is something else we could do. . . ." Devan hesitated, then spoke in a rush. "No one cares about our mistresses, since they aren't for public display. I'm a little young—usually men wait until after they're married . . . but it's been done before."

Nisha stared at him in horror. She had to swallow before her voice would come. "You want me to be your mistress?"

"Of course." The light returned to Devan's face, and he gestured as he spoke. "It's the perfect solution. No one in the court would ever have to see you, no one will care about your foot, and we can be together, just the two of us. And my father won't be nearly so furious about me falling in love with an untrained and casteless girl if I don't marry you."

Nisha flinched, but Devan didn't notice.

"I have money, enough for a comfortable apartment for you near the palace. You wouldn't ever want for anything. There will be servants to shop and clean and cook. I'll come as often as I can. You'll be safe there."

I'll be trapped there, Nisha thought. The picture Devan was painting didn't make her feel safe or loved or wanted. Instead it made her insides twist.

Devan sprang to his feet. "I'll do it now," he said. "You won't even have to go back inside these walls. I'll speak for you before the Redeeming and take you back to Kamal with me tonight."

Nisha held out her hand. "Devan, don't."

"Don't?" Devan gave her a look of puzzled hurt and sank back down. "Don't what? Don't want you? Don't try to find a way for us to be together?"

He touched her face, curled his icy hand over her cheek in a way that had, moments before, made her feel special. "I love you. Don't you want to be with me?"

"Not like that," Nisha said. "I would die, Devan. Maybe my body wouldn't, but inside . . . inside I wouldn't be the girl you loved anymore. I'd turn into a shell. Please don't ask me to do that. There has to be another way."

Devan met her gaze for a moment longer, then looked away. "There is no other way. The Flower caste has always been perfect, Nisha. Only common people are cripples."

At those words, something inside Nisha broke like a clay pot. All the anger and humiliation leaked out, leaving only a cold emptiness behind.

"Is that how you think of me now? As common?"

"No, of course not," Devan said. He rose again. "But you have to understand–"

Nisha understood all that she wanted to. "Did you ever care

about me?" she asked, the words rising from a deep place inside her and spilling out before she even knew what she was going to say. "Or was it all a game, something to amuse you as long as it was convenient?"

Devan flinched. "*Me?*" he asked. "What about *you*? What were you doing in that quarry anyway? If you had trusted me, if you had waited, I would have come for you. But instead you go wandering around in the forest as if you were a damned Kildi and ruin everything. I can't take you as a wife, and being my mistress isn't good enough for you. What am I supposed to do?"

Devan slammed his palm against a tree trunk.

Shame filled Nisha, and she touched the tiger mark under her collarbone. No one wanted her. She wasn't loyal enough to her family to be a Kildi, and she wasn't flawless enough to become Flower caste. She didn't belong to the City, she didn't belong to Devan, she didn't belong to the cats, she didn't belong to anyone, anywhere. Devan's words flayed her to the bone.

Tac, who'd been standing several paces away and staring into the forest, came back at Devan's angry shout. He crouched down and took Nisha's hand. His touch was a lifeline, and she clung to it as Devan stepped closer to her again.

"You tell me, Nisha," he said. Tac growled what sounded like a warning, but Devan ignored him. "What am I supposed to do with a girl who limps like a beggar's brat?"

It happened so fast that Nisha barely saw it. One moment she was holding Tac's hand; the next, Tac had sprung up and backed

Devan against a tree. The gleaming point of a dagger rested on the courier's throat.

The young nobleman's eyes were wide with fear. "Call him off, Nisha," he said, his voice cracking. "Please, I'm begging you."

Nisha wasn't sure whether to laugh or cry. But she had no more tears, and it wasn't that funny. "Let him go, Tac," she said through dry lips.

Tac lowered the dagger. The look he gave Nisha was one of mixed frustration and grief, as if he had taken her heartbreak and made it his own. Then he spun and punched Devan full in the face.

The nobleman crumpled against the tree. A thin dribble of blood marked the corner of his mouth.

No one moved. From somewhere in the forest, a monkey hooted.

Finally Devan pushed himself up. He carefully brushed the dirt and twigs from his tunic, pulled out a handkerchief, and wiped his cut lip.

"I would have given you the world," he said without looking up. "I would have braved my family's judgment, all for you. A wife untrained in court ways, they would have accepted given time. But this . . . I'm sorry, Nisha."

Then he turned and walked to his horse. Nisha watched him as he led the mount through the open gate of the City, until the flash of his tunic was lost beyond the stone walls. He never looked back.

Tac knelt in front of Nisha. His brown irises held gold flecks in the light, and he raised his eyebrows, asking if she was all right.

"You shouldn't have done that," Nisha said. "But I'm not sorry you did." She took a ragged breath. "Will you take me to Sashi now? Please?"

The young man shrugged his broad shoulders. Then he picked up Nisha as if she were an injured fawn and carried her inside the estate walls.

29

SASHI WAS STANDING by the window, her dark hair falling over her face, when Nisha pushed open the door from Tac's arms.

At the sound of footsteps, Sashi turned her face toward them. "Who is it?" she asked dully.

Nisha gestured for Tac to set her down. Her left foot felt sore and bruised, but it held her weight. She clung to Tac's arm to avoid falling over. "Sashi, it's me."

Sashi's face hardened. "I don't want to talk to you." She threw the words at Nisha like they were daggers.

"I'm so sorry, Sashi." Nisha fumbled for words. "I shouldn't have said anything to Matron, but I did because I trusted her . . . I told her not to do anything, to wait until I knew more. I never, ever thought they'd take it this far so quickly."

Sashi shrugged and turned to the window. "It doesn't matter what you thought," she said. "And you should know better than to believe anything Matron says. She doesn't care who has to suffer as long as the City of a Thousand Dolls is safe."

Her voice grew hot enough to sear Nisha like a brand. "How could you possibly think I killed anyone, Nisha? All these years we've known each other, how could you even think it for one second?"

"I didn't want to! But when you wouldn't tell me about the blood, I didn't know what to think."

Sashi pressed her lips together until they turned white. "You should have trusted me," she said. "A friend was hurt, and I . . . helped her and promised not to tell anyone. And I never will. Not that it matters now."

"A friend?" Nisha stared at Sashi, her brain racing. A friend. Someone who knew the House of Jade. Someone who was bleeding . . . bleeding because of Nisha. "Sashi, was that *Zann's* blood on your asar?"

The blind girl turned away, but not before Nisha saw the truth in her face.

"It was, wasn't it?" Nisha asked. "Zann is a servant in Jade—of course she would go there when she was hurt. You helped her, and that's how you got blood on your asar. She came to you after we ran into each other in the maze."

"That's not how she told it," Sashi said with flat precision. "She said you attacked her."

Nisha's jaw dropped. Tac stiffened beside her.

"I didn't attack Zann," Nisha said. "I was running, and I didn't see her." Something in Sashi's voice gave her pause. "What else did she tell you? Why are you protecting her?"

"Because she needed it!" Sashi snapped. "You didn't see her, Nisha. She was so frightened. She thought that perhaps you had been sent to hurt her."

"I would never hurt Zann. You know that, Sashi."

Sorrow twisted the blind girl's mouth. "I wanted to believe that. But she made me promise, promise that I wouldn't tell anyone I'd helped her. She was afraid whoever was coming after her would come for me, too. "

"Sashi," Nisha said carefully, "Zann might have done something terrible. I need to know if she told you anything else."

Her friend shook her dark head. "No. I promised, Nisha. If you ever believed me, believe me now. I don't think Zann hurt anyone. She was too frightened."

Nisha opened her mouth, then shut it again. Sashi never told secrets, no matter how hard she was pushed. Nisha had made the mistake of not trusting Sashi once, and she wasn't going to make it again. "I'm going to get you out of here, Sashi, I promise."

Anger flashed across Sashi's face. "You think you can just fix this, don't you?" Her voice rose. "I have no future anymore, Nisha! They'll never set me up in a healer's practice now. I'm going to have to beg in the streets because you didn't think of anyone but yourself!"

"Sashi, please," Nisha said. Her eyes were dry and hot. "This was all a big misunderstanding. I know I made a terrible mistake, but I will fix it. I'll get you out of this, I swear. You're my friend."

"Friend!" Sashi's laugh was cynical and sick-sounding. "Since when do you know how to be anyone's friend? You think you're the only girl in this City who feels alone." She took a deep breath, her face cold and set. "Leave. I never want to see you again." She turned away from Nisha, a gesture as final as a door slamming.

"I will get you out of here," Nisha whispered fiercely to her friend's unresponsive back. "I will."

She looked up at Tac and voicelessly asked him to help her out of the room. When the door had shut behind them, he lifted her back into his arms. She didn't say where she wanted to go next, just huddled in his arms. He carried her into the hedge maze, making his way to the center fountain.

The fountain was as loud and dancing as it had been the day that Jina died. Tac set Nisha down lightly on its wide stone lip, steadying her with a gentle hand. She gazed down at the crystal clear water, at the blue of the lapis stones that inlaid the basin.

She felt like she was drowning, like the cold water was filling her lungs. What she wanted right now—more than anything—wasn't Devan or a family, it was the cats. She hadn't seen a single one since her return, not even from a distance, had heard no comforting voices in her head. She had broken her promise.

Now she was alone.

A hand touched Nisha's shoulder, startling her so much that she almost fell into the water. Tac sat down next to her. He squeezed Nisha's shoulder, as if to say, *You have me.*

His kindness undid her, unraveled her as if she were a torn weaving. She was suddenly weeping, deep, choking sobs that seared her throat. Tac pulled her close until her head rested on his shoulder.

When her sobs subsided, Nisha pulled away. Her chest ached and her eyes were blurry, but she was no longer drowning. She tried to meet Tac's gaze and found herself blushing.

"Thank you," she said, looking away. "You don't have to be so kind." Something loosened within her. "I'm still going to beat you the next time we fight."

Out of the corner of her eye, she saw Tac smile.

The sheltering walls of the labyrinth surrounded Nisha. It seemed right to be here, where Jina had died, where Nisha had first realized that death and pain were following her. Here, in the heart of the City, nothing had changed. And yet . . . everything had changed.

Nisha had changed.

It was time to stop running, stop handing the problem off to someone else. This time Nisha would stay and fight. This time she would figure it out.

Somehow.

She looked down at the fountain pool and touched her fingers to the surface. The water flowed like silk over her skin and rippled into a thousand splintered pieces. Then there was a flash of black. As the water calmed, it reflected a girl in a black-hooded robe standing on the opposite side of the fountain.

Nisha looked up to see who it was. The dark-headed girl's head was bent. Nisha could see bits of a yellow Music asar under the dark overrobe.

"Hello?" Nisha said softly.

The girl's head jerked up, eyes wide. Zann's face was painted with clumsily applied performance makeup, dark kohl paint ringing her eyes.

Nisha's mouth fell open. "Zann?"

The two girls stared at each other for a moment. Then, clutching her overrobe around her, Zann bolted toward the hedges. The yellow of her asar flashed like a trapped bird as she ran.

"Wait!" Nisha called. Forgetting her foot, she lunged forward. Only Tac's strong arms prevented her from hitting the ground.

Nisha knew, with a sudden, sick certainty, that it was *her* Music asar Zann was wearing. And if Zann had broken into her room, it could mean that she was the one who'd left the message.

Half wild, Nisha struggled against Tac's grip. "We have to go after her. We have to!"

Nisha! A spotted blur streaked across the grass, and Esmer skidded to a stop at Tac's feet.

Nisha went limp with relief. *Esmer,* she sent. *I'm so glad to see you.*

The older cat's eyes slid away from hers. *We saw her. Zann is headed for the House of Music.*

Stung by the cat's abruptness, Nisha allowed Tac to lift her.

Esmer trotted ahead of them. *We won't lose her. That Music asar has your scent all over it.*

I'm not worried, Nisha sent. *Not about that.*

There was a moment of uncomfortable silence.

I'm sorry, Nisha sent. *I'm so sorry I broke my promise.*

Esmer gave a heavy sigh. *I know, Nisha. It was foolish of Jerrit to ask it of you.*

At the mention of Jerrit, Nisha sat up straighter. *How is he? Is he healing all right?*

Jerrit is much better. He had to go away for now, but he said to tell you he still remembers his promise. The gray cat's mind-voice sounded grimly amused.

Nisha let out a breath. Jerrit still cared about her, wasn't angry with her. For now, that was enough.

She leaned her head on Tac's chest. *I'm surprised you and Jerrit still trust me.*

I would trust you all the way to the Mountains of the Dead, Esmer sent flatly. *But among our kind, the oath of the Long-Tailed Cat is taken very seriously. If a tribe is found to be harboring an oath-breaker, it's scattered, their young taken to be raised by other clans.*

The spotted cat paused. *Jerrit is young and rash. He didn't think about what would happen if you broke the oath. And believe me, he's as sorry about that as you are.*

Esmer gestured with her tail at the copper-edged doorway in front of them. *We're here.*

They followed Esmer through the front door of the House of Music and were greeted by Vinian. The Music Mistress was holding a handkerchief to a little girl's bleeding nose, and she looked torn between anger and tears.

"Oh, Nisha," she said when she spotted them. "What is going on? Is that your asar Zann is wearing? And what happened to you?"

Nisha ignored the questions. "Vinian, where did Zann go?"

"She ran in and went for Bindi's sitt-harp." Vinian gestured at the novice, whose nose was still gushing. "Bindi tried to stop her, and Zann elbowed her in the face. Thank goodness the older girls are already at the pavilion, or who knows what would have happened."

"It's all right, Vinian," Nisha said. "I'll talk to her."

Do you have a plan? Esmer sent.

No, Nisha sent back. *But I'll improvise.*

Nisha and Tac followed Esmer across the recital hall. Nisha wondered for a moment at his strength after he carried her up the long flight of stairs to the roof without tiring. But his arms were full, and it was Nisha who pushed open the trapdoor that led to the roof.

The door fell open with a loud rattle, and Nisha poked her head out of the opening.

Zann was sitting in the corner of the flat roof. She had shed her overrobe somewhere along the way to reveal the saffron asar wrapped perfectly around her, fitting her like a second skin. Her performance makeup was smeared and stained her face like a mask. The skin around her wrist cuffs was red and inflamed, as if she'd been clawing at them. She bent over the sitt-harp, never looking up.

Nisha recognized the song Zann was trying to play. It was the "Song of the Empress Veil," an intricate epic known for its sorrowful tones and difficult fingering. Mastering it had been Zann's greatest triumph. But now her folded paper harp pick stumbled across the strings, and what should have been a golden trickle of notes came out jerky and sharp.

Even with rough playing, the song still held a haunting echo of loss. It made Nisha think of Jerrit, and a stab of longing went through her. She pushed aside both the hurt and the longing for her friends. There were other things to worry about now.

"Zann," she said, nodding for Tac to carry her onto the roof. "Zann, I need to talk to you."

"Go away," Zann said, speaking to her hands, pausing the song. Her fingers clutched the folded triangle of paper. "I'm trying to concentrate." Another wrong note like the screech of a crow, and Zann cursed under her breath.

"Zann," Nisha said, trying to sound calm and unthreatening. "I need to ask you about the asar you're wearing."

"No." Zann's voice was a growl of frustration as she tried to position her fingers on the sitt-harp. "I don't have time to talk to you. I have to get this right. Why isn't it working?"

Nisha tried a different approach. "Why do you need to get it right, Zann? Why is this so important?"

Zann gave a humorless laugh. "You have no idea. You don't know what I had to do to get this asar, so I could get to a harp and have one more chance to play this song."

Nisha and Tac exchanged a glance, and Tac stepped closer.

"What did you do, Zann?" Nisha asked, digging her fingers into Tac's arm. "How did you get the asar?"

"Someone gave it to me." Zann unfolded the harp pick, smoothed out the scalloped edges, then refolded it and tried to play the song again. "That was the deal. If I helped them, I would get a Music asar."

Nisha's stomach lurched. "Who is 'them'? What did you do?"

Zann, bent over the sitt-harp, didn't answer.

"Zann!"

"What?" Zann looked up. The smeared makeup and her red eyes made her look like an evil spirit in a story. "Why won't you leave me alone? You took my music away once—isn't that enough?"

Familiar guilt tugged at Nisha's insides, but this time she ignored it. Zann had made her own decisions, and Nisha had lost too much today to carry Zann's losses as well. Instead of shrinking back, Nisha made her voice intentionally harsh.

"If you want me to go away, Zann, tell me what I want to know. What did you do to earn that asar?"

Zann opened her mouth as if to refuse, then softened. "I had to do it," she said, so quietly that Nisha could barely hear her. "You don't understand what it's like, to walk past this House, to hear the dancing and the singing and the sound of bells and drums, knowing you'll never be allowed back in. I would have given anything for the chance to play one more song. So when they came and asked me for a favor, told me they'd get me an asar so I could sneak in and play music, I couldn't say no."

"Zann, what did you do?"

A tear tracked down Zann's painted face. "I stole the *gunia* seeds from the House of Jade," she said. "I offered to help the healers making face paint that day. When no one was looking, I sneaked a few of the *gunia* seeds into my pocket. I swear I didn't know what they were going to be used for."

She breathed. "After Jina died, I wanted to tell someone. I tried to tell Sashi when she helped me clean up my bloody nose, but . . . I couldn't. All I told her was that I'd done something bad. Sashi promised to help me, but she was arrested. I couldn't tell anyone else. They would lock me up, and all hope of playing music again would be gone."

Tac had been inching closer, carrying Nisha as she talked, and now they were within touching distance of Zann.

"Zann," Nisha said as gently as she could. "Who asked you to get the seeds? Who poisoned Jina?"

Zann's fingers closed around the paper harp pick, crumpling it. "You'll never believe me. No one will. It's just my word against theirs."

"I'll believe you, Zann." Nisha reached out one hand. "I promise. Just tell me."

"No!" Panic had replaced the sorrow on Zann's face, and she scrambled to her feet. "Stay away!" Zann lifted the sitt-harp over her head. "I paid too much for this. I won't let you take it away from me." More tears leaked from her eyes, and the crumpled harp pick fell from her hand. "Please go away. Please."

She took a quick step, away from Nisha, and her foot turned on a loose piece of brick. She staggered and fell backward, the sitt-harp flying from her hands. Slowly, inevitably, the instrument bounced against the rim of the roof and fell out of sight.

Zann gave a single shriek that sliced through Nisha like a sword.

"No!" she cried. Then she ran toward the edge of the roof.

"Zann!" Nisha flung herself out of Tac's arms. Her fingers touched Zann's sweaty hand, her wrist–

Strong hands caught her just before she hit the rough brick of the roof, and her outstretched hands grasped only emptiness.

She heard a soft thump.

"Zann," Nisha whispered as Tac pressed Nisha against him. He held her tightly as she stared into the cold, hollow air. "Oh, Zann."

30

NISHA WAITED IN one of the low chairs in Matron's study. Tac had gone to find Matron—or Josei, Nisha wasn't sure—and she was alone. Through the open door of the study, she could see servants running back and forth, their faces focused and set, platters of food and jugs of wine in their hands, preparing for the masquerade.

Pavilion Field was full of people. Nisha had seen it as Tac carried her into the Council House. The sounds of music and laughing, the murmur of voices, the clang of staffs and swords. Everything Nisha had been waiting for. Now it seemed hollow, empty.

Her mind felt stuck like a cart wheel in mud. Zann was dead. If Nisha had done something different, said something different, could she have stopped it?

Mistakes, she thought. *I am making mistakes and I am losing everything.*

She rubbed her hand over her face. Her leg ached and the blank eyes of the dead girls spun in her head.

Atiy.

Jina.

Lashar.

Zann.

Zann, stroking the sitt-harp like it was the most precious thing in the world, playing with the paper harp pick–

Nisha's thoughts were interrupted by a loud argument in the hall. Peering through the door, she saw Kalia confront Matron. The woman's usually spotless white asar was disheveled, and she held a girl by the arm.

Chandra.

Nisha held herself perfectly still. Instinct–and the sharp twist of Kalia's mouth–told her not to move.

"You mean to tell me you know nothing about how my assistant got into your library?" Kalia hissed. "I told you, I don't want her in there."

She flung Chandra to Matron's feet and the girl crouched there, quivering, her face gray.

The corners of Matron's mouth tightened almost imperceptibly. "Kalia, if you can't control your own assistant–"

"I can't control her with you undermining me! I know you let her into the library, and I know it was you who gave her that botany scroll I found under her bed."

Matron's expression didn't change. "I really don't know what you're talking about."

Kalia stepped forward and grabbed Chandra's arm again. "What I want is for you to stop interfering. Or maybe I'll just take *your* assistant."

"That's not why you want Nisha," Matron said. "You want Nisha because you want to take her away from me." Her face took on a peculiar look of anger and regret. "You've wanted to take away something I cared about since I was appointed as Matron and you weren't. We were allies, friends before."

Kalia's knuckles went white, and Chandra whimpered. "That was another time, *Madri*." She spit out Matron's given name. "Now the Council's on my side."

"Oh, Kalia." Matron sighed. "Everything is about power with you. Power has always been the tar'Vay curse; you love it too much. I should never have given you more."

The expression on Kalia's face made Nisha shrink back in her chair. "You're about to fall, Madri," Kalia said. "Akash and I will see to it. And when you go down, Nisha will, too."

"Enough." Matron's voice was a shard of ice, sharp enough to draw blood. She took three deliberate steps that brought her face-to-face with Kalia.

"I may have been forced into my role as Nisha's protector," she said. "But that doesn't mean I don't take it seriously. I won't let anything happen to her."

"Not even if it's the only way to save the Houses?" Kalia asked in a silk-and-daggers voice.

Matron didn't answer.

"I thought so. As for you," Kalia said, hauling Chandra to her feet, "you and I are going to have another *talk*."

Kalia dragged her shrinking assistant away, Matron staring after them. Then she turned and saw Nisha through the open study door. For a moment, her face looked old and sad. Her smooth mask then dropped into place, like the closing of a window. She walked into the room to stand across from Nisha.

"I heard about Zann," she said.

"How could you do it?" Nisha cried. "How could you let that woman take Chandra away? Kalia could kill her!"

"Kalia has never seriously hurt an assistant before," Matron said, sounding far less sure than Nisha would've liked. "What happens to one girl is not my biggest problem right now."

"What if that girl were me?" Nisha asked quietly.

Matron flinched. "Nisha, try to understand. I have to think of the greater good, the survival of this estate."

"This place doesn't deserve to survive!" Nisha said. The anger felt good and drove out the grief she'd lived with for days. "I don't understand how you can stand to lead the City. All the manipulation, treating girls like pieces on a game board. Stefan was right about you."

"So you saw your uncle?" Matron's voice held a curious twinge of satisfaction. "What did Stefan have to say?"

Nisha gripped the arms of her chair. "He said this was an evil place. And I think he's right. There's nothing good here."

"Nothing?" Matron pointed at Nisha, her thin, bony finger

aimed straight as any dagger. "There are almost a thousand girls here, girls we feed and clothe and keep safe. Do you know what people were doing with their baby girls before the City of a Thousand Dolls? They were leaving them to die. Infants still wet from afterbirth were left in the forests for the wolves to eat. Children barely old enough to walk were killed by their own parents, smothered in the night and burned in the cremation fires." She pulled out a scroll from her shelves and slapped it on the desk.

"Do you want to read about it? It's all written down, the stories passed from matron to matron so we never, ever, forget why we are here."

Nisha stared at Matron as the woman went on ruthlessly.

"Do you know what will happen in the Imperial Court if the City falls? The citizens of the Empire accept the two-child law only because we tell them that the City of a Thousand Dolls is a safe place for their daughters. If there were no City, the Emperor might lose the support of the people. That's what our opponents in the Imperial Court don't understand: opponents who don't like the money spent on the City, and opponents who oppose what we do. Shut down the City, and you open the doors to war. *Another* war."

Nisha felt as if Matron's words were a river, sweeping her away. Was this what the world was like? Pain and anger on every side and no way to find a right answer for any of it? Were there no certainties anywhere?

"I understand your questions, Nisha," Matron said, her voice gentler. "But we do good things here. We are the only people in the Bhinian Empire who dare to take a child born in one caste and train her for another. We're the only ones *allowed* to."

Matron waved a hand. "This place takes money, Nisha. Raising all these children, feeding them, training them as novices, all of it requires money. And we get it from the clients who pay for these girls. Some girls are sacrificed for the greater good. I understand if you have a hard time accepting that. But don't you dare sit in judgment on it unless you're ready to accept the alternative."

Nisha couldn't find words to respond. It was true–she'd always known this. The City of a Thousand Dolls took in those no one else wanted, gave them a caste, a home. These walls had sheltered Nisha from the danger that had killed her parents. Here, girls born into lower castes could marry royalty. Even Sashi, who might have been rejected for her blindness, had had a future because of the City of a Thousand Dolls. A good one.

If Nisha could save it for her.

She jerked back to the present. "Matron," she said, "Sashi isn't the killer!"

Matron looked sharply at her. "What?"

"I saw someone at the quarry, just before the boulder fell on me. It had to be the murderer stopping me from asking questions. There's no way Sashi could have done it."

"If someone pushed that rock onto you, it would clear Sashi," Matron agreed. "But how can you be sure someone was there at all? Perhaps the boulder just rolled over on its own. It could have been a terrible accident, Nisha. The quarry is a dangerous place."

Nisha frowned. "No, I'm sure it was pushed, and I know I saw someone. A shadow—someone close to my size."

"Perhaps you did," Matron said. "But that's not a lot to go on. With Zann's death, we cannot afford any more mistakes." A spasm of pain crinkled her eyes. "What happened on that roof?"

Nisha closed her eyes. Her words came from a leaden place in her chest.

"Zann stole the seeds for whoever poisoned Jina. She gave them to someone in exchange for a Music asar, so she could sneak into the House of Music. But she wouldn't tell me who it was."

Matron folded her hands in front of her. "Nisha . . . is it possible Zann herself killed those girls? She snapped."

Nisha looked at Matron. "You should have seen Zann on the roof. She was so tormented just for getting those seeds. Someone manipulated her."

"But Nisha, how can you be sure?" Matron asked. "Zann had clear motive to hate the City. She had free run of the House of Jade. It would have been very easy for her to put the poison in Jina's seeds. And she could have pretended to be running errands, sneaked into the House of Beauty, and stabbed Lashar."

"And Atiy? Why would Zann kill a girl she'd never met?" Nisha shook her head. "No, I can't let you put this on Zann. Not when she can't defend herself anymore."

"Nisha, without someone else to take the blame, the Council won't drop the charges against Sashi," Matron said, each word as blunt as a mallet strike. "At the very least, Akash will insist that we throw her out of the City."

"Sashi is innocent!" Urgency made Nisha's voice high and harsh. "If you turn her out, she'll have no way to survive!"

"Quite possibly," Matron said, meeting Nisha's eyes. "It's a pity that Zann couldn't have confessed to the killings, isn't it? Then we could know with certainty that Sashi wasn't involved."

Nisha felt a stubborn flame rise inside her. Zann might have resented her and have stolen the seeds that killed Jina, but Sashi had been right when she said Zann hadn't hurt anyone. Nisha had no intention of seeing either of them take the blame for three murders. Besides, if Nisha said that Zann was the killer, she would be damaging more than Zann's memory. She would be leaving the real murderer free to kill again.

"I won't give up," Nisha said, meeting Matron's eyes without blinking. "I will find out who did this."

Matron looked away. "Very well," she said. "But in the meantime, I need you. The masquerade is tonight, and we'll be shorthanded without Zann."

The change in subject startled Nisha. "But . . . I can't go like this." She waved at the heavy cast on her foot. "That place will be full of Flower caste." Her eyes blurred at the memory of Devan's cruel words.

Matron's eyes fell on Nisha's foot. "You can sit at the Redeeming table and take fees. Your foot will be under the table covering, and no one will see it."

Nisha grimaced. The Redeeming table was set up in the House of Flowers foyer, at the base of the marble staircase. Someone from the Council House took Redeeming fees for the girls bought throughout the evening. Nisha had always volunteered for the kitchens to avoid the Redeeming table.

But as long as Matron needed her for something, the Council might leave her alone. If Nisha agreed, she would be safe, at least for the evening.

The only thing she had now was time, and not very much of it. She would save every second, no matter what she had to do.

"I'll do it," she said. She looked down at herself. She was still wearing the skirt and blouse the Kildi had given her, and they were dirty and smudged from the long trip through the forest. "But I have to change."

Matron nodded. "You have a few hours. I'll send someone for you."

Nisha turned to see Tac in the doorway.

"Get some rest, Nisha," Matron said. "You'll be very busy tonight."

This is what the Lotus Throne decrees:

First: No girl in the City of a Thousand Dolls shall be judged by her birth. Upon entering the City, each girl will be considered casteless until she is spoken for, at which time she will receive the appropriate caste mark and be given a place in the Bhinian Empire.

Second: Let all who would claim a girl pay an agreed-on price, to compensate the City for her training. No girl shall be spoken for without the formal exchange of coin.

Third: If a man pays in advance, the girl shall be trained as he specifies. If he comes to claim her and finds her unsatisfactory, he may demand the return of his money or ask to be given another girl instead.

Fourth: Once a year, the City shall host a great Redeeming Ceremony. The girls shall display their training and beauty so that all who come may honor the wisdom of the Lotus Throne in creating and maintaining such a city. At that time, any who seek a wife or apprentice may choose from the available girls.

Fifth: If a man wishes to claim a girl before she reaches her six-teenth year, he must appear before the City Council and petition for her early release. The Council may refuse or grant such a request as it wishes.

Sixth: No girl shall be sent from the City before the time of her first blood.

Seventh: Once a girl has been spoken for, she is the responsibility of the one who speaks for her. She may not be returned to the City, nor is the City responsible for her future conduct.

From a scroll written and sealed by the Second Lotus Emperor,

establishing the rules of the Redeeming

31

NISHA TRIED TO rest. But once back in her room, she tossed and turned on top of her bedroll. Her foot still throbbed, but the blinding, bone-deep pain hadn't returned. Whatever the Kildi healer had done was working.

When she heard the soft knock at her door, Nisha sat up gratefully. Even the swirling, glittering crowd at the masquerade was preferable to being alone with her own thoughts. She reached over and pulled the washbasin off the small table by the bed, squinting to see herself in the rippling surface.

"Come in," she said, dipping her fingers into the water and trying to wash the smudges off her face.

Tac walked in, carrying a bundle of fabric in his arms. A smile wrinkled his eyes when he saw her, and Nisha scowled at him.

"Don't look at me like that," she said, gesturing to her fractured reflection in the bowl. "I look awful."

Tac's smile widened. He put the fabric down and sat next to Nisha on the bed. Wetting the edge of his tunic sleeve in the water, he washed the dirt marks from her forehead and nose. His hands were gentle on the side of her face, and his breath touched her hair. Nisha didn't move, afraid if she did he would vanish. Tac ran his wet fingers through her hair, smoothing it down. Then he handed her a hair tie.

She reached out and took it, their fingers brushing. "Thank you."

Bracing herself against the floor with her good foot, Nisha plaited her hair into one thick, loose braid. It wasn't formal, but it would have to do. "Will you bring me a gray asar out of that chest?" she asked.

But the young man shook his head and picked up the fabric he'd brought.

When Tac unrolled the fabric, Nisha's breath caught in a gasp. It was an asar, almost the same shade of gray as she usually wore. But instead of thick, plain cotton, this one was patterned silk, with a border of crimson *asboka* flowers.

"Is that for me?"

"Indeed it is," came a voice from the doorway, and Josei appeared, Nisha's red scarf in her hand.

"Sorry I'm late," she said to Tac. "I had to answer some questions about my girls from potential buyers. It's a madhouse out there. We've never had so many nobles at the Redeeming. Is she ready?"

Tac gestured to Nisha, and Josei looked her over. "Not bad at all." She took the fabric from Tac's hand.

"Now get out. We don't need you for this part." Tac nodded and left, shutting the door behind him, and Josei turned to Nisha.

"What's going on?" Nisha asked.

Josei gave what Nisha was starting to think of as her fox-grin. "You didn't think we'd let you go to the masquerade looking like something the spotted cat dragged in, did you?" She waved the asar in her hand.

"All kinds of things can be weapons, Nisha, as Rajni reminded us. And at the very least, you will be able to hold your head up out there in the middle of all those nobles."

Nisha felt an answering smile creep across her face. She wouldn't have to show up at the masquerade looking defeated in front of Devan and all the others. She would go defiant. She would have that victory.

Soon she was transformed. The gray-and-crimson silk flowed from one shoulder and pooled around her, hiding her foot. The slim tunic underneath was the color of the darkening sky, and Nisha's throwing knives were hidden easily by the long sleeves. She wrapped her red Kildi scarf around her head, hiding her braid. As a finishing touch, Josei handed her a mask of painted ceramic with the face of a black tiger.

Nisha paused, running her fingers over the mask. The tiger's face was both calm and powerful, the face of a predator who had nothing to fear. It was so far from how Nisha actually felt that she was reluctant to put it on, as if she would be lying. Instead she held it in one hand and looked up at Josei.

"I'm ready," she said.

The House of Flowers was full to bursting and crowded with more people than Nisha had ever seen at a Redeeming before. All the doors had been thrown open to allow people to move freely, and they swirled through the place like a river over jutting rocks. Crowds watched the dancers in the mirrored hall, dined in the banquet room, and gossiped in small groups in the spacious foyer. The throne room was especially full, as lesser nobles scrambled to get close to the High Prince.

The whole place smelled of spices and rice wine, orange blossoms and vanilla.

And then there were the masks, a constant stream of painted faces, some angry, some solemn, some with ferocious grimaces. Few people wore smiling masks. Frightening masks were much better than smiling ones at scaring away evil spirits. And no one wanted evil spirits at a party.

Tac carried Nisha in through a small side door and paused in the shadow of the staircase. Despite her new asar, she felt out of place, a blot on the bright crowd. She wished for Josei, but the House of Combat Mistress had been called back to the Pavilion Field to help her novices with another demonstration.

Nisha hadn't seen Esmer or any of the other cats. The thought that they might have left for good was a painful one. But there was nothing she could do about it. For now, at least, she still had a job to do.

Nisha and Tac watched from the shadows as someone stepped to the Redeeming table and offered to speak for one of the novices. The servant looked up the girl's price in a scroll and took the money offered. Once the transaction was complete, another servant climbed up the large marble stairway above the crowd and rang a large gong.

The gong's low vibrations silenced the room. The servant on the stairs called the name of the novice, a girl from the House of Music, who had just been redeemed as the wife of a wealthy merchant. The novice came forward to greet the client, and everyone went back to eating and drinking.

Matron was standing at the bottom of the staircase, next to the Redeeming table. She raised one eyebrow when she saw Nisha.

"You look better than you did before," she said. "I approve." She motioned to the servant attending the table. "You're relieved. Go help the kitchen staff."

The servant slipped away. Tac lowered Nisha into the stiff wooden chair and arranged her asar so it flowed over her feet. Then he stood behind her chair and folded his arms across his chest.

Matron nodded in satisfaction. "There are people I must speak to, Nisha. Have your guard here fetch me if you have any trouble." With another nod to Tac, she slipped away into the bright whirl of people.

Nisha ran her fingers along the table covering, embroidered with silver. From where she sat, she could hear the music from the dancing hall, the stately thrum of drums and bells, the flowing melody of the double-reed flute, the rippling notes of sitt-harps. She could imagine each step the dancers were taking, each arch of the spine, each flicker of the fingers. Her feet itched to join them, but her cast bound her like a chain, tying her to the chair.

A woman in a green-and-gold-embroidered asar walked up. Her mask was orange and black with a wide mouth and hooked nose. Her hands were painted with elaborate designs in dark-green dye, the sign of a practicing healer.

"I would speak for the Jade novice Danna," she said formally. "I will take her as an apprentice."

Nisha nodded, keeping her eyes cast down. Nervousness fluttered in her stomach as she unrolled the scroll and found Danna's name. The price next to it seemed huge to Nisha, but the woman paid it without comment. Nisha gestured to the announcer, who walked up the stairs and hit the gong.

"The novice Danna," she said in a carrying voice, "has been redeemed as apprentice by Uditi the healer."

Nisha put the gold in the strongbox next to her and marked the healer's name on the scroll. There were already quite a few girls marked off, since many craftsmen and merchants preferred to pay for their girls early and take them back to Kamal or their homes before dark.

This isn't so bad, she told herself. *I can do this.*

Tanaya appeared in a flutter of silk. "Nisha!" Tanaya's light hair glowed in the sea of dark heads. "What on earth are you doing over here? Have you seen the prince? I'm so nervous."

Some of the tension in Nisha's shoulders relaxed. At least Tanaya was safe. "You look beautiful," Nisha said, meaning it.

Tanaya's asar was of richly embroidered scarlet silk, edged with gold, setting off her clear skin and black-brown eyes. A cluster of rubies nestled in her shining hair, matching the golden collar of rubies around her neck. Tanaya's delicate hands tangled in the fabric of her asar, and she bounced up and down on the balls of her feet.

"I'm so nervous," she repeated. "What if he doesn't want me?" She looked up and saw Tac behind Nisha's chair. "Since when do you have a bodyguard?"

"He's . . . here to guard the strongbox," Nisha said. She didn't like lying to Tanaya, but explaining Tac would mean explaining her foot, too. "He's one of Josei's assistants."

"Too bad he's not guarding you," Tanaya said with a wink.

Nisha suppressed a surge of annoyance. Tanaya had acted the same way when she'd realized Nisha cared about Devan. Did she think Nisha was desperate enough to throw herself at any man who appeared? Tanaya probably didn't realize that Nisha even knew Tac.

"It seems like everyone has a bodyguard today," Tanaya said, oblivious to Nisha's frown. "Have you seen all the warriors?"

Now that she was looking for them, Nisha could see dark-clothed shadows standing at intervals along the wall. Swords gleamed at their waists. "Where did they all come from?"

"Many of them are Prince Sudev's private guards," Tanaya said. "But I know the members of the Council brought their own warriors too. Wouldn't do for someone to try to kill the High Prince, I suppose."

"I suppose," Nisha said, not really listening. As if her thought of Devan had conjured him, she saw the young noble across the room. His mask was pushed up above his eyes, and he was laughing. Other young men flocked around him like jeweled parrots.

Nisha closed her eyes briefly to shut out the sight of Devan's smile. Tanaya kept talking.

"I sneaked away from Indrani to come and say hello. I feel like I haven't seen you for a week. Indrani keeps fussing, trying to make sure everything is perfect, making me practice my bow one more time. Anyway, I have to go. I'm going to be late."

Tanaya whirled away and a piece of paper fluttered to the floor, skittering to rest against the leg of Nisha's chair.

"Tanaya, wait!" Nisha bent down to scoop up the scalloped paper. "The way you drop these poems, I'm surprised you don't . . ." Her voice trailed off as her fingers rubbed along the grain of the rice paper.

The same kind of paper as the note she'd found under Lashar's body.

Everything around Nisha slowed, stopped.

She remembered: Tanaya playing with her ruby necklace, a necklace that matched the marks on Atiy's neck.

Tanaya, claiming to be in her room all day the day Lashar died, but smelling of lavender, distinctly like the House of Beauty.

Tanaya, who trained in every House.

Tanaya, who could go anywhere she pleased.

Zann playing the sitt-harp with a folded paper pick, a paper with scalloped edges.

It all made a horrible sense.

"Did I drop another one?" Tanaya took the poem from Nisha's unresisting hand. "I always write when I'm nervous." She paused. "Nisha, what's wrong?"

Nisha looked up at the girl who had always been her hero, feeling something inside her shatter. She hadn't known a heart could break so many times in one day.

"Why, Tani? Why did you kill them?"

The paper fell from Tanaya's hand.

32

FOR A MOMENT, neither girl moved.

Then Tanaya bent down swiftly. Even over the other scents in the foyer, Nisha could smell the rich scent of the night-queen flower. Their faces were inches apart.

"I don't care what you know," Tanaya whispered. "If you're smart, you won't say anything."

"I know you killed Atiy," Nisha said softly, her words heavy with certainty. "Jina. And Lashar. Zann had your paper, Tanaya, the paper you use to write poems. She had it on the roof right before she killed herself. Zann never went to the House of Flowers. She wasn't allowed in. How did she get it?"

"Shut up," Tanaya hissed, looking around. "Do you want everyone to hear you?"

"Tanaya," Nisha said, her voice forcing the other girl to meet her eyes. "Tanaya, please. I know you left the note in Lashar's room for me. Only you would tear it so I wouldn't see the scalloped edges. Someone who stole the paper would never think of that."

For a moment, she thought Tanaya would deny it and walk away, but the older girl just shook her head.

"You have no idea what happened the day Atiy died," she said. Her eyes flashed to Tac.

"He won't tell. He can't speak," Nisha said. "Help me understand. Please, Tanaya."

The *please* sucked the vitality out of Tanaya. She slumped, her voice so low that Nisha had to lean forward to hear her. "After I helped you dress, I went to the House of Pleasure for my *achaneh* dance lesson," she said dully.

Nisha nodded. *Achaneh* was a private dance that the wives of the royal family learned for their wedding nights. The House of Pleasure was the only House that taught it. Tanaya stared into empty air.

"As I was leaving the practice room, I bumped into Atiy going in. I'd never met her before, never even seen her, but she . . . she was wearing the exact same necklace that I was."

Tanaya's hand crept to the collar of rubies and gold at her throat. "I persuaded her to come up to the roof with me—I don't remember how—and I asked her where she got it. She said she was training to be the secret mistress of the prince. My prince!"

Tanaya's whisper became a hiss. "Can you imagine? All these years of studies and lessons I went through, all that training?

And some mousy little whore thought she was going to share Prince Sudev with me? I tore the necklace from her neck. We struggled, and she tripped."

Tanaya spread her hands. "I swear, Nisha. I swear, by the Ancestors and by the Five Sacred Rivers, I did not mean to kill her."

Partygoers swirled past their corner, but the chatter and laughter felt unreal and far away. No one took any notice of them.

"All right, I believe you. What about Jina?" Nisha asked in a low voice.

Tanaya's face was still stiff with fury and hurt pride. "Jina was in the stairway when I was coming down from the roof. Was it my fault she was poking around where she had no business?"

"So you *killed* her?"

"No." Tanaya straightened. "Atiy was an accident, and you can't prove that I had anything to do with those other girls."

"Tani." Nisha held out her hand. "You know I'll have to tell Matron about this. Come with me. Turn yourself in."

"You think I'm afraid of you?" Tanaya's smile mocked her. "In a very short time I will be a princess, and you will still be a nobody who no one wants."

The dead, frozen butterfly in the quarry. Tanaya had crushed the butterfly as carelessly and ruthlessly as she had killed those other girls. Just like she had pushed the boulder onto Nisha the moment she was defenseless.

"Is that why you tried to kill me?" Nisha whispered, the words digging their claws into her throat. She moved her foot so the heavy cast slipped out from under her asar. "Is that why you did this to me? Because I'm a nobody?"

Tanaya's smile turned sad. "I had to protect myself. And no matter how you or I feel about it, I'm still the more important one. I don't make the rules, Nisha. You're alive, and you should be grateful for that and learn from your mistakes. This isn't a fight you can win. Trust me."

With that, Tanaya walked away. Nisha stared after her, her eyes burning. Matron's words echoed in her mind.

Sometimes, Nisha, people are not who you expect them to be.

Tac touched Nisha's shoulder, and she jumped. His eyes were as troubled as her own. *What do we do?* they seemed to ask.

Nisha didn't know. Tanaya's cruel words were also true. She was the most important novice the City of a Thousand Dolls had ever trained. No one would believe Nisha over her.

But if she did nothing, Sashi would die.

Nisha bit her lip and looked up at Tac. "Can you find another servant to take the table? I need to find Matron."

Tac carried Nisha through the crowd. She had pulled the black tiger mask down, and the ceramic was cool on her hot face. She felt safer behind the mask, less conspicuous, but more than anything, she wished for a breath of fresh, free air. She longed for the feel of grass bending under her bare feet and the vibrations of purrs in her ear.

But those things were gone for Nisha. And whatever happened next, she had to make sure they weren't gone for Sashi, too.

As Tac scanned the crowd for Matron, Nisha sneaked a glance through the open door of the throne room. She wanted to see the man Tanaya had thought it worth killing for.

Then she saw him. Prince Sudev was handsome, a slim man not quite thirty, with hair and eyes as dark as ink and the shadow of a beard under his high cheekbones. He leaned forward on the throne, chin resting on his fist. Sometimes he covered a yawn with one perfectly manicured hand. Black-clad bodyguards stood to either side, hands on hilts, eyes wary.

The prince's long blue-and-silver tunic shimmered like a moth in a darkening forest. His teeth flashed in frequent smiles, but his eyes looked like they had forgotten how to smile a long time ago.

Every time his eyes wandered in her direction, Nisha shrank down. Instinct told her it would be very dangerous to draw the prince's attention. She wasn't here to see him. She had to talk to Matron.

Matron stood in an alcove outside the throne room, talking to a man with the two earrings and gold chains of a successful Bamboo caste merchant. Her eyes widened in surprise when she saw Nisha.

"Excuse me, please," she said to the merchant.

The man nodded and moved away, and Matron pulled Nisha and Tac farther into the alcove.

"What are you doing here? You had strict instructions to stay at the Redeeming table." Matron lowered her voice. "Nisha, I have seen the prince throw a man in prison because he was offended by his scarred face. He's the most spoiled and unpredictable of all the Imperial family, and you cannot let him see you. You know it's an insult to appear before a member of the Imperial family while injured."

"I'm sorry, Matron, but I had to find you. I know who killed Atiy."

"What?" Matron stiffened, looking around the room. "Who was it?"

Nisha pushed up the tiger mask and took a breath. "It was Tanaya. She fought with Atiy on the roof. She said they were fighting over the High Prince."

"She *told* you?" Matron's hand flew over her mouth.

Nisha nodded. "Just a few moments ago. Matron, I think she killed Jina and Lashar, too. I didn't tell you before, but someone left a note addressed to me under Lashar's body. A note telling me to go to the quarry. The edges were torn, so I didn't realize at first that it was the same paper Tanaya likes to use to write her poems. And Zann used the same kind of paper for her harp pick on the roof." Nisha felt her voice crack with hurt. "I confronted Tanaya about the paper, but she refused to talk about it. She says Atiy was an accident, but you should have seen her face. She's behind the deaths, Matron. I'd stake my life on it."

Matron's face was the color of ash. "Ancestors defend us. Nisha, you have to get out of here."

"What? Why? What about Tanaya?"

"I will deal with this," Matron said hurriedly. "But you have to leave, now. Tac, you have to take her away, somewhere safe. Hurry!"

"I don't understand–" Nisha started, but her words were cut off by a smooth voice.

"Nor do I." The designs of Akash tar'Vey's brown-and-black tunic glittered like scales as he approached them. "But Tanaya was right to warn me just now. She told me you were spreading vicious rumors and trying to cause trouble."

Nisha couldn't keep the hurt from her voice. "Tanaya told you that?"

Matron held out her hand. "Akash, Nisha has done what we asked. We asked her to look into these deaths."

"And she provided us with a most convenient solution," Akash said, and straightened his sleeves. "A blind healer no one will miss. We did not ask her to fling accusations at the most important novice in the entire City."

He bent closer to Nisha, his breath smelling of rice wine. "I am willing to overlook this as an unfortunate delusion caused by your accident. But you must never speak of this again."

Despair was followed by a hot flash of anger. "Don't you even care that Tanaya might have killed three girls? What if she is guilty?" Nisha's words were high-pitched and desperate, a grasp after reason.

And Akash's reply caught her completely by surprise.

"Of course she's guilty," he said. "Which is why we needed another suspect. It's the only reason I allowed the Council to agree to Matron's proposal. That's why I held off your buyer and permitted you to investigate. You were never supposed to find the truth, Nisha. You were supposed to find a scapegoat. And you did an excellent job."

Nisha felt like she'd been punched in the throat. "You used me? You used me to set someone up falsely so you could protect the real murderer?"

Akash waved his hand, the gold of his flower tattoo clearly visible. "It was a distraction. And a better option than trying to cover up Tanaya's involvement. Even getting rid of Jina left too many unanswered questions."

His words were like a slap, and Nisha reeled.

Matron gasped. "*You* killed Jina?" she asked. "It wasn't Tanaya?"

Akash shrugged. "Tanaya came to me in private after Atiy's death and told me what she'd done. She also told me that the only person who'd seen her come down the stairs after Atiy's fall was Jina. She wasn't sure if Jina had seen her, but that's not the sort of thing you take chances with."

Nisha's mind flew back to Zann's expression on the roof, the look of trapped despair. *You'll never believe me. No one will. It's just my word against theirs.*

"Zann wasn't just talking about Tanaya," Nisha said, her words soft with horror. "She was talking about both of you. You manipulated her and bribed her into getting those seeds. Because not even Tanaya could get into the private stores of the House of Jade without someone noticing. Did you at least have the courage to put the seeds in her bowl yourself? Or did you get another person to do it?"

"I don't see how that's relevant," Akash said, a scowl creasing his handsome face, a face that reminded her too much of Devan's.

"So Zann gave you the seeds," Nisha said, each word costing her. "And Tanaya gave her the asar. And then . . . what? You thought you'd just use me to make sure no one suspected? But it didn't work, did it? Because Tanaya killed Lashar. I know that for sure."

Akash's scowl deepened. "She's not as . . . manageable as we thought. I never would have told Tanaya about Lashar had I known she was so determined. But once you take a life, it becomes that much easier to take another. Even if it's the life of a friend." He cast a meaningful look at Nisha's cast.

"Really, Nisha, why would I bother to bargain with you? I had the Council convinced, I had a buyer, I could have gotten rid of you as easily as that." He snapped his fingers. "But covering up death is such a messy business. The chance that you could bring me someone else to accuse was too irresistible."

Nisha felt like she was suffocating. The whole conversation was taking on the quality of a nightmare. Any moment now, she'd wake up in her own bed with the cats curled up next to her. *Let me wake up. Please let me wake up.*

Matron was staring at Akash in disbelief, visible, dark-red anger rising in her face. "You never told me any of this, Akash."

Akash snorted. "Of course I didn't. For all your talk about sacrificing to save the City, none of us really believed you would hand us an innocent girl. You are far too sentimental for that."

He enunciated as if each word were a cold iron bar.

"You can't tell me you didn't suspect anything. You knew that the necklace Atiy was wearing was missing, that it was twin to Tanaya's. Who else would have taken it? And Lashar's death should have confirmed it! We were considering transferring her to High Prince Sudev as a replacement mistress. We were just about to inform Rajni. Who else benefited by her death but Tanaya?"

"I didn't want to believe it," Matron stuttered. "I thought after the snake attack that I must have been wrong–"

"A masterful stroke," Akash crowed. "I was most impressed when she told me she wanted the krait to throw suspicion off herself. I may not like you, Matron, but you do train your girls well. Tanaya is every bit the intelligent and cunning wife who Prince Sudev needs. It's a pity that she had to show her talents in such a way, but still, she's a credit to you."

Matron winced, and Akash's mouth widened in a cruel smile. "Though if it had been up to me, I would not have pinned our hopes on one girl. My predecessor should have made sure at least three girls had the proper training. Then we could have simply replaced Tanaya instead of trying to clean up her mess."

He shrugged. "No matter. We have a girl in custody for the killings, and Tanaya is more than ready to become a princess. Once the ceremony starts, she's the Imperial family's problem."

Akash tar'Vey had coldly covered up Atiy's murder, plotted Jina's death, and left Tanaya free to kill again, had even given her the name of her next victim–Lashar. And now he was going to destroy Sashi, all to protect himself and his own power. Nisha knew that she had never hated another human being as she hated Akash tar'Vey.

She tried to force herself out of Tac's arms and put her face as close to Akash's as she could stand. Staring him right in the eye, she willed him to believe her words. "I won't let you do this. I'll tell everyone. I'll tell the High Prince if I have to."

Akash smiled broadly, showing his teeth. "Oh, I doubt that very much, Nisha."

Akash snapped his fingers again, and two heavyset men in black tunics appeared and took hold of Tac's arms.

"*You* are no longer my concern either. Where you're going, you won't be able to tell anyone much of anything. As I told you, we have had an offer for your bond. The buyer raised her offering price and I accepted. She is most anxious to claim you."

And Kalia tar'Vey, glowing in spotless white and her eyes alight with triumph, stepped out of the crowd. Dangling from her hand was a mask painted with the face of a laughing girl.

"Hello, Nisha."

33

FEAR CONGEALED IN Nisha's chest. She couldn't move, couldn't breathe. All she could do was stare at Kalia's satisfied smile.

Tac tried to pull out of the guards' grip, but he couldn't, not without dropping Nisha.

As if from far away, Nisha heard Matron arguing in a low, urgent voice, heard the distant chatter and laughter of the oblivious crowd.

Kalia came closer and ran a cold finger down Nisha's cheek. Nisha jerked her head away, and Kalia laughed.

"I told you I was becoming more powerful than Matron. And you've been very, very bad to cause our family so much trouble."

Nisha did the only thing she could think of. She spit.

Kalia touched the spit on the shoulder of her asar and wrinkled her nose. "Nisha, don't be disgusting."

She grabbed Nisha's hair, sending pain shooting through her head. She put one smooth hand on Nisha's exposed neck and tightened.

Matron moved forward, but Akash grabbed her and jerked her back.

Kalia spoke to Nisha, but her eyes rested on Matron. "You belong to me now."

Nisha tried to speak, but all that came out was a choking noise. Her scalp and neck throbbed. Her vision blurred around the edges. After what seemed like an eternity, Kalia released her hair and patted Nisha's cheek.

"I'm glad we understand each other. But I think you'll have to do with restricted food and water for a while. If your mouth is dry, you can't spit."

Nisha was too busy taking in great gulps of air to answer. Kalia turned to Akash, who was still holding Matron's arm and shoulder tightly.

"Akash, may I ask you to please see that Nisha is delivered to my rooms?" She looked Tac up and down. "And do see if you can separate her from her guard. I have a feeling he would prove troublesome."

"Of course, cousin," Akash said, nodding to her. "It was a pleasure doing business with you."

Kalia disappeared into the crowd. As soon as she was gone, Akash waved his hand at the black-clothed guards. "Take her away."

"No!" The shouted word came from Matron and Nisha at once. Nisha kicked wildly, and Tac pulled hard against the men holding him.

The tiger mask slid from Nisha's head, shattering on the floor.

"Nisha?" There was a sudden silence, and Nisha looked up to see Devan standing on the edge of the crowd, staring at their small circle.

Devan's eyes jumped from Nisha to Akash, and confusion creased his forehead. "Uncle? What is this?"

Akash straightened his tunic and cleared his throat. "Nothing you need to concern yourself with, Devan. Just some City business."

"City business," Devan repeated. "What kind of City business involves hauling away injured girls as if they were criminals? What has she done?"

He came close to Nisha, his wonderful dark eyes creased with worry. "Are you all right, Nisha?"

Akash looked from Nisha to Devan. "How do you two . . . Of course." Grim amusement and recognition filled his words. "*She's* the girl your father was worried about. The mystery girl you kept hinting at. He thought she might live in the City and that was why you wouldn't give up the courier job." He laughed. "You really thought your family would accept this girl as your bride? Oh, nephew, you're a fool."

Devan flinched. He opened his mouth to respond, but just then the deep sound of a brass horn filled the room. All eyes turned to the staircase, where one of the prince's advisers stood.

"The Imperial Redeeming Ceremony will now begin!"

As if the words were a magic spell, the crowd turned and started to push into the throne room as one.

The press of people shoved against the men holding Tac, pushing the guards off balance. Taking advantage of the distraction, Tac pulled out of their hands and pushed as far away as he could. But the crowd made escape impossible. Tac and Nisha were swept into the throne room. Behind them, several people deep–just as stuck–were Akash, Devan, and Matron.

"Can we get away?" Nisha asked Tac. He shook his head, hopeless frustration written all over his face. Nisha followed his stare and saw that the men who had tried to drag her away were guarding the doors. Even if she and Tac could push against the tide of people, they wouldn't make it outside without being caught.

A cold calm came over her. Like the rising of the White Mist, it filled her, blocking out the noise and jostle of the excited crowd. Nisha felt disconnected from her body, from the fear that still twisted her stomach. Two words ran like sparks through her blood.

Save Sashi.

And with those words came an idea, a mad idea. It could get her killed. But it would be worth it if Nisha could undo her mistakes, if she could rescue the one truly innocent person in this whole mess. At least she would have tried.

"Get me closer," Nisha whispered to Tac. "I want to be in the front." *Please,* she added in her mind. *Let me do this.*

For a moment, she thought her friend would refuse, but

instead he nodded, and started to move with the crowd toward the throne. Servants were already clearing a path to the small side room, where Tanaya was waiting.

"Nisha." Devan shoved his way through the tightly packed people in Tac's wake. "Nisha, what in the name of the Ancestors is happening? Why was my uncle trying to take you?"

"Because he can," Nisha said with bitterness. "That's what I was trying to tell you earlier, Devan. I'm a nobody, and this is what happens to nobodies. We get taken away and sold."

Devan looked stunned, as if she'd struck him. "I–I didn't know."

"You didn't want to know." Nisha was tired and no longer angry. Devan couldn't save her, but that was all right. She no longer wanted to be saved.

"It's all right, Devan," she said, allowing a thread of tenderness to creep into her voice. "You can't help me now, and I don't want you involved."

Nisha nodded to Tac, who started moving away.

"Wait, what are you going to do?" Devan whispered. "Nisha! Nisha, come back here."

Nisha didn't turn around. Her entire attention was focused on the slowly opening side doors. The musicians, who had squeezed into the throne room ahead of everyone else, began playing a sprightly tune.

The crowd cleared a path, revealing two tiny, wide-eyed girls from the House of Flowers. The girls' hair had been brushed until it shone, and they wore blue-and-silver-embroidered asars.

They looked so young as they walked, dropping petals of white star jasmine. When the girls reached the base of the throne, the music changed.

The drums and other instruments died away, leaving only a lone bamboo flute playing. And when Tanaya stepped out from behind the doors, Nisha couldn't stop a gasp.

Tanaya was flawless. Not a hair was out of place, not a wrinkle marred her shimmering scarlet asar. Thin bands of gold spiraled around her upper arms, and rubies shone from her hair and neck. She carried a golden fan painted with red flowers, and her slippers were encrusted with gems.

Approving murmurs followed Tanaya as she walked toward the throne. Every movement was perfect, every step graceful. She seemed to float past the crowd like a vision.

Nisha swallowed. It seemed incredible, insane, that the beautiful, once-kind girl in front of her could also be so ruthless. But Tanaya's mocking words echoed in her ears. She had dared Nisha to try to stop her.

Fine, then. She would. She could feel the daggers in her wrist sheaths, but she didn't want to kill Tanaya. She didn't think she *could* kill Tanaya. And if Tanaya died unaccused, it wouldn't help Sashi.

The solution was obvious. Now she just had to wait for the right moment.

It came shortly after Tanaya knelt before the high prince. Tanaya's head bent just enough to show the arch of her neck, and her fan fluttered to touch the prince's feet in an expression of freely given submission. She brought the fan back with a snap, pressed her hands together, and went still.

Prince Sudev stood and stepped closer to the motionless girl before him. He walked around her several times, his eyes taking her in. The tension in the room pressed against Nisha's skin. She—and everyone else—watched and waited.

The prince returned to his throne and sat for several moments, his fingers drumming on the wooden arm of the chair. "She is suitable," he announced into the silence. "I will accept her."

A sigh blew through the crowd, a breath of relief, of satisfaction.

Nisha spoke loudly. "I wouldn't do that."

Tanaya's head jerked up, and a gasp ripped through the room. Prince Sudev's eyes narrowed. "Who said that?" he demanded.

Nisha nudged Tac, who reluctantly stepped forward.

"I did, High Prince Sudev," Nisha said. Fear thrummed through her, but she'd gone too far to stop. "I have an accusation to make against this girl."

"An accusation?" Prince Sudev leaned back. "Really. And I was afraid this ceremony would be boring."

Nisha opened her mouth, but another voice overrode her.

"Forgive us, Your Highness," Akash said, pushing his way through the crowd until he stood just near Nisha and Tac. His smooth voice was high and cracked around the edges, his smile brittle. "Pay no attention to this poor disturbed girl. She is no one, a charity case. We will take her back to her room."

"It's a little late for that, don't you think?" the prince asked. "If this 'disturbed' girl is brave enough to interrupt a royal ceremony, perhaps we should hear what she has to say."

"I would like to speak," Nisha said clearly.

"Shut up!" Akash said in a strangled whisper. "You don't know what you're doing!" He looked back at the prince. "She's a charity case," he repeated. "No one important."

Sudev raised one eyebrow. "Now that *is* interesting, Akash, since you've never struck me as a particularly charitable person. The law is clear. Any person who comes to the Lotus Throne with petition or accusation will be heard. This may not be the Lotus Throne," he said, looking down at the carved chair, "but I think I will hear her anyway."

He gave Nisha a stare that reminded her of a hunting cat right before it pounced. "You may proceed with your accusation."

Tanaya was standing now, hands on her hips. "Nisha, do you know what you've done? You'll be killed for this."

"It's likely," Nisha said. *But I'm not doing this for me.* She took a deep breath.

"I believe you should know, Highness, that this girl you are taking as wife confessed to me not an hour ago that she caused the death of a girl named Atiy."

Interest sparked in the prince's eyes. "I know of Atiy. And you say Tanaya is responsible for her fall?"

Nisha nodded and continued in a high, clear voice. "Tanaya claims it was an accident, but she was struggling with Atiy at the time. Soon after, two other girls in the City died under mysterious circumstances. One, Jina, was the lone witness to Atiy's fall. The other was a girl named Lashar."

Another spark of recognition flickered in the prince's face, but he only nodded.

Nisha's throat was dry, but she managed to finish. "I heard her confess to causing Atiy's death with my own ears."

She let the words settle in the silent room. Maybe the prince would believe her, but perhaps not. She had spoken the truth before everyone in the City and done all she could think of to clear Sashi's name.

Prince Sudev considered her for a moment, his palms pressed together and his fingers on his lips. Then he looked at Tanaya. "Do you have an answer to this remarkable accusation?"

"She's lying," Tanaya said, her back straight. "She's jealous of me and doesn't know any better."

The prince raised one eyebrow. "It is certainly possible." His eyes shifted lazily between the two girls, as if weighing them against each other. Tanaya lowered her gaze, but Nisha met the prince's eyes steadily, without flinching. They stared at each other for a long moment.

"Interesting," Prince Sudev said. "No one has looked me in the eye like that for many, many years." He looked back at Tanaya, who was still standing with her eyes appropriately cast down. "Most . . . interesting.

"This is a case," he continued, "of one girl's word against another. Can you give me any reason to believe you over my promised wife? Do you have any witnesses to this alleged confession?"

Nisha slowly shook her head. "N–"

Then a deep voice spoke close to her ear. "I heard it," Tac said.

"I was standing right behind her when Tanaya admitted to causing Atiy's death."

Nisha stared at Tac. "I thought you couldn't talk," she whispered.

Tac shrugged.

Tanaya's hands clutched at her asar, wrinkling the smooth silk. "Lies," she said. "They're in it together. And the law states that three citizens are needed to make a formal accusation."

"Lovely *and* clever," the prince said, running his gaze down Tanaya's body. "Very well. Is there a third person present who is willing to stand and accuse this woman?"

There was a moment of silence before a slim figure in a brown-and-gray tunic stepped forward out of the mass of people.

"I will be the third witness."

Nisha turned to see the Shadow Mistress standing next to her. The Mistress pointed at Nisha.

"I have been following this girl since she returned to the City. She has no knowledge of this, as I can remain unseen when I choose. I was standing in the shadow of the staircase when Tanaya confessed. I also believe, from my own investigations, that Tanaya murdered Lashar."

"This is becoming very interesting indeed," the prince said. "And who are you?"

The Shadow Mistress raised an eyebrow at him. "We have a history that you do not remember, Highness. But for now it is enough to say that I am a teacher in these Houses. And that I am sworn to serve the Emperor and his family in all things." She pulled up her sleeve, revealing a flower tattoo inked darkly into her skin. A black lotus.

Fear whispered through the crowd, and the nobles standing closest to the Shadow Mistress edged away.

An angry flush stained Tanaya's cheeks. "You're nothing but a hired killer, a base assassin. How dare you accuse me?"

"Assassin I have been," the Shadow Mistress said in her cold, soft voice. "And assassin I will stay. To kill a stranger for the good of the Empire is a dark act. But to murder two innocents just because being a princess isn't enough . . . that is the action of a spoiled child. And spoiled children in positions of power are dangerous."

"A worthy distinction," Prince Sudev noted. "And if what you say is true, then it would seem my future wife has taken it upon herself to eliminate my mistresses."

He turned his unsmiling eyes on Tanaya. "Did you kill those girls?"

Tanaya still stood tall, but she was beginning to shake. "It wasn't like that. Atiy was an accident. And the other one . . . I was trying to protect my future, our future. They said you would be mine," she said. "They promised."

"Did they?" The prince leaned forward. His voice had gone very quiet and sent prickles down Nisha's spine. "That was poor judgment on their part, since I belong to no one. Did you think to lay exclusive claim on a prince? How stupid of you."

Tanaya hunched her shoulders, shriveling under his matter-of-fact cruelty. She began to cry.

The prince went on, "I am heir to the Lotus Throne and the future ruler of the Bhinian Empire. I can't have a wife who's been publicly accused of murder."

The words fell onto the room like ax blows. The devastation on Tanaya's face turned to fury.

"You did this," she hissed, turning to Nisha. Her hands bent into claws. "You sneaky, manipulative bitch! I should have drowned you like a kitten when I had the chance." With a feral cry, Tanaya sprang toward Nisha's throat.

The crowd gasped like spectators at a play, and the bodyguards reached for their weapons.

They weren't faster than the Shadow Mistress.

One moment Tanaya was leaping at Nisha; the next, the Shadow Mistress had her in a chokehold, one arm twisted up behind her back.

"Only an amateur loses her temper," the Shadow Mistress said. She flung Tanaya to the floor and wiped her hands on her tunic with a clear expression of contempt.

Tanaya lifted her head, eyes burning with desperation. "Please," she begged the prince, crawling toward the base of the throne. "I have worked my whole life for you. Don't throw me away now."

"A true Flower noble never begs. And while elimination of rivals is not unheard of, a true noble never, ever gets caught," Prince Sudev said quietly. He snapped his fingers and raised his voice to say, "Take her away."

"No! I won't let you do this. I won't!" Tanaya scrambled to her feet and reached up to the ruby hair ornament that crowned her heavy gold waves.

Nisha stiffened. She remembered Rajni and Josei speaking over Lashar's blood-soaked body.

That's her hair ornament.

It's a dagger. You arm your girls?

Time turned slow and murky. Nisha watched Tanaya draw the slender blade from her hair. She felt her own dagger slide out of her sleeve, felt the heaviness of the hilt as it hit her palm. The world narrowed to just Nisha and Tanaya, the way it had when Tanaya had thrown her daggers at Nisha in fun.

Tanaya lifted her arm to throw. She was fast.

But for once Nisha was faster. Her own dagger flew in a blur of liquid sliver. The honed edge of the knife sliced deep into Tanaya's arm, sending her throw wide. Tanaya's hair ornament clattered across the marble floor, and the room filled with the sharp, metallic smell of Tanaya's blood.

By the time Tanaya's hand dropped to her side, she was surrounded by the guards and a blade was pressed to her own throat.

No one moved. No one breathed.

With a theatrical sigh, Prince Sudev stood and stepped off the dais. Tanaya's elaborate hairstyle had come loose and fell around her face in heavy tangles. Her face was tight with fury, her clothes rumpled. Red blood streamed freely from her cut arm and dripped onto the floor, almost matching the color of her asar. And still she was beautiful.

The prince walked to Tanaya and ran a finger down her cheek. "Such a pity. You would have made an excellent wife for me."

Tanaya opened her mouth to speak, but the prince laid a finger on her lips, silencing her.

"*Shh*. You have no idea how close you are to death right now. I could have you executed where you stand." Tanaya shrank back, and the prince smiled.

"But my father prefers to be consulted on such matters, so your punishment will have to wait until I get back to Kamal." He gestured to the guards. "Tie her well before you tend her wound. She is more dangerous than you can possibly know." He gave Tanaya a mocking smile. "Though I find that to be true of women in general."

A nervous titter rippled through the crowd. Nisha closed her eyes, not wanting to see Tanaya–the girl who had defended her, the girl who had been her friend–dragged away. When she opened them again, Tanaya was gone.

34

THE PRINCE FOLDED his arms. "Can anyone tell me why I shouldn't have this whole place torn down for endangering my royal person?"

No one answered. Akash tar'Vey looked sick, and Matron frightened beyond words.

Sudev raised his head, his eyes resting on Nisha. "Ah, my brave rescuer," he said, holding out his hand palm down. "Come here."

It wasn't an invitation, it was a command, and Nisha knew it. Tac stepped forward.

The prince's tone never changed. "I would prefer you faced me on your own feet."

Swallowing, Nisha held on to Tac and slowly slid her feet down to the floor. Balancing on her good foot, she leaned against him.

"Tell me," the prince said, pointing at Nisha's cast, "is that temporary or permanent?"

"Temporary," Nisha said, holding her head up. "If the Ancestors are willing. But only time will tell for sure."

Prince Sudev wrinkled his nose. "With such a disability, you are to be commended for your reflexes. You defended me most excellently and saw the dagger before even my trained guards did." He glanced at the black-clothed soldiers behind him, and they shifted uncomfortably. The prince went on.

"A man should know the name of those who save his life. What are you called?"

"I am Nisha Arvi." Nisha pressed her palms together and bowed as low as she could without falling over. Tac kept a steadying hand on her shoulder.

"Arvi?" The prince's eyes narrowed. "Aren't the Arvi a Kildi clan?"

The crowd murmured. Nisha felt the back of her neck get hot, and she couldn't stop herself from touching the gray silk that covered her tiger mark. "Yes. My father was a Kildi. Emil Arvi, Master Trader of his clan."

The murmurs turned to uncomfortable whispers. From the corner of her eye, Nisha saw Devan's eyes widen. Akash appeared equally taken aback. Matron looked resigned.

The prince did not seem surprised or shocked. His eyes swept up and down Nisha, finally coming to rest on the red scarf over her hair. His voice was lightly mocking. "So, Nisha of the Arvi clan, I owe you a life-debt."

"What? No!" Nisha looked around frantically. Life-debts were for warriors and nobles. She didn't think royalty could even owe a life-debt.

"But I do," Prince Sudev corrected her. "No one is exempt from a life-debt. But I dislike owing anyone anything, especially not to a daughter of the Kildi. Name your price."

Nisha gaped at him. "What?"

Prince Sudev spoke slowly. "I wish to repay my life-debt to you. Name what you wish, and if I can give it, I will."

Nisha grabbed at her chance. "If it please you, Highness, I wish to save my friend. She was falsely accused of Tanaya's crimes and imprisoned. I want her released, and I want the City to find a healer in Kamal for her to study under. It will be as if she had never been never suspected."

"Reasonable," the prince said. "It will be done. It can be the last thing this City does. I intend to speak with my father about shutting down this estate."

"You can't!" Nisha said more loudly than she'd intended. "Please don't," she amended. "The City of a Thousand Dolls isn't perfect. But if you just shut it down, there will be no place for people to bring their unwanted girls."

"What the people do with their extra brats is hardly my problem," Prince Sudev said quietly. "My father may have an attachment to this City, but I do not. And if I don't respond to this"–he gestured to the puddle of Tanaya's blood on the floor– "this insult, I will lose face. I hope you're not suggesting I lose face, daughter of the Arvi?"

"Of course not, Highness," Nisha said, her brain working furiously. "But I may have a less dramatic solution for you. What if you punished only one person: the one who allowed Tanaya to continue to kill, who silenced witnesses and knowingly hid information from you?"

"And who would that be?"

Nisha looked over to where Akash tar'Vey was trying to inch his way out of the crowd. "The new Head of the City Council, of course," she said, pointing. "That man. Akash tar'Vey."

Akash froze and looked at Nisha, his expression a mix of hate and fear.

Nisha didn't waver. "I think he would make an excellent . . . scapegoat."

A smile touched the prince's mouth. "You are more ruthless than I would have given you credit for. And you amuse me."

He nodded, and guards started closing in on Akash from each side.

"No!" Akash tried to run, but the fascinated crowd pressed too close, and he could only stare like a trapped deer. "Mercy, Highness. Mercy!"

Prince Sudev rolled his eyes. "I hate it when they beg. Take him away," he called to the guards.

Nisha shivered. The prince gave her another mocking smile. "Not so ruthless, then? If it comforts you, his punishment will be lighter than what he deserves. My father will not allow me to anger a family as powerful as the tar'Veys. Now, who should be this unworthy man's successor?"

That question at least was easy to answer.

"Someone who puts the welfare of the girls here above all personal considerations," Nisha said. "The Matron of the Houses."

"Done." The prince shrugged. "Now I have saved your friend

and your precious City. Is my debt repaid?"

Nisha thought of Zann and a wave of reckless courage swept through her. She had risked her life and freedom, and she was still alive. She could risk a little more. The words tumbled out of her mouth. "I want your personal promise that no girl will be spoken for against her will."

An angry mumble arose from the crowd of assembled nobles, and the prince waved a hand to silence it.

"An interesting suggestion," he said, his mouth twisting upward. "But how will this place stay profitable if girls can turn down potential redeemers?"

"What if the girls could repay the City for its estimated losses?" Nisha said, the idea crystallizing even as she spoke it. "If a girl refuses her Spoken, she will be set up in a trade somewhere in the Empire. Girls here are trained in all sorts of skills. Every novice here is an expert, and each could earn her own money if she were allowed. The girl will pay a percentage of her wages to the City every year until it equals the amount that the Spoken would have paid for her. And if she finds a husband before the debt is paid, the Council can set the remaining amount as a bride-price."

The angry murmurs softened into approval.

"It will be done." Prince Sudev's look turned from amused to thoughtful. He eyed Nisha, appraising her again. "Are we even now? Or is there something you want for yourself, Nisha Arvi? I can hardly believe that you are concerned only with the welfare of others. I would offer you a position in the palace. Perhaps not in the court, but we could find you a position in the royal archives. . . ."

Nisha had saved her friend and helped the girls who would continue to fill the City of a Thousand Dolls. She'd kept her promise to herself. But the thought of spending her days in a tiny room filled with dusty books made her sick. She didn't want to work in the archives, and she didn't want to work in the palace. She wanted to be free.

"Your Highness, Akash tar'Vey sold me to his cousin, Kalia."

"Did he now?" Prince Sudev said. "That is more like the Akash I know." He sighed. "Well, we can't have nobles acting like slave merchants—not publicly, anyway." He gestured to another set of guards. "Find Kalia tar'Vey and hold her. I don't care how much the tar'Veys yell. They have a lot to answer for after today."

Nisha held Tac's arm tightly, dizzy with relief. It was over.

She was free.

But Sudev wasn't done yet. In a few steps, he was close to Nisha, close enough for her to see the white lotus flower that marked the base of his neck.

"My offer is still open," he said.

Nisha stared into his dark eyes. "I told you. I just want my freedom."

The prince turned away abruptly, and the first hint of real anger edged his voice.

"It is all very well to speak of being free, but as you have seen, freedom means nothing without the protection of caste. And you have no caste mark. I would strongly suggest that you accept my help, daughter of the Arvi. Unless, of course, someone here wants to speak for you."

Nisha looked around, her gaze finding Devan. The young nobleman was staring at her as if he'd never seen her before. Devan looked out the door where they had taken his uncle, then back at her. His mouth opened–

And Nisha shook her head at him.

No.

Even if Devan still wanted to speak for her, it couldn't be as his wife. And she couldn't be his mistress, either. That cage might be kinder and more comfortable than the one that the prince was offering, but it was still a cage. Atiy might have been happy in that life–probably would have been, if she'd had the chance–but Nisha wasn't Atiy. Or Tanaya or Jina or any of these other girls.

She was just Nisha. And she needed to be free.

Thank you, she thought at him fiercely, sending him the words she knew she'd never get to say. She hoped that even though he couldn't read her thoughts as her cats could, he might see the message in her face. *Thank you. For everything.*

Good-bye.

Devan held her eyes for a long moment, their shared history flowing between them like a muddy river. Then he turned and pushed his way through the crowd, toward the door.

Prince Sudev's eyes traveled over the gathered crowd. "No one? No one will speak for Nisha Arvi, limping orphan girl?"

The crowd tittered, and Nisha felt herself turn red with shame. The prince turned back to her.

WE SPEAK FOR HER.

A collective voice resounded in Nisha's mind with a power and authority she had never imagined. She saw the mouths of those around her drop open as they heard it and a river of spotted cats flowed into the throne room. Cats spread out along the edges of the crowd as Esmer trotted to the middle of the room, her tail high, catlike confidence radiating from every step.

Nisha stared at them. So did the prince.

"Cats?" someone sputtered from the crowd. "Cats don't talk!"

And as Nisha watched, her cat-friend, her cat-mother, disappeared. In her place stood an elegant gray-haired woman wearing a simple brown tunic. Her voice was soft and thin in the open air as she spoke.

"Not generally, no," Esmer said. "But we are not cats. We are a tribe of cat-Sune that has made our home here for these last ten years in order to fulfill a sacred trust laid on us by the girl's parents. Now we step forward and speak for Nisha Arvi. We will claim her and adopt her as one of our own."

The older woman nodded to Josei's assistant, who was still standing next to Nisha. "It's all right now, Jerrit," she said. "You can talk again."

Nisha swayed, her head swimming. "Jerrit?"

The crowd fell apart.

35

NISHA COULDN'T STOP staring at the young man
holding her up. Her eyes traveled over his broad hands and strong
arms, the arms that had carried her all day. She studied the way
he stood, the fall of his hair. His human eyes were more brown
than gold, but the wide grin was pure Jerrit.

Forgive me, he sent. The touch of his mind on hers was so familiar and comforting that Nisha almost burst into tears. *It was the
only way I knew to protect you.*

Jerrit glanced at the older woman. "Esmer didn't think that
my walking around in human form was a good idea," he said out
loud. "But I told her I was doing it whether she approved or not,
so she finally agreed."

"I'm just so glad you're here," Nisha whispered. "I thought I
wouldn't get a chance to say good-bye."

"Well, you won't have to say good-bye anytime soon," Jerrit said. "Watch."

Nisha couldn't speak. A fierce, impossible hope had her by the throat. She took his hand and squeezed it.

Esmer stood in front of the prince, her arms folded. "Will you accept?"

The prince scowled like a small child deprived of his toy. "I have to think about it," he said. "No Sune has ever purchased a girl from the City before."

A wicked grin spread across Esmer's face. "Would it help if I told you that the girl's mother was also a Sune, and a legend among our kind?"

Time seemed to stop for Nisha. She could hear her heart beating in her ears, but everything else around her, the astonished nobles, the surprised prince, faded away.

A Sune.

My mother was a Sune.

It didn't seem possible.

She wasn't a spotted cat, Jerrit sent, answering the question that hovered on Nisha's lips. *Your mother was one of the tiger-Sune. I don't know the story very well, but I believe she gave up her cat form when she met your father. Or maybe before that. It's a little confusing.*

A tiger.

Nisha was half tiger.

She touched the mark under her collarbone, the tiger that had set her apart ever since she could remember. It seemed to warm under her hand. Was that why her mother joined the Arvi? Because their symbol reminded her of her past life?

Do the Kildi know? Nisha asked.

Jerrit shook his head. *I don't think so.*

More questions were bursting out of Nisha's skin. *Am I going to change? Does it hurt?*

Slow down, Jerrit sent, a warm laugh accompanying his mind-voice. *Remember what Josei told you? Half-Sune don't change until they're finished growing. It's usually not until eighteen at the least. You have a couple of years yet.*

Half relieved, half disappointed, Nisha dragged her attention back to Esmer and the prince.

"Well," the prince said finally, "that does alter things." He craned his neck until he spotted Matron in the crowd.

"You there, new Council Head. Come and talk with me."

Matron made her way slowly through the crowd. Her head was bent in respect, but Nisha saw a gleam of satisfaction in her eyes. The two retreated to the dais with Esmer, where they spoke in low voices. The Shadow Mistress stood nearby, watching them.

"Did Matron know? About my parents?" Nisha asked.

Jerrit looked surprised at the question. "Yes, of course. She was the one who agreed to let us stay in the City. She took you as her assistant and promised Esmer she would protect you as best she could."

Nisha felt dizzy and leaned against Jerrit for support, the way she always had, even before she'd known who he was. "Why would she do that for me?" she asked.

"Not out of choice." Jerrit grinned. "Your father blackmailed her into it."

"He *what?*"

Jerrit nodded, clearly amused. "Yes. He'd learned a few secrets about the City in his years of trading between here and Kamal. He had discovered that Matron had been funneling City funds to a school in Kamal that takes in older orphans. Only the Council Head has ever been allowed to take City money for any purpose other than running the City. So Matron was basically embezzling the money. When your parents realized they were in danger–from what, they never said–your father came straight to Matron. He threatened her with exposure if Matron didn't take you in and protect you as best she could until he could come and get you."

"But they died. . . ."

Jerrit rested his forehead on hers. "Yes. And Matron refused to send you back to the Kildi without knowing who killed your parents."

Nisha's gaze drifted to Matron's stiff figure. "She saved me."

Matron looked over to see Nisha staring at her, and raised one eyebrow in grim amusement.

Nisha looked away, her gaze falling on the Shadow Mistress. "And you," she said. "You were following me?"

"From the moment you found my House and I knew what you were about" was the woman's quiet reply. "Before that, you didn't need me. You were safe here. But when I heard your story, I knew you were in danger. And I, too, had made a promise. Your mother was one of my closest friends."

"My mother?" Nisha whispered, feeling the words flutter like songbirds in her throat. "You knew my mother? You knew she was Sune?"

"Of course I did." The Shadow Mistress slid her eyes away from Nisha's, her face unreadable. "I owe her my life many times over. But when I gave up my name to come here, I never expected to see her again. Then one day, there she was, in my House. She said her daughter was sitting at the gate, and that she and Emil were in danger and were going to try to reach someone who could help them. She wouldn't tell me any more, but she charged me to protect you, to swear by our friendship and by the debt I owed her. When your mother left, she dropped this scarf."

Nisha reached up to touched the red scarf over her hair.

"But . . . if you were watching me, why didn't you help before now?" Nisha asked, trying to understand. "They were going to sell me."

A flicker of anger crossed the Shadow Mistress's face. "When I promised to protect you in the City, I didn't know that you would be here for ten years. I am oath bound to the Emperor. He sent me personally to this estate under a solemn charge of obedience, and I could not directly oppose the Council's decisions. I chose my battles, and perhaps not as well as I could have. But I would not have left you in their snares long."

"Somehow, I didn't think the rules applied to you," Nisha said.

The Shadow Mistress bent down, looking at something on the floor. "The rules apply to everyone, Nisha. Even your parents."

"How did you know her?" Nisha asked, thinking again of her mother's mysterious past. "She wasn't an assassin, was she?"

The Shadow Mistress gave her a brief, sad smile. "All you need to know is that, legend or not, your parents were the best people

I have ever known, and that they loved you more than they loved life itself."

Something deep inside Nisha relaxed, opened like a flower unfurling. She was not flawed or untrainable. She had not been abandoned. Her parents had done everything they could to keep her safe.

She had been loved.

The Shadow Mistress straightened, picking up a scrap of scalloped rice paper off the floor. She handed it to Nisha. Tanaya's handwriting was clear and sharp.

Mirrors reflecting
Doubling the laughing crowd
Lies set in glass

I see no bright eyes
Peering out from this jeweled mask
I, too, am a lie

Nisha crumpled the paper and let it drop to the floor.

"You shouldn't be standing," Jerrit said suddenly. He picked Nisha up as if she weighed nothing, his body warm and strong against hers.

Nisha leaned into his warm chest for a moment, then punched him in the arm as hard as she could.

"Ow!" Jerrit said. "What was that for?"

"You lied to me!" Nisha said, torn between tears and laughter.

"You were there the whole time, and I was so worried. I thought you hated me, that I was never going to see you again—"

"I know," Jerrit said. "You don't know how many times I almost spoke to you. But if I had, Esmer would have made me go back to cat form until it was all over. Matron made us swear that we would tell you nothing about us, or your parents, until your sixteenth year, after your first Redeeming. She didn't want you to go looking for your parents until you were older. And I had to protect you."

His voice roughened and he held her tighter. "If anything had happened to you," he said, resting his face in her hair, "I don't know what I would have done."

A warm quiver started up in Nisha's belly, and she spoke quickly to cover it.

"My parents sent you with me?"

Jerrit nodded. "I don't remember much, since I was so young at the time. I have no idea how your parents even knew about our tribe. I do know that Esmer personally promised to look out for you until you left the City, and that we moved in the day after you did. You can ask Esmer, but I think she took another oath of secrecy for that."

The reminder of her broken oath to Jerrit made Nisha squirm. "Jerrit, I'm sorry I broke my promise—"

"That's all over now."

"But how can it be over?" Nisha said. "Esmer said you can't take back oath-breakers."

"We can't, so we decided to go with you."

"What?" Nisha choked on the word. She must have misheard him. "You cast *yourselves* out?"

Jerrit nodded. "When a tribe decides not to be a part of the Marjara-Sune–the cat clans–they are Sundered. No cat-Sune will speak to them or even acknowledge their existence."

"But why?" Nisha said. "Why do that for me?"

"Because if we go voluntarily into exile, we keep our honor. We won't lose our young, and we won't have to worry about hostile tribes because no one's allowed to acknowledge our existence." Jerrit laughed, and it was a deep sound, almost like a purr. "And unlike breaking an oath, being Sundered isn't permanent. It is reversible."

"Then you can go back," Nisha said. "You can undo it."

"We could. But we won't." Jerrit's voice became very tender. "Esmer offered the rest of the tribe a choice, Nisha. They could remain with us and be Sundered, or they could go freely and join another tribe. Do you know how many of our tribe wanted to stay?"

"How many?" Nisha whispered.

"All of them," Jerrit said, holding her closer. "Every single one. So you see, you're stuck with us."

Before Nisha could fully absorb his words, the prince approached them, followed by Esmer and Matron. Prince Sudev looked sullen, Matron looked grimly satisfied, and Esmer smiled brightly.

"In light of the respect my father has for the Sune, I have decided to be gracious," the prince said. His voice was anything but gracious and made Nisha very glad she wasn't going to work in the palace.

Prince Sudev turned to Matron. "The City is yours. I trust nothing like this evening's . . . debacle will happen ever again."

"You can be sure it won't," Matron said.

The prince's cold gaze moved to Nisha. "Now I really must insist that you declare us even. I am losing patience with this game."

An idea struck Nisha, one that made the corners of her mouth twitch.

"Thank you, O Gracious One. You have been very generous in repaying your life-debt."

She settled back in Jerrit's arms, feeling safer than she had in days. The City of a Thousand Dolls would continue, with its dizzying mix of good and evil, but now the girls would have at least some choices. It wouldn't give Zann, Atiy, Jina, or Lashar their lives back, but it was something.

"But there is one more person I'd like you to help."

Bracing herself on her good foot, Nisha leaned her elbows against the stone that lined the top of the wall. Thick frost soaked her heavy wool tunic, but she couldn't have cared less.

The view was as vast as she'd imagined, a broad carpet of treetops as far as the eye could see. The branches had shed their leaves, and a delicate cover of frost crusted each thin twig. In the soft light of day, the trees glittered like diamonds. White tendrils of morning mist wove through the branches, evaporating in the open air.

Nisha took a deep breath, savoring the feel of the cold, sparkling air. Jerrit put a hand on her shoulder, and she smiled up at him.

Where are we going? she sent. She was amused to still find herself communicating with Jerrit in the old way.

We thought we'd stop by Stefan's camp, Jerrit sent with a grin, *if that's all right with you.*

He's still there? The thought startled Nisha. *I thought they were packing up to leave.*

Jerrit began to laugh, and sent, *Aishe refused to go. Esmer says she sat down in the middle of camp and threatened to bite anyone who tried to move her. She said she wasn't going to abandon a member of their family for a second time, even if everyone else was.*

A smile pulled at the corners of Nisha's mouth. *That sounds like something Aishe would say.*

They stood in companionable silence for a moment and listened to the carefree chatter drifting up from the two wagons outside the main gate. Nisha could see Esmer's gray head as she supervised the loading of the bigger wagon.

The Sune woman Rashi, her dark-brown hair pulled back, argued playfully with small, red-haired Valeriana. Other Sune in human form loaded the wagons with things Nisha had never known the cats possessed.

Her own bundles were in there somewhere, along with the sack that the Kildi had given her. It felt good to see her things bundled together with the others', as if she weren't leaving home at all, but taking everything with her.

Well, almost everything.

Nisha's gaze was drawn to the smaller of the two wagons. A slim, green-robed figure sat stiffly upright in the front. A familiar ache started in Nisha's chest.

"Sashi still won't talk to you?" Jerrit asked, following her gaze.

"No." Nisha shook her head. "I tried again this morning. She wouldn't answer her door. She still hasn't forgiven me, and I don't blame her."

"She has her own life to figure out," Jerrit said. "And you can't change what's been done . . ."

"No matter how hard you want to," Nisha finished. Her eye caught a cheerful figure in an off-white asar. Chandra ran to hug Esmer, then patted the sturdy cart horses, and finally clambered into the smaller wagon, settling in among the bundles and plants.

"That was a good thing you did," Jerrit said, "asking the prince to send Chandra with Sashi as an assistant. You probably saved her life."

There were so many lives she hadn't saved, Nisha thought. Her eyes drifted again to her friend in the wagon seat. It didn't feel like enough, and she wondered if it ever would.

Nisha watched as the wagon master swung himself up beside Sashi and clucked the horses into action. As the healer's wagon pulled away, Chandra looked up and saw Nisha.

Even from the wall, Nisha could see the smile that lit up the girl's face. Chandra waved, and Nisha and Jerrit waved back, watching the wagon until it was lost in the trees.

"I hope she's happy," Nisha whispered, more to herself than to Jerrit. She felt stiff and tired and a thousand years old.

Jerrit fidgeted for a moment. "We found this outside the main gates, by the way." He handed her a small bouquet of star jasmine. Nisha's heart gave a painful thump at the sight of the note tied to the stems.

She unfolded the rice paper. No poem, no elegant phrases, not even a signature. Just two simple words.

Forgive me.

Nisha put the white flowers down on the edge of the wall.

"I'm sorry about Devan," Jerrit said. "I know you cared about him."

"I did," Nisha said, leaning her head on his shoulder. "Maybe I always will. But I don't belong in his world. I don't want to belong in it. I wouldn't have been happy, not with people watching everything I do, waiting for me to make a mistake."

"Well, if you don't belong there, then where do you think you belong?" Jerrit slid his hand over hers, and their fingers entwined like vines in a garden.

Nisha smiled up at him. There were so many new pieces to her identity, sometimes she didn't even recognize herself. Half Kildi and half Sune, orphaned and adopted, wounded and free. The only thing she knew for certain was that she was loved. And for now that was enough.

"I don't know where I belong yet," she said. "But we'll figure it out, won't we?"

Jerrit laughed and scooped Nisha up into his arms, so their faces were inches apart. His chest was warm, driving out the chill of the frost.

Nisha half hoped her foot didn't heal *too* quickly.

"Come on," Jerrit said, touching her forehead with his own. "Can't keep the tribe waiting."

"My tribe," Nisha said, savoring the words. She leaned her head back against Jerrit, feeling his heart beat in time with her own.

My family.

Acknowledgments

IT WOULD BE impossible to thank all the people who made this book a reality, but I'm going to give it my best try.

To my husband, Dan, the most brilliant, supportive person I know. Thanks for the hugs, the editing advice, the late-night cookie runs, and all the other million and one ways you made this possible. I love you madly.

To my parents, who taught me to read and never took a book out of my hands because it was too hard or grown-up. Because of you, I am at home in the written word. Thank you for never giving up on me.

(Special thanks to Dad and his tribe of cats, past and present, including Macduff, Fizben, and Pascal. It's *your* fault there are cats in every book I write.)

To my sisters, who have two of the biggest hearts I know and remember all the embarrassing stories. Thank you for being the amazing women you are.

To my astonishing and hilarious agent, Jennifer Laughran. Of all the surprising things on this improbable journey, you were the best surprise of all. Thanks for the perspective, the cheers, and the awesome book recommendations.

To my tireless editor, Sarah Dotts Barley. Because of you, my book is better than I could ever have made it by myself. Thank you for all your hard work, enthusiasm, wonderful ideas, and for loving Nisha and Jerrit and all the rest just as much as I do.

To everyone at Andrea Brown and HarperCollins, especially Erin Fitzsimmons, the designer, who made my book look more epic than it actually is (no matter what she says); Renée Cafiero and Valerie Shea, who helped me find lost days and educated me on the ways of the comma; Colin Anderson, who created the completely amazing jacket art; and Taryn Fagerness, foreign rights agent extraordinaire. A book is a work of art made by many hands. I was lucky to have yours. Thank you.

To my Starbucks coworkers and customers in the Pullman, Moscow, and Five Mile stores. You made my days go smoothly and put up with my tireless book blather. Thanks for making me feel so supported. You guys are the best.

To Neysa, Sarah, Amy, and the rest of my original critique group. You saw this book in its rawest form and did not run screaming. Thanks for sharing the ride.

To all my in-real-life friends who've walked the last year with me, thank you. Thanks to Arwen for the pizza-and-movie nights and the marathon book-reading days. Thanks to the Moscow Library YA book club–Sofia, Haley, Jamie, Addie, and Hailey– for being the coolest people I know. And thanks to my family at Real Life for letting me pounce on you and bombard you with book news at seven in the morning. I owe you all the coffee in the world.

To all my wonderful blog readers, Twitter pals, and Facebook friends. You guys make me laugh every single day, and I'm so lucky to have an extended family like you. You make the Internet a warm and friendly place, and that's no small feat. Thank you from the bottom of my socially awkward heart.

And finally to my tenth-grade English teacher, Mrs. Mallory, who, when she found out I was writing a novel in her classroom, suggested I form a writers' club. If it weren't for you, I wouldn't have believed that I could do what I'm doing right now. Thank you.